TWO
FALLEN
WORLDS

lost

by

Derya LITTLE

First Printing, 2018

ISBN: 978-1987535280

deryalittle@gmail.com
deryalittle.com

Dear Shohag,

Pray for me!

[signature]

−for my amazing husband,
who patiently reads every page I write.

The Seven Marks of Kaya

Riser: Can lift immensely heavy weights
Pacer: Can run up to eighty miles per hour
Healer: Can heal external and internal injuries
Reader: Can influence the behavior of plants and animals
Seer: Can discern the truthfulness of a person's mind
Strider: Can walk through solid objects
Waver: Can manipulate water

Day 1: Earth

The dad wrestled with a sandy blond boy and a little girl with curly brown hair. He could almost hear their laughter of joy through the double glass window. The messy toy room was warmly lit with three yellow light bulbs, making the scene even more unrealistic.

James rolled his eyes as he thought about how families like that did not last long in the real world. Seeing this father play with his children was nothing more than watching a cheesy family movie on a Saturday night - one was more fleeting than the other.

He started to walk away, but couldn't help glancing back one more time. The well-worn soles of his brown boots stepped through the muddy, unkempt lawn in a hurry. He had only a few hours left before sleep.

It had stopped raining about ten minutes earlier, so the dark pavement and narrow sidewalks were still wet. It was James' favorite time of rain, a little after the slush and a little before the mud. Other than the short-lived window of fragrance and calm, the climate in Seattle did not have much to praise. Wet and wetter or gray and grayer were the daily weather reports.

Surrounded by the refreshing crisp air of the evening, James walked the deserted streets. The little convenience store he had cased earlier was only two blocks away. He hurried past the quaint single-family houses and then the townhouses that stayed quiet in the night. The street light at the corner was something to be avoided. He took a mental note. Around the corner, a young couple walked out of the store carrying bags of groceries, engaged in a deep conversation.

What was their worry, really?

"Should we make the pasta with white or red sauce?" Maybe there was something much more important than the color of their food, he thought.

"Should we rent a movie or finish the crappy murder series?"

James watched them with what seemed to be disgust, but if you squinted your eyes and paid close attention, it was clear that the disgust was only a cover-up for envy.

"Trivial worries of trivial lives." He shook his head and pushed open the old metallic store door. It was time to take care of his own trivial life.

He pulled a piece of blank paper out of his pocket to give the impression of checking what was on the list his imaginary mother gave him. In his actual unwritten list, a can of chili, a small jar of peanut butter, and something for dessert, maybe some biscotti cookies, appeared. The crinkled paper was a tool to acquire the contents of his mental list. He pretended to look through the shelves as if he could not find the one ingredient his imaginary mother desperately needed to prepare a gourmet meal for his equally-imaginary family. Possibly cardamom, or chia seeds. He didn't know what one needed to cook gourmet meals.

He picked up a can of chili with a bright red label and stuffed it inside the makeshift pocket between the outer layer and the lining of his coat. Where was that cardamom? His eyes darted between the blank paper and the labels, as he strolled through the store.

The tiniest peanut butter jar resided on the middle shelf, making it much easier to snatch and bag without many hand movements. Two down, one to go.

Did she actually need that stupid spice? Who cooks with cardamom anyway?

The small white package of brown cookies with a burnt taste sat on a higher shelf. He picked up one of the fancy packages next to it, read the ingredients, and decided that he did not like coconuts in his cookies. As he put the colorful package down, he swiped the humble biscotti, and with an expert hand placed it in his side pocket that had a giant hole at the bottom. He would have loved to have some Fritos with his chili, but the package would make too much noise. Also, one did not have the luxury of a feast every night.

He wore the expression of someone who was disappointed at not having found cardamom for his beloved mother and her gourmet recipe, then stepped out to the wet and cold Seattle night.

Mission was accomplished. Dinner was served.

Maggie was working on one of her riddle books when James arrived with his loot. The first time he shoplifted, the guilt was so overpowering that giving away everything he had stolen was the only cure. No need to mention going hungry for two days. On the third day, though, the hunger had punched him in the face so hard that he had not felt his conscience tickle since then. Still, the hidden pockets never contained more than what he needed, and the only luxury he was willing to steal was Maggie's occasional biscotti cookies. She at least deserved that much.

She lifted her head up from the book and without a greeting proposed James' daily riddle.

9

"Take off my skin - I won't cry, but you will! What am I?"

"Really? Stop being patronizing. That wasn't even hard!" James said.

"Well, tell me the answer then, smarty pants."

"It's an onion, obviously."

"Tomorrow's will be so hard, you are gonna owe me three packages of biscotti!"

James fished out the brown cookies from the depths his coat and threw them in front of Maggie. She ripped the package open and took a tiny bite from one little cookie. She believed in savoring the moment.

"*Two* packages of biscotti. But it's still gonna be a hard riddle."

James unloaded the contents of his coat, while Maggie brought out two small plastic bowls and two silver spoons. It was obvious that the shiny ornate cutlery did not belong to the temporary dwelling of two homeless teenagers. They were the only things Maggie brought with her from home, and she made sure that they were used daily. Life was a little more civilized when you ate with silver spoons.

In the chill of early spring, they shared cold chili in a can with a red label, and nibbled on crackers smeared with generous helpings of peanut butter. Neither of them liked crackers, but both liked peanut butter. It was a good trade off.

All in all, it was a protein-rich, nutritious dinner. They'd had worse nights.

After the meal, James and Maggie laid down in their respective corners in the little shelter made from thick cardboard and pieces of tarp, eating their share of brown cinnamon cookies. James did not know what cardamom tasted like, but the taste of cinnamon was all too familiar.

Maggie returned to her coverless book about acrylic paint. James Knox covered himself with a military-grade blanket and went to sleep watching his only friend eat stolen cookies and read torn apart books.

Day 1: Kaya

A moment later, James of Seattle woke up. Sunlight seeped through plain beige curtains. He rolled over and wrapped the fluffy comforter around his body, his eyes remained closed as his mind adjusted to being awake. He could feel the presence of the little plant that was nestled on the window sill. It was a comforting sensation. One of the perks of living on Kaya.

Unlike the ghastly weather of Seattle, the brightness of his room promised a sunny and dry day in Aqui. Stretched out in his simple, but comfortable bed, he thought about the first day he woke up on Kaya instead of Earth. It had been almost three years to the day.

One night, he went to bed at home with his parents in a small town not far from Seattle. But instead of waking up in their suburban home, James found himself in a place that served as an inn for orphaned teenagers. Everything about him was still the same, even his name and his memories from Earth. But, there was more. Much more. He also possessed the memories of a life that was lived here on Kaya. It was as if his mind occupied two bodies in two worlds.

The James of Earth was slightly shorter and much skinnier than James on Kaya, but other than that, it was the same person that looked through the brown eyes in the mirror every day. He had two lives. One here on Kaya, far far away from Earth with a different sun, different moons, and different stars in the night sky, and one on Earth where he slept next to Maggie during a cold Seattle night in a comatose state.

He stretched his numb muscles and rolled over to get up. Whether it was Seattle or Aqui, he was always hungry in

13

the mornings. He grabbed yesterday's towel from the back of the chair and headed for the community bathrooms he shared with the rest of the floor. After taking a nice, warm shower and getting dressed in the simple Kayan attire of comfortable brown cotton pants and a beige shirt, he went down two floors to find the spacious kitchen.

The orphanage was called House of Sevgi, named after its founder who had a heart for taking care of those without family. It looked like a building that would have belonged to the age of the Roman Empire on Earth. White marble walls and floors gave the impression of extravagance, and white lilies carved along the ceiling took the coldness of marble away. During the day, long wide hallways were awash with sunlight that flooded through high windows. At night, oil-lit torches cast gloomy shadows for the residents of the Inn.

The walls of the hallway glowed white this morning, making the short walk a more pleasant experience. James entered the roomy kitchen, where an early riser had already lit a fire to boil water. There was no one in sight. He woke up on Kaya at seven in the morning every day, but even then, he was usually the last one to eat and the last one to head out the door.

In the quietness of the warm morning, breakfast was oatmeal made with rolled oats and a generous amount of sugar. They did not have maple syrup on Kaya. Pity.

Joan shuffled in. At least James had the presence of mind to shower before showing up in common areas. Joan didn't care. Her straight blonde hair threatened to defy gravity, and her eyes looked like they had inhaled yet another book through the night. She poured the last of the oatmeal into a ceramic bowl and grabbed a spoon from the drawer. James was not sure whether her eyes were open or not.

Joan grumbled something similar to good morning as she dragged herself to the chair across from James and started eating. Her eyes began to open ever so slowly as the tasteless oatmeal reached her stomach.

"What's your first class?" she asked, food still in her mouth.

"Math, you?"

"Sciences." She swallowed. "I read Thecla's biography all night. She was a fascinating woman who is on a fast track to becoming my latest hero."

Thecla was the founder of the order of Healers who lived on an island off the coast. That much James knew about the sisters who taught half of the classes, and no more. However, he was not going to pry Joan, since a history lecture was not the best way to start the day.

Also, he was running late.

As usual.

For Joan's sake, he wished they had coffee on Kaya.

His days in Aqui began early. The first period started at eight in the morning. Each class was forty-five minutes, then a fifteen-minute recess in between that gave students enough time to move around and reset their brains.

The grand school building twinkled in the morning sun. The Inn's strong but simple wooden door provided the perfect view from the top of the hill. A stone cobble walkway connected the Academy with the Inn, for a commute just shy of a mile. Surrounded with fruit trees and fragrant raspberry bushes, it was a short, but pleasant trek.

The Academy of Aqui was much older and more glamorous than the Inn. It was built over six hundred years earlier to support the university that currently laid in ruins in the capital city. The sturdy and elegant architecture could easily host five thousand students, but currently provided education for a mere thousand between the ages of seven and seventeen.

The bell tower that chimed at the beginning and the end of each period stood to the very right of the long building. The tower always reminded James of an elongated cupcake with swirly icing on top. In reality, it was a tall, round building with carvings along its outside walls. The roof was also made of carved marble spanning around to a point at its apex. The bell tower was doubtlessly the most beautiful part of the Academy. The rest of the building was much simpler (except the main gates), even though hand-carved depictions of Kayan history framed the windows and the doors. Just by looking at the walls, one could learn a lot.

The magnificence of the main gates could be easily mistaken for the entrance to a palace. James climbed the white steps and went through the timeworn doors that were swung open every day by the headmaster himself.

Math students of the day were already busy with finding their place in large tomes or placing blank parchments on their desks for note-taking. Leo leaned his chair against the wall, talking to Elgar. Unlike James, Leo hated being late or rushing. Early on in their friendship, they had established that neither would wait for the other in the mornings. It was a system that satisfied everyone.

Not a minute had passed after James' arrival when Sister Ita of the Theclans entered the room with her long, light blue habit swishing behind.

James picked up his pencil, ready to write down Sister Ita's lecture, as if another body of his did not lay asleep millions of miles away.

On this sunny spring day, mathematics, arts and marks went by, some slower than others. School was school. James enjoyed a few and disliked others, but even the most boring class was preferable to the unwanted thrill of shoplifting in Seattle. He did not complain.

After school, students older than twelve headed down to their designated work areas. The hour between book-reading and hard labor was a daily blessing.

James cleared off his desk, one that had been hand-crafted by a master carpenter centuries ago, scratched in places but still ornate.

Leo walked over with a brown satchel dangling from his shoulder and pointed at the book James was packing in his own satchel.

"I think Joan was reading this book last night. I saw her light on after midnight."

"Yes, I saw her at breakfast. She said it was the biography of Thecla."

"I know that she wants to learn as much about the Theclans as she possibly can, but how is she gonna stay awake at the mines all day long? T6 Healer or not, she needs rest."

"I guess, sometimes you have to make sacrifices," James said. The thought of hungry nights after he let Maggie eat the last of their scarce food nudged his mind. "It's worth it."

"Stop the melancholy, my friend, you can visit the realm of coolness later," Leo said, jumping off the desk.

His friend's customary lightheartedness brought James back from the memories of another world.

"The only place I wanna be, my good man, is where delicious meat and potatoes are served at this very moment!"

Leo brandished one of his smiles that sent the girls of the Academy a little crazy, and led the way to the lunch room.

After a sleep-inducing meal of hearty beef stew and sautéed greens, older students slowly walked the path down to the stables where horse-drawn carts waited for them. James and Leo had been lucky enough to get the same work assignments this year. Today was the spinach fields. The younger students would at first help with light housekeeping chores, and then spend most of the afternoon playing and reading. Life got slightly harder once you turned twelve.

On a nice spring day like this, spinach fields were much more enjoyable than working in the coal or marble mines. Even though after a couple of hours James' hands looked like they were permanently dyed in dark green, the luxury of talking to Leo almost uninterrupted for four hours made up for his ogre hands.

There was something magical about working with living things. He felt like an old farmer who had tended the soil for decades. His Reader mark made it possible for him to feel the fragile presence of the greenery that stretched in front of him and the gentle strength of trees beyond. The Marks were some of his favorite things about Kaya.

"I don't know if I'm ever gonna be able finish that book about Healers. I start yawning as soon as I look at it," Leo said, pulling out another thick spinach plant.

"You can check my report to see if that helps. Although, you might need to beg Joan or Elgar for a summary," James said. He didn't mind reading about Healers.

"Joan will never let me forget it, and Elgar's summary is probably longer than the book itself. I'll just see what you wrote." It was amazing that Leo could devour thousands of pages about some obscure king, but not want to read a book about the founder of the famous Healer order.

The rest of the afternoon, James and Leo talked about mundane things like assignments, tomorrow's classes, which professor they disliked the most, and the terrible dinner they had at the Inn last night. The typically peaceful day was slowly coming to an end as the Kayan sun started to disappear beyond the forest.

Time to go home. Leo pulled the heavy cart that contained the labor of everyone around them with the ease of a toddler pulling a toy wagon, following the crowds pouring to the plains where strong horses waited for their load. James watched his friend with admiration for both his strength and humility about being one of the most gifted Risers in Aqui.

The Riser mark gave a person the ability to lift, pull, or throw weights well beyond their natural limits. Leo was a Tier 6 Riser, and many suspected that before he turned seventeen and stopped improving, he would hit Tier 7, which was the Perfect Mark.

By the time they arrived at the Inn and washed the stubborn green off of their hands, the sun had gone down. Twin moons of Kaya, one full, one crescent, peeked in the horizon in the company of stars that did not belong to the Milky Way. It was Elgar's turn to cook, and both James and Leo felt grateful for it. After Joan's terrible squeaky eggplant dish yesterday, they were looking forward to a bowl of one of Elgar's improvised soups and a thick slice of freshly baked honey bread.

All seventeen of those who lived in the Red Wing were gathered around the kitchen already. Some served themselves soup out of the black iron cauldron over the fire, others grabbed slices of bread, and still others were busy with munching down the goodness that filled the kitchen with a spicy aroma. James loved the Inn.

Soon their voices became part of the many conversations that got mixed with clinging spoons and moving chairs. A long day of school and work made sleep evermore enticing.

The weariness combined with chay, the yellow relaxing tea Kayans drank after every meal, was more than enough to send James off to bed. Even though he did not want to leave the warmth and the food behind, he headed for his room after giving Leo a pat on the back.

There was no escaping from what had been faithfully happening for the last three years. It was well before midnight, but he went to sleep.

Day 2: Earth

"So, what did you do yesterday?"

Although he had not told anyone in Aqui about his dual life —even Leo— Maggie knew about the world far, far away. Together, they had concluded that it was another planet because the night sky had a different set of stars. Also, there were two moons. Big giveaway.

James didn't care about Maggie knowing his secret. He had very little to lose if people on Earth decided that he needed to be locked up for inventing such tales. Besides, there was no one more trustworthy than Maggie. She was the little sister he never had. When they found each other not long after James ran away from home, she became the blessing that made the homeless life a little more bearable. They shared everything, the good, the bad, and often, the ugly.

He sat up and looked over to Maggie's side of their "home." She had settled down on the floor wearing her usual tattered brown boots, orange-striped leggings, and a pair of those funny-looking gloves without fingers that went up to her elbow. What did she call them? He couldn't remember. With dirty lime green, cut-off gloves and muddy leggings, Maggie was a young teenager through and through in appearance. But, life's cruel curveball had made her wise beyond her years without consent.

She patiently waited for James' account of the previous day on Kaya. The little girl inside the wise mind cherished hearing stories from another world, and never, ever doubted the truthfulness of James' boring adventures.

"Spill it out," she said and packed her sketchbook inside her doodle-covered messenger bag.

"Same old, same old," he said, feeling hungry again, "school and then work at the spinach fields." He did not want to share how much he loved living the boring life on Kaya. That life was his consolation. All Maggie had was the dark, dank days of northwestern America.

He told her in detail how the biology professor, Lady Elwin, made them memorize and differentiate twenty-three species of asparagus and how he and Leo had a conversation about the possibility of life on other planets.

"I still think you should tell Leo about Earth," Maggie said.

"Oh, that would be a cheerful conversation. Where should I start? The sleeping on the floor? The soup kitchen? The stealing?" James replied.

"No need to be a jerk about it," she said with one of her piercing scowls.

"I know, I know, sorry. I don't think it's a good idea, Maggie. I have too much to lose there, if they think I've lost a few of my marbles. To be honest, when I'm there, all I want is to forget my life in Seattle...I don't know...Why taint my friends' lives?"

"I understand, but what kind of friendship is that?"

"One of a kind?" James said with a smile, hoping to get out of this uncomfortable conversation.

Maggie chuckled. "Well, as long as you keep me informed."

Maggie's enjoyment of hearing about every minute detail about his life in Aqui brightened the darker winter days. She made charts and schedules to remember names and to understand Kayan life better. Her hands waved in the air with excitement as she talked about overgrown plants, and the color-coded poster she made depicting the seven marks of Kaya hung behind her fluffy hair. Seer, Reader, Pacer, Strider, Waver, Riser, and Healer, all written in rainbow colors, seals drawn with the expert hand of the homeless talent.

She would have been quite the artist, if she had not grown up in an abusive home. For the time being, her amazing talent did nothing other than decorating their paper and tarp shelter.

The day he told her about the marks that every Kayan possessed, Maggie thought about which ones she would have liked to have. Usually, everyone possessed at least two strong marks on Kaya, and some level of the rest of the five marks. There were few who were blessed with three strong marks. James was one of those lucky people, since he was a Reader, a Pacer, and a Seer. As a Reader, he could sense the presence of other living things and often impose his will on them. As a Pacer, he could work and run much faster than others. As a Seer, he could discern if somebody was lying or telling the truth.

Maggie was not impressed with James' marks, not that he had any choice in them. It was like being born with musical talent or being completely tone deaf. Strider and Healer marks were the ones she was interested in.

"I mean, who doesn't wanna walk through walls, or heal others?" she said, after having finally made up her mind about imaginary marks.

Despite her admiration for Striding and Healing, she could not hide her amazement when James' told her how Leo pulled the heavy carts with ease. "One cannot have it all," she sighed.

"It's Sunday," Maggie said, bringing him back to reality of life on Earth. St. Michael's offered dinner for the needy after morning Mass.

"Still early, and it looks like it's gonna rain," James said sticking out his head to check the skies.

"I'm gonna work on my drawing of the Academy then."

James nodded and stretched his legs a bit. It was a good time to finally finish Jane Eyre. Soon raindrops started to tap on the tarp roof, making them feel peaceful and dry despite their many troubles.

By the time James and Maggie arrived at the church social hall, there was already a line. In spite of that, before long their plates were heaping with warm food cooked by church ladies with gray hair. They kept to themselves most of the time, even though people seemed friendly. Part of it was James' unwillingness to be found, in case his parents stopped their constant fighting long enough to look for him, and part of it was his dislike of grown-ups, even though he was on a fast track to becoming one. The irony did not escape him.

He grabbed a book from the little shelf of children's books. Both of them enjoyed looking through the heavily-illustrated pages as they ate. Minimum effort, maximum entertainment. Today's title read *Blockhead: The Life of Fibonacci*.

In the welcome company of the spicy meatloaf and crunchy potatoes, the young Fibonacci boy told them about his obsession with numbers and how a certain series of numbers found themselves in the most unlikely places in nature. By the time the apple cores replaced juicy red fruits, the children's book had lost its allure, prompting Maggie to ask questions about Kaya again. They dawdled for a while, picking at the empty plate with their forks. Once it became clear that there was need for more seats, the time to head back to the streets had come. With full bellies barely after noon, they did not have to worry about what to eat tonight for now.

Wandering around downtown and asking random strangers for change occupied most of their day. They tried to stay out of sight of any official-looking person, because they would either be sent to foster care or returned to their families. Neither of them had had much luck with either.

Late afternoon came and went, and once again they were hungry. A growing body was a pain to feed.

It was Maggie's turn to come up with dinner, but thankfully a random stranger had given them five bucks. With all the change from panhandling added up, they almost had ten dollars to splurge on dinner.

James wanted to go back to the store where he saw the happy young couple from the day before. A can of prepared food of their choice, and this time some Fritos, were on the menu. Some fruit for Maggie was not beyond reach, either. James enjoyed them as well, but she delighted in devouring nature's candy. It was a love affair.

Grapes were on sale.

Maggie walked to the check-out line with the confidence of someone who could pay for their food. The cashier girl commented on Maggie's gloves, and there was some girly banter about colors and knitting that went over James' head. Maggie paid, and the cashier handed her the receipt. Final pleasantries were exchanged.

As they walked out of the now-familiar convenience store, James stuffed a crumpled-up dollar bill next to the cash register without either Maggie or the cashier noticing.

Day 2: Kaya

The first breath he took in this far away world always felt like the breath of life. It was the last school day of the week. Two days of weekend and pleasant laziness awaited.

The school week was a day shorter on Kaya. Four days of work and school, then two days of weekend. It was a preferable arrangement, because free time in Aqui was more agreeable than the endless idleness of homeless life.

A warm shower and then breakfast as usual. James loved the daily routine, although his room reflected a certain degree of messiness. Everyone was gone, even Joan, and he didn't expect to see anyone else before school.

Other than another sleepy resident from the west wing of the Inn, the paved path to the Academy was empty. He wished there was more time in the mornings to eat with his friends and walk with them, but what time he woke up or what time he fell sleep in either world was not something he could control.

On Earth and on Kaya, James fell asleep at midnight and woke up at seven in the morning. There were no exceptions. His mind had to live a combined day of thirty-four hours, but it was never tiring. The fact that sleep came, whether he wanted or not was, considered a form of narcolepsy in both worlds, and nobody thought much of it. After all, sleep disorders were common no matter where you were in the galaxy.

Today's classes were literature, sciences, and philosophy.

Sister Eata, the literature professor, walked in, the hems of her blue cotton robes of the Theclan order lightly fluttering in the morning breeze; a simple garment, much like the rest of the Kayan attire. The Anchorites of Thecla also went barefoot winter and summer and wore a neck band that was made of raw wool. The purpose of this ugly and unusual accessory was to give slight discomfort to remind the wearer of the sufferings of those they served. Theclans were Healers. Since they had to be proficient in other avenues of knowledge as well as Healing, the sisters also volunteered to teach, like the brothers. Between the willingness of both orders to fill the ranks, the Academy did not want for professors.

"I am going to assume everyone has done the readings," she said after slamming the pile of marked assignments on her desk.

"Just to remind you: last week, we talked about how there were ancient texts warning against people like Haydar and their potential dangers. Today, we are going to examine the cryptic messages and hidden meanings in poetry."

Sister Eata retrieved the box containing her colored chalks.

"Any ideas?" she asked, holding a long piece of yellow chalk.

"I think these were written by those who had visited Kaya from other worlds," Andrew said.

"There is no proof of that," Elgar said. Always the voice of reason.

"Not that we would know it," Andrew replied. "The aliens would not be able to cross the Ambit to visit Aqui, even if they somehow managed to make it to Kaya."

"Let's suppose there were aliens." Elgar geared up for an argument. "If they make it to Kaya, the Ambit might not hold them back."

"I don't think so," Andrew said.

"Settle down," Sister Eata interrupted. "We are not talking about spacemen. Who is going summarize the text for me?"

Leena took up the challenge. "The ancient texts talked about how the seven marks were all perfected in each Kayan. Before Haydar's infamous experience centuries ago disrupted the order, everybody possessed all seven marks in its utmost level. There were no tiers to measure the level of one's mark. Depiction of mark mastery and a perfect Kaya were the main theme of this work."

James could not imagine being a tier seven Healer or a Riser. Superman would look like a mere human on Kaya.

Some of the students speculated that maybe the marks remained perfect outside the Ambit.

Most did not dare to hope.

The Ambit, the shimmering transparent boundary that formed an impenetrable cage around Aqui, came up when Haydar's hunger for power went wrong. The ingredients and resulting reaction of his experiment became airborne, infected everyone in its blast radius, and took their marks away. Not only were countless people instantly incinerated, but an unknown and unexplainable phenomenon occurred, trapping the residents of the region called Aqui within its boundary.

Nothing could get in. Nothing could get out.

If you tried to leave, the Ambit transported you to another random part of Aqui. James remembered the first time he went ambiting with Leo. During one of the idle days on the beach, they decided the make the hike to the closest

Ambit point. The shimmer of their cage reflected the light at certain points like a thin layer of water. The boundary that held James and all those he knew on Kaya captive was kind enough to give the illusion of freedom with its transparency.

Ambiting was easy. It required two simple ingredients, a body and a giant magical, mostly invisible dome. Check and check. To make sure that they would come out at the same place, James and Leo linked their arms a few inches away from the shimmer and jumped forward.

A strange sensation of falling and diving into ice old water enveloped them, and then the warm air welcomed them again. Instead of the hills that led down to the beach, they found themselves on the other side of Aqui covered with thick forestry, having to walk or hitch hike for nearly fifty miles. Still, it was much better than exiting out in the middle of the sea. Because of accidental ambitings, the fishermen had to patrol the seas along the Ambit once a day to make sure nobody was stranded in the sea.

The reason why many people tried ambiting only once in their lives was not hard to guess. It was the inescapable proof that they were all prisoners inside this shimmery dome. Instead of constantly being reminded that they would have to spend their whole lives in a giant circle that stretched for about two hundred and fifty miles, the people of Aqui did their best to ignore their golden cage.

James pulled his thoughts back to the present and joined the heated conversation about the upsides and downsides of living in a world where everyone could walk through walls, all had super speed and super strength, and everyone died of old age.

But human nature was human nature, even on Kaya. The people of perfect marks were not able to prevent Haydar from trying to weaken others so that he could be the most powerful above all. The marks of millions of Kayans could neither foresee nor stop the devastating bomb Haydar's experiment had become.

James was not as optimistic as his friends, maybe because the other half of his life had witnessed the imperfectness of human beings.

Sister Eata did not interrupt the arguments, letting imaginations and at times pessimism run amok. Before the class was over, she handed out new parchments to read for the week and told them that there was a solution to every problem. She enjoyed being cryptic.

Sciences and philosophy were not nearly as interesting as the literature class. Talking about mating habits of various bugs or rules of rhetoric lost its appeal for James in approximately thirty seconds. Sister Elwyn, the science professor, was always overly excited about her subject matter, while Brother Erfyl, the philosophy professor, managed to compose sentence after sentence without any change in facial expression or intonation. Trying to imitate Brother Erfyl was a popular pastime activity at the Inn.

Lunch brought a little more excitement than usual. He served himself buttered, fluffy rolls and steamed vegetables and settled next to Elgar.

"Look at the misguided youth. I think adrenaline drowned out their common sense," Elgar said, still scribbling on his notebook.

James watched as one of the Goners elbowed Claire in the ribs. Clearly, their plan was not thought through well, because Claire happened to be a T5 Riser and a little cranky that day. Not a good combination.

Goners were the youth who turned somewhat suicidal during puberty because of feelings of entrapment and hopelessness about having to live in the Ambit. They were reckless and violent, and many would get injured or die as they rushed from one thrill-seek to another.

James did not have much sympathy for them, because life in Aqui, trapped or not, was still a piece of paradise. Just like any other Aquite, he felt claustrophobic at times when he laid down and watched the Amber shimmer a few miles above, but the hopelessness had never overtaken him. Maybe it was his weird luxury of having to live on Earth which made him appreciate life on Kaya in return. A blessing in a thick disguise.

Claire would not respond to their harassment normally, but she had been agitated for the past few days, since the last family she had, her aunt, had passed away recently. She was in need of an outlet, and the Goners had provided one on a silver platter.

Seeing that things were about to get out of hand, Leo quickly walked over to Claire's side. With two Risers like Leo and Claire, and not one among the Goners, James knew that it was not going to be a pretty sight, if Sadwen and his crew did not back up.

They did not.

"You know, the Goners aren't bad kids, they are just really stupid," James said, mouth full of dinner rolls.

"Well, the thoughtlessness that comes with stupidity is bad. Sometimes really bad," Elgar said and pointed at the unfolding scene with his pencil. "Case in point."

He was right, this was clearly one of those times, because Sadwen pushed Claire back when she shoved his arm out of the vicinity of her ribs. Leo had already reached out to stop Eoban and Fina. As far as James knew, Sadwen was a T6 Waver and a T3 Strider, impressive but not good enough to take down a strong Riser. With ease, Claire lifted

Sadwen who was at least fifty pounds heavier than her. She was mad, and he had a mean look on his face. Again, not a good combination.

Wavers could move water at will. Depending on the strength and skill of the performer, waving could be one of the deadliest of the marks. Sadwen, even though not a killer, did not mind hurting others to bring some measly amount of excitement to his life. James watched the hot lentil soup rise to the air unbeknownst to Claire. But before Sadwen scorched her, Elgar's hand made a Waving motion guiding the boiling soup back into the copper cauldron.

"Just leveling the playing field," Elgar said and turned the page on his math book. All of this took place in a matter of seconds, which was long enough for Lord Ywi to storm in the dining hall through the kitchen wall and take all five of them to detention. Elgar was far enough from the action to be spared from Lord Ywi's extra creative detentions.

Leo and Claire were nowhere to be seen for the rest of the afternoon. Neither did Sadwen nor his reckless bunch show up at the fruit orchards. It must have been a particularly creative day for their headmaster.

Lord Ywi taught the arts classes and ran the Academy. He was the headmaster whom everyone admired and feared at the same time, personable enough when sketching the portrait of one of the students perfectly or playing any of Kaya's beautiful instruments flawlessly, but outside of the classroom, he ruled with an iron fist. In addition to his strong triple marks, he was a genius educator who always came up with the best punishments for unruly behavior.

To everyone's surprise, Leo and Claire showed up at dinner in rather good spirits. As they gobbled up the chicken noodle soup Elgar had made after work, the story of Sadwen, Eoban, and Fina trying to learn how to knit a scarf all afternoon made the whole kitchen burst into laughter. That was their punishment, and punished they were. Leo and Claire on the other hand, were tasked to write a five-parchment essay on how to help those who lose hope and purpose. Sure it was annoying, but it seemed like Leo and Claire enjoyed spending the afternoon together despite having to find ways to benefit the Goners. They both seemed a bit lighter on their feet.

Wrapped in the laughter of his friends, James thought it was a good day. Belly full, arms sore from reaching up to pick peaches all afternoon, sleep was more than welcome.

Day 3: Earth

Maggie's sketch book was safely nestled against her chest like a teddy bear. Only a few valuable things deserved a place in this transitionary life of theirs. They didn't haul shopping carts or big rucksacks around, mostly because, both James and Maggie knew —and hoped— that homelessness was just a phase in their future of endless wander. While James made things happen, Maggie imagined the things that needed to happen.

James' only precious belonging was an old, heart-shaped locket that belonged to his grandmother, hiding a tiny picture of his family, taken well before the unbearable screaming and drinking began. Even though at age sixteen, he was much more realistic, some might even say pessimistic, than before, he still held a glimmer of hope that his parents would one day break out of the prison of their own making.

Childhood images of playing with his little brothers in the backyard, drinking watered-down juice and the occasional ice tea during hot summer days had started to fade. Bright sunny days and their happy family of five seemed more like a mirage than memories from a time long gone. All that remained was the oppression of the fateful day his baby brother was run over right outside of their house by a teenager who thought speed limits were for losers.

Five-year-old Jake was instantly killed, leaving behind a family in ruins. His mother soon succumbed to drinking and smoking, even though she had never had a cigarette in her life before and only drank occasionally with friends. Guilt and what-ifs overwhelmed her. She was tending the flower garden when Jake rushed to the street after a run-away ball. As the car that changed their lives forever turned the corner much faster than it should have, James' mother was too far and too late to save her baby. All she could do was to hold his little body as he passed on to the next life.

His mother kept asking herself the same questions over and over again. Why was she so far away? Why didn't she see the ball rolling into the street? Why was she so slow? Why wasn't she paying attention? Soon after the heart-breaking funeral, his mom ripped out all the flowers she took care of for more than a decade and became a recluse. For the first few months, all she did was clean the house and fix dinner for the family, most days without uttering a single word. Then, the walls of her bedroom became the only things that she talked to. After that, more and more empty bottles piled on the red floral carpet of her bedroom.

The smell of cheesy potato soup was forever replaced with the rank of neglect and cheap sour wine.

His dad grieved by becoming a workaholic. The man took every overtime he could get and volunteered for any out-of-the-city opportunity as if he did not have a family.

Maybe he didn't.

All that was left after Jake's death were two boys, a woman, and a man that happened to be living under the same roof. The family was gone long ago.

Jesse was eight years old, and James twelve when Jake left the Earth for good.

Jesse was a smart boy who enjoyed playing football and proudly declared math as his favorite subject at school. He didn't play anything that involved a ball after Jake, but he studied harder, read more, and rarely talked. Sometimes, James would hear him cry in his room. Two brothers became strangers.

James, on the other hand, stopped enjoying anything related to school. Reading remained the only thing that would keep his mind from constantly wandering towards Jake's direction. He read anything he could find. The atmosphere inside the house had become so stifling that when weather permitted he would spend hours outside, reading at the picnic table, going inside just for natural urges and food. Nobody seemed to care about anybody in the Knox household anymore.

It was a dark and unhappy place.

A year after Jake's passing, his mother and father exchanged the silent treatment for screaming matches. They fought every time his father was home. Every single time. Jake was gone, happiness was gone, and now peace was gone. James was fourteen years old.

One day, he took the bus to Seattle and never went back.

It was that easy.

Maggie stirred under the space blanket and opened her eyes at the pace of a turtle.

"It cannot be seen, cannot be felt,
Cannot be heard, cannot be smelt.
It lies behind stars and under hills,
And empty holes it fills.
It comes first and follows after,
Ends life, kills laughter."

James loved the riddles Maggie found and memorized just for him. Even when it took a while, he would always find the answer. She would never yield or give up, and day after day, there was a new riddle that she found or conjured up from the depths of her amazing memory. The day he couldn't find the answer before midnight would be the day he promised to give his mother a call.

"You know, I'm a Tolkien fan. How could you possibly think I wouldn't know the answer?"

"Everyone remembers the one with teeth, I thought, maybe you forgot about this one. Since you are such an old man."

James threw his pillow, made from an old sweater, at Maggie.

"It's the dark!"

She giggled and rubbed her eyes to shake off the sleep. Just like every morning, they were hungry again. A large cup of hot coffee wouldn't hurt either.

Alas, it was Monday, and nobody liked Mondays. Even the charities that passed out hot coffees and breakfast sandwiches didn't like Mondays. James and Maggie usually spent this unpleasant day at the library.

Contrary to general opinion, libraries were not boring places, especially since the dawn of the world wide web. Most public libraries now had computers connected to the Internet. These were the devices people like James and Maggie used to participate in the ever-growing cyber world. For obvious reasons, they didn't Tweet or Instagram, and they still checked their Facebook pages, but never posted anything. It was a simple way of staying informed about their family and friends. Not that there was much to learn.

Also, these book-infested buildings were wonderful places for people-watching. The characters in a public library were more colorful than one might expect. James and Maggie enjoyed the company of the usual suspects like the green-haired woman who read all the newspapers every day and the old man who was adamant about learning C plus plus for some crazy reason. Their oddness became familiar and comforting.

Then, there were kids who threatened to trash the entire floor that was devoted to children's books and the play area. James liked watching toddlers play. They reminded him of Jake who loved hiding behind the shelves, driving their mother crazy.

Back then, his mom hated it when her children were out of sight. James had been gone for two years now. Did she care?

He shook his head to erase the thoughts about his mother, because nowadays thinking about his family brought nothing more than misery and a longing for the happy days. Simple toddler watching was more pleasant.

Another reason the library had become one of their regular spots was, of course, their love of imaginary worlds. Reading was self-medication for both. They traveled from one adventure to the next in the pages of a novel, and the hardships of their own lives became a little more manageable.

Maggie worked on finding new riddles and learning the latest coloring techniques from the all-knowing Internet. James perused a few fantasy novels. The riddle from that morning had stirred his mind about Tolkien.

They even had two slices of pizza, apples, and small containers of milk that were left over from a program that catered to younger children.

That evening was Maggie's turn to get dinner. They left late in the afternoon to case a new store, so that neither they nor the cashier would get in trouble for the periodically-missing food.

There would be no Fritos tonight.

Day 3: Kaya

"I could not be more ready for a lazy weekend," Leo said and plopped himself on the chair. The clothes and towels covering the chair did not seem to bother him.

James had just opened his eyes.

"You're sitting on my underwear," James said.

Leo jumped. "You've got to clean this place once in a while. That's just disgusting!"

He picked up the heavy chair with one hand and turned it upside down, a messy pile of towels and clothes falling to the floor. James had not mopped the floor for over a month.

"There, now you need to get your pretty hands dirty," Leo said and sat back on the chair with a satisfied smile. "Get out of the bed; we have some obligations to fulfill."

Leo was right. The weather had been getting warmer, so the plan for the Fiveday was to hike up the stream not far from the Academy and go swimming where the weak creek formed a sizable pool for all five of them to enjoy. There was nothing like a lazy weekend spent with friends.

Kayans worked four days and rested two days. Short work week and long rest days were even more important in Aqui, because people needed to be given as many opportunities as possible to forget that they were, after all, living in a giant cage. Thankfully, the peninsula they were all trapped in provided ample amount of scenic views and adventures to kill time and increase the endorphin levels.

Especially on a sunny day like this, nobody even wanted to talk about the Ambit.

"I thought I'd have a little time to read before we left," James said, stepping on the cold marble floor barefoot.

Leo grabbed the book from his nightstand and waved it in the air. "Enough with the fantasy stuff, come back to reality."

"Oh, because the reality is filled with fun people like yourself?" James said.

"People like myself are the only ones who would put up with you," Leo said as he threw James a shirt. "Now, get ready."

After ample amount of nagging, Leo and James found themselves in the kitchen. Joan and Elgar were heatedly discussing something over the plates of what seemed to be cold scrambled eggs.

James grabbed half a dozen of eggs from the basket that the picker of the day brought from the chicken coop at the back of the Inn. After making some cheesy and still warm scrambled eggs, he piled some on Leo's plate and settled next to Elgar, whose toasts James unashamedly stole.

They were still talking about the texts assigned during Sister Eata's class.

Elgar, the only T6 Waver James knew, continued so excited that his seal medal bounced on his chest:

"But, all over the literature, there are prophesies and directions about how to restore the balance. Don't you think Haydar's experiment upset the balance?"

Joan was not as enthusiastic about restoring anything. It sounded very Jedi-like. James was sure she would have made fun of Elgar if the legend of Star Wars had reached Kaya.

"Yes, yes, Haydar was definitely out of line, but how could people who lived thousands of years ago know about something that was going to happen long after they were dead and provide the means to undo it?"

Elgar was not persuaded, "I am sure our nature did not change much since then. More than likely, they were the ones who put up a mechanism or a spell that keeps the Ambit up to curb possible contagions."

As he chewed a bite from yesterday's bread, James put in his two cents. "If that's the case, there must be a failsafe device."

The unexpected contribution startled both.

"Well," Joan said, "if the Ambit were devised by the Fathers of Kaya, instead of simply being another terrible side effect of the Dispersal, I am sure they would have given us a way to get out of this prison after so many centuries." She pushed the eggs around with her fork. "It's kind of cruel."

James couldn't help but agree. There should be a way out of this glorified stockade, but for now he was content with his life in Aqui. Since the day he woke up in two worlds, he always preferred his days on Kaya to those on Earth. The relative ease of life in Aqui with friends, warm food, and lack of drama made James wish that time went by faster in Seattle and slower here. Even though he occasionally wondered what the rest of Kaya looked like, the Ambit never bothered him, as it did the other Aquites, especially the younger ones. His own friends were no exception to this.

Elgar agreed that an invisible cage was indeed a cruel punishment for a crime committed four hundred years ago by someone who was not related to anyone in Aqui.

"You are right, maybe it's cruel. But maybe they didn't think it would take this long for us to figure out how to take the Ambit down. Maybe it can only be taken down from the inside."

"That's a lot of maybes," said Joan, clearly tired of talking about this dead-end subject.

But Elgar was relentless. "We should talk to Brother Aelred."

Joan's eyes shot wide open, "Are you crazy? He hasn't seen, let alone talked to, anyone for decades except a few brothers in the castle. What makes you think that he'll come out of his recluse for you?"

"Just a thought," Elgar said, shoulders slumped.

Leo chuckled at the suggestion of meeting the Abbot. "That would be a cheerful conversation with one of the brothers. They are gonna think you lost your mind reading all those science books."

In response, Elgar gave him a second shower with the ice cold water in the pitcher.

But Leo and Joan were right - it was impossible to get an audience with the man.

Brother Aelred was the Abbot of the castle monastery that contained all the books, parchments, and documents that were saved from the blast. The Dispersal was how the Aquites referred to the explosion of Haydar's experiment, because that was when the virus or the contagion was spread throughout Aqui, and possibly the rest of Kaya. Nobody knew what happened behind the Ambit.

There was so much destruction after the explosion that most of the books and valuable documents were eradicated, in addition to the loss of most of Aqui's scientific minds. Innovation and development had been slow as manpower diminished through the years. Secondary infertility was another rampant side effect of the Dispersal.

The Maelite order, to which Brother Aelred and all the brothers who teach at the Academy belonged, preserved and duplicated by hand the books and parchments that were salvaged. Originals and rare documents were still kept at the castle monastery, which sit on the skirts of the Zita mountain range. It was called the Castle of Kaans, named after the title of the ancient kings.

Years before James' birth on Kaya, Brother Aelred had decided to spend the rest of his days in contemplation and had been living in his quarters in the castle ever since. Other than the two brothers who helped run the monastery, no one had talked to him for decades. He had to be around sixty years old now.

Brother Aelred remained to be somewhat of a legend since he was the only known T7 Waver and also a T7 Strider. James wondered what he did with all that power as he lived his days behind cold stone walls.

Anyway, this was not a day to worry about depressing things like magical boundaries or contemplative monks. It was a happy day to enjoy the cold and refreshing waters that came down the mountains.

They headed out as soon as Claire and Leo, who had joined the breakfast group during Elgar and Joan's heated discussion, finished eating. While Leo washed and dried plates, Godric walked in with a few books tucked under his arm. He declined the offer to join them in the spring pools, since he had to work on his Seer test that he was taking next week.

The five of them left for the Zita Mountains, outlining the region of Aqui in the north. The magnificent range was so high that you could always see snow at the peaks, summer or winter. James didn't think it would be possible to go over them even if the Ambit did not spit you out somewhere else.

45

You would have to travel to the East, where the mountains leveled down, or to the West where the heights yielded to the sea. There was only one passage that led through the mountains, and even that was too treacherous.

The Castle of Kaans was built on the skirts of the Zita for a good defensive position. The kings of old, Kaans, resided there as the army lived off the arable lands of Aqui. Nowadays, the castle hosted the quiet and studious monks of the Maelite order.

As they hiked up toward the spring pool, James and his friends could see the Western tower of the Castle. After almost two hours of walking through the narrow and at times dangerous mountain path that was formed by hikers and traveling monks over the years, they finally reached the beautifully clear and refreshingly crisp pool. The source where the water seeped through the mountains was surrounded by rocks that could be easily climbed and used to jump into the pool below.

The five of them spent hours climbing, jumping, swimming, and drying in the sun. It was one of those rare days that the troubles and worries of life seemed distant and blissfully out of reach. Time became a useless tool in the midst of fun and friendship. When it was time to head back to the Inn, nobody had the energy to hike. Thankfully, they were young, and it was downhill. Leo took the lead, and Elgar brought up the rear.

The Kayan sun had been lost behind the mountains long before they finally arrived at the Inn. Godric had already made dinner for them. They piled in the kitchen, exhausted, sun-kissed, and starving. The scent of Godric's herbal flatbread, seared beef, and sour plums made James' stomach groan with yearning.

During the scrumptious and simple dinner, the cook of the day told them about the pages he had to memorize to pass his Seer test to become T6. As a strong seer, he should have gathered that the only thing his friends were interested in at that moment was food and sleep.

They were soon satisfied on both accounts.

Day 4: Earth

"Alright! Who is ready for some serious shower action?" Maggie yelled rather than said, as soon as James stirred.

"Your attention to personal hygiene is just heartbreaking," James said.

"It is not easy to maintain this gorgeous complexion. Also, my hair stinks," Maggie replied.

"You could say that again!" James said.

"At least I am not making Mrs. Jackson hold her nose every time you pass." Maggie threw his boots. One of them landed on his face. James picked them up and started to get ready for their day of cleanliness, homemade food, and television.

"I am so glad that we bumped into your cousin. It's so good to exfoliate once in a while. Homeless life is hard on one's pores," Maggie said, flicking her curly black hair with the drama of a bad actress.

It hadn't been long since James and Maggie had bumped into his cousin Sarah during a daily panhandling session. Before James could make a quick getaway, Sarah caught up with them. He did not want anyone in the family to know where he was, but Sarah promised not to tell anyone, if they accepted her help. That was when Maggie and James had started going to Sarah's apartment, which she shared with two other college students. They had three hours every Tuesday morning for showers and breakfast. These homeless teenagers never forgot to grab the lunch bags and the cash left for them on the kitchen table. It was the only time during the week that the apartment would be empty.

Only then, Maggie and James could enjoy the comforts of indoor plumbing in peace.

They both appreciated Sarah's generous and selfless gesture every week. James knew that she had to work hard to make it through college. Every penny or meal she provided for them probably meant that she had to work more hours or spend less for herself. She never tried to persuade him to return home and always kept her silence and distance. Their only communication was the concise notes left on the kitchen table.

"I think it's time Sarah bought a shampoo that is more friendly to my hair," Maggie said. Her hair was puffed and frizzled from its weekly treatment of shampoo and conditioner.

"Beggars can't be choosers," James replied.

"But look at this!" Maggie said and fluffed her hair even more. It was true. She had a magnificent mane. James couldn't keep his chuckle in.

"I am glad you find my girly problems entertaining. Do you have any idea how hard it is for a black girl to deal with her hair?"

No, James didn't have a clue.

"I'll have you know that there is a whole industry devoted to it!" Maggie continued with mock indignation. She whipped her hair in the air for effect and left the room. That mane needed to be tamed.

They left Sarah's place smelling like lavender and dressed in clean clothes. The short mornings they spent at this small and humble student apartment was the only reason James and Maggie retained some level of hygiene, and they were eternally grateful for it.

As usual, James recounted everything that happened in Aqui to Maggie in detail, including Elgar and Joan's discussion about the Ambit. Maggie agreed with Elgar. However, unlike James, she was excited over the possibility of taking the Ambit down.

"I don't think it's magical," Maggie said and took a bite off the golden apple Sarah had packed for them. "I mean, there is no evidence that Kaya is any more magical than Earth."

James was not so sure. "How about all the marks? Some of them could easily be called magical. Just because nobody carries wands or wears pointed hats does not mean that there is not some form of magic involved."

Maggie rolled her eyes in the way that only young teenage girls can. "You have been reading all these fantasy books way too long. Your brain is mushed."

"My brain is just fine, young lady. But, for the sake argument, let's say you are right. Although I'd have hard time explaining Waving scientifically, or Seeing."

"I've been thinking about that," Maggie replied. The apple core flew in the air towards a nearby trash can.

"It could be that Wavers are able to manipulate water, because most of our bodies are made of water. Maybe, they can somehow use the attraction between the molecules. Seeing is probably easier to explain. They might be able to sense and interpret brain waves."

James always knew that she was smart. Hearing her talk about things that are beyond comprehension as if they were matters of fact made him proud of her. But, just like any good older brother, he would not let it go. "How about Striding?"

"That one is problematic indeed," Maggie yielded.

"You should have seen Lord Ywi walk into the dining hall through the kitchen wall as if it was thin air. Even after having lived on Kaya for so long, it is still so hard to wrap my head around."

"That's it!" Maggie jumped in excitement and started to walk backwards, waving her hands. "Maybe, they have a way of adjusting their own density, like us walking through the air. The air is still there, but we are just too dense for it stand against us. Ha! I told you we could find some explanation for every one of the marks."

She took a deep breath and continued nonstop, "So, if we can explain things with our limited earthly minds, the ancient people of Kaya must have been able to conjure up some tech that would put up a containment system like the Ambit, and then install a failsafe device to take it down."

"But..." She seemed to be talking to herself rather than James. "Because nothing can come in or go out, only people from the inside can decide whether or not the threat was eliminated, and then they could take the boundary down."

Even in his big brother shoes, James could see the logic in Maggie's ongoing monologue about the Ambit. She was right. There was no reason to suggest that Kaya was a magical land. It bore remarkable similarities to Earth, like sentient beings exactly like humans other than the marking abilities. The plant and animal life were essentially the same, give or take a few. For all intents and purposes, Kaya was not any more enchanted than Earth. Lack of magic and fairies also meant that the Ambit was nothing more than a glorified Berlin Wall that would come down eventually.

For the first time since he woke up in Aqui, James was excited over the possibility of living in a different part of Kaya.

The thought of freedom was captivating.

He could not wait until he talked to Elgar and Leo.

Day 4: Kaya

Sixdays were always lazy. Unlike Fivedays, James and his friends almost never planned anything for the Kayan version of Sundays. It was the last day of the week and they all either hung around the common room or took a walk in the woods when the weather was agreeable. Today was a lounge on the fluffy cushions kind of day.

After finishing his math assignment, James took a long warm shower in the marble laden bathroom assigned to the boys. He needed to work on his Pacing today, but first things first. Shower, breakfast, and then Elgar. Nothing should come before breakfast. Except shower.

He touched one of the indoor plants nestled in a big ornate clay pot in the corner of the hallway as he passed it. When a Reader touched plants on Kaya, he could feel the life within them more vividly. Being aware of something other than yourself was like a slight electric shock. It was, of course, much stronger with animals.

Godric was eating while he studied in the kitchen. James mumbled a quiet good morning for the sake of politeness, because he did not want to disturb his friend. Mark tests were one of the most important things in the Academy. Everyone's marks would solidify around the time they turned seventeen, some earlier, some a bit later, but once you reached your eighteenth birthday, your marks would remain in the same tier for the rest of your life.

Each Aquite was born possessing some tier of all marks. These extraordinary abilities were similar to senses or artistic talents. But regardless of the tier you were born with, you had to work hard to develop and control these extraordinary gifts. Nobody knew what marks they possessed before they reached puberty. Once in a while you would see an occasional child Waving or Striding involuntarily, but they had no control and usually would not be able to duplicate the experience.

James was a T1 Strider, which meant that he might be able to walk through a wall to save his life, but he did not count on it. If the tier of a mark was below three, it would be nearly impossible to develop. It was possible, but extremely hard to improve T3 marks. T4, T5, and T6 were the only ones that were assigned to be developed.

The Initiation of Youth determined the tiers of their marks. Professors from the Academy tested and eventually allocated every child two or sometimes three marks to study and develop. Then, the Minister of Education presented each child a seal medal, rectangle for two marks and triangle for three. This way, everyone's gift was known.

James touched his own triangular seal medal, aged metal branded with Pacer, Seer, and Reader seals. It was hung around his neck with a length of twine cord. One of the few private possessions people owned and cherished in Aqui. Everything else was borrowed and passed on.

If you worked hard and used your abilities often enough to improve your control, it was possible to step up a tier, but laziness and lack of practice meant that your senses and handle on the mark would dull, and you would be stuck in your initial tier. Some were comfortable with that. James knew that Godric was not. So after breakfast, he left him alone in the kitchen with his books.

Holding the big hand-written book titled "Chronicles of Ancient Fathers" in one hand and a steaming cup of chay sweetened with honey in the other, James pushed open the common room door with his shoulder.

Even though it was getting rather warm outside, big rooms in stone buildings still needed some fire to break the chill of the long night. The morning blaze, undoubtedly built by Ebru when she woke with the birds, had already turned into orange with only a little crackling. It was perfect for roasting chestnuts, but there were no chestnuts on Kaya. No coffee and no chestnuts. Nothing is perfect.

He settled on one of the giant cushions haphazardly thrown next to the hearth. There were no enormous couches in Aqui, but rather big, soft cushions that are placed either on the floor or on wooden divans made up for the lack of La-Z-Boy technology. Not that he currently enjoyed the fluffiness of a couch in Seattle, anyway.

Before James finished his tea while reading the big tome, Elgar walked in carrying a couple of books and a handcrafted wooden box that contained the Bakhita pieces — a game similar to chess.

Elgar put his books and the Bakhita on the table in front of the window and settled down to read as he nibbled on lemon drops out of a bowl on the table. He hadn't noticed that there was someone else in the room.

Before long, Leo and Joan walked in laughing and eating freshly-baked pastries. How did James miss the cinnamony goodness while he was in the kitchen? He got to his feet and snatched the extra piece of pastry Leo was carrying in his left hand before his best friend knew what was happening.

"Give it back!" Leo bellowed as he chased James around the room, but by the time he caught him, the pastry was already on the way to James' digestive organs.

"Where did you get these?" asked the thief, clearly not satisfied with one piece.

Leo threw himself on the divan, a little out of breath. "Ebru just took them out of the ground oven. We are gonna have them for lunch. What are you doing in the common room so early anyway? I thought you were gonna practice your Pacing."

"I need to talk to Elgar when he returns back to our world. Actually, I'm glad you are here, too."

"It sounds serious." Leo mocked James' hand gestures, but still moved to the table where Elgar was lost in his book.

James wished Claire was there, too, but they would have to fill her in later. Once everyone took a seat around the scratched but still sturdy wooden table, and Elgar finally came back to the room from the depths of his imagination, James cleared his throat.

"Last night, I thought about what Elgar and Joan were talking about during breakfast." He hated to take credit for Maggie's ideas, but since no one on Kaya knew about his double life, Maggie would have to go uncredited for the time being.

Elgar shortly explained the discussion about the possibility of taking the Ambit down to a confused-looking Leo.

In the past, James and Leo had talked about one day being able to explore the rest of Kaya. When they studied the atlas that mapped out the rest of their world, the continent and oceans surrounding their invisible cage was not any closer than Earth. As far as they were concerned, life outside of the Ambit was as implausible as life on another planet. At least one of them knew better.

"I think, the Ambit is just a weird machine to quarantine the contamination of the Dispersal," James said. No comprehension dawned on anyone's faces.

"I mean, if it's just a device to control the damage caused by Haydar, once the threat is gone, it should be taken down. Right?" James said.

Some wheels started to turn in some of the heads.

"Buuuttt...Only the people on the inside would know what is going on." James said. Very. Very. Slowly.

"Yes!" Elgar said with wide open bright eyes.

"Yes! That means there should be a way for *us* to take it down."

"Give the man a candy," Leo said, handing Elgar one from the bowl.

Elgar bowed and accepted his reward.

In their history or science classes, the phenomenon that made the Ambit remain intact and invincible for so long was either declared inexplicable or sometimes even magical. James never wanted to believe that Kaya was an enchanted world, but it was easy to blame it on magic when reason fell short. Now, after having talked to Maggie, he knew that the Ambit had become a puzzle to be solved, not a spell to be bound under. For the first time since he woke up on Kaya, James Knox wanted to be free from the golden cage. This newfound desire fueled his passion.

Joan was not ready to jump on the bandwagon just yet. "Let's assume everything you said about the Ambit and a failsafe device is right. How would we take it down without having the slightest clue about its mechanism?"

"Whoever put up the Ambit must have left instructions on how to take it down," Leo answered.

"Yes, but where?" Joan asked, continuing to play the party-pooper.

Where, indeed.

None of them had any idea about the location of such valuable information. The region of Aqui was only a few hundred miles long, but it still was too big of an area to look for something that could be as small as a book or a box. Despite the gloom Joan's realistic questions brought to the discussion, they were all exhilarated about the prospect of seeing what lay beyond the beautiful lands they grew up in.

From then on, the conversation swiftly turned into where they would go or what they would do if their pleasant captivity came to an end. Even Joan had a few ideas about traveling Kaya and learning different Healing techniques. As much as she loved the sisters of Thecla, the endless possibilities of acquiring knowledge from those who had been Healing longer than the sisters was too appealing to dismiss. At the end of the hour, they decided to at least explore Maggie's idea that had managed to travel through galaxies.

They agreed on reading anything and everything about the Ambit and the Dispersal over the next few days. Leo kindly volunteered to debrief Claire about their discussion.

Of course, everything would have to wait until after a lunch of delicious cinnamon goodness baked by the mother of the Inn, Ebru. James ate six pastries with fresh goat's milk. He needed his energy.

Out of all three of his strong marks, Pacing was the only one that came natural to him. He didn't know why, maybe because he was a good runner even on earth. Before he decided to leave school and family for his hopefully-temporary escape, he ran almost every day, even when the track team did not practice. Jake's passing had put many things on hold, including the pleasure of running. Here on

Kaya. Pacing was the way James unwound, processed his thoughts, and explored Aqui.

He remembered the rush of energy and newness when his marks were first unlocked about four years ago. The desire to pace everywhere instead of walking like civilized people was overwhelming. Unfortunately, using your marks unnecessarily was considered rude and impertinent. One of the reasons the Goners were disliked so much was that they practiced their marks frivolously. Older Pacers informed him that the temptation to pace to the bathroom decreased significantly over time. It was a relief to hear that he would not be condemned to a Forrest Gump style of life for long.

Fresh, crisp spring air filled his lungs on the porch as rosemary bushes brought him a fragrant greeting. James the Pacer bounced back and forth on his heels, did a few simple stretches, and took off without ceremony. He was gone. High-tier Pacing was as close as one could get to flying. It was a feeling unlike any other.

The wind deafened him, and his vision blurred slightly. Speed and sheer exhilaration made his heart beat faster and faster. He could lose contact with the ground any moment, but gravity was stubborn.

Four years ago, when his marks flooded his body and mind, he could run thirty miles per hour. Now, he was about to hit fifty miles for almost three hours, above average for a T6 Pacer, who was close to T7. The desire to perfect this mark filled his whole being. He ran and ran until his whole body begged him to put some more pastries and sausages in his belly.

"You always overestimate your stamina, James," Ebru said. She was clipping pieces of rosemary for the evening roast when James returned.

"I know," James replied, "I'm always a mile off. One of these days..."

"One of these days," Ebru said and handed him a boiled egg. She always kept boiled eggs and apples in the pockets of her apron.

On Sixdays, Ebru and her husband prepared a marvelous meal for the residents of the Inn. They all ate together after sunset in the big dining hall located right below the spacious common room. As soon as he crossed the threshold of the Inn, James could smell deliciousness and once again felt grateful for this current family.

Inn families volunteered for at least three years to look after and oversee the youth whom fate brought, one way or another, to the House of Sevgi. Most of the families shared the vision of caring for orphans, much like the first founder and builder of the Inn, Sister Sevgi of the Theclans.

The current family had three members: Ebru, her husband Arin, and their five-year-old daughter Oya. Inn families were charged with guiding the residents so that they could learn how to live independently as self-sufficient members of Aquite society when the time came to leave the Inn at age eighteen. Ebru and Arin had evolved into good friends and older siblings over the last year. James and Leo sought their wisdom and advice relating to school work and, on occasion, troubles with friends. Teenagers were teenagers everywhere, and some liked to cause trouble, while others tried to avoid it. During one of those vexing occasions, Arin had been apt at promoting cool-headedness.

Ebru was a free-spirited Reader, who spent most of her days running around with Oya, teaching her about flowers and playing with various forest critters. She was an excellent cook, when she wanted to cook, but her desire for culinary endeavors was temperamental. To everyone's delight, this Sixday was a day she didn't mind spending in the kitchen. James smelled her famous irresistible roast that was baked for almost a whole day in an underground oven, encased in a dish that looked like a big clay ball. Roasted potatoes, rosemary parsnip, and some glazed peaches accompanied the mouth-watering roast.

Busy clanking of cutlery told James that Ebru's all-day labor was appreciated. As they enjoyed some watered wine to wash down the meat in the hum of the background noise, James started to dream about his bed and that lovely fluffy comforter.

Day 5: Earth

Maggie was gone. It was unlike her not to be watching over him while his consciousness was still on Kaya. He peeked out of their paper shelter without leaving his mattress, which was also made of layers of cardboard and tarp. There she was, talking to their neighbor.

Since Mrs. Jackson, their elderly neighbor and friend, did not have a nice cousin who let her shower, Mrs. Jackson looked like she hadn't been to the vicinity of a bath for a long time. Even though she always made sure to keep her face clean either with rain water or baby wipes, the state of her clothes gave away her current living situation. It was safe to guess that Mrs. Jackson was in her late sixties, and had probably spent most of her life on the streets. She looked like she was always cold. Maybe that was the reason that, summer or winter, she was always dressed in layers upon layers of mismatched clothing. Mind you, one did not follow the current fashion when one's clothes were donated or picked up from who knows where. Her signature piece of attire was the wool-lined winter hat with ear flaps. It was made for someone with a bigger head, but Mrs. Jackson cherished that comfy warm headgear more than any other piece of clothing she owned.

Maggie handed Mrs. Jackson something and skipped back towards James. It was refreshing to see someone skipping in a dark concrete street, especially one that hosted a few of the homeless of Seattle along with their meager possessions and the trash cans that provided warmth during cold nights. James was once again grateful for the luck that brought Maggie into his life.

"So, did you tell them?"

"Oh, yes. We had a long and edgy conversation about the possibility of taking the Ambit down."

He was hungry, and wondered if Maggie had given Mrs. Jackson the last of their peanut butter and crackers.

"And?"

James was still thinking of his grumbling tummy. "I need some food first. What did you give Mrs. Jackson?"

"The rest of our peanut butter and crackers. She hasn't eaten since the day before yesterday."

The shame of grudging a few crackers from a hungry old lady kicked in quickly despite his ever-starving morning stomach. His face muscles changed from disappointment into purpose. "Let's go find some food, then."

It was Wednesday, and the pickings were slim. They would have to walk all the way to one of the food banks run by a gospel mission. James wished he could Pace there and back in a matter of half an hour. However, his good old human legs would have to carry his body at the walking speed of an earthling. The tendency to become whiny when hungry was an annoying quality to possess for a homeless guy.

The food bank distributed canvas bags filled to the brim once a month, and it was always a treat. They both received their share of goodies including dry cereal, canned meals, chips, apple sauce, cookies, and juice. Usually, the food lasted three days, if they didn't eat much. It was worth the two-hour walk.

Breathing in the crisp morning air, James' brain slowly started to function normally. Maggie was patient enough to wait until the hungry, cranky boy left and a pleasant conversationalist emerged.

The excitement he felt yesterday resurfaced, and James finally felt awake enough to tell Maggie about the previous day in the Inn's common room. Once he finished listing Joan's many objections and questions, he looked at Maggie expectantly.

Maggie was thinking.

She did not express any opinion for a whole thirty seconds. "Well?" James asked. "What do you think?"

"I think Leo is right. There must be some kind of instructions somewhere. But I don't have the slightest idea where it might be or what it looks like. What do you think?"

James indeed had spent most of his Pacing hours thinking about where the instructions would be written or hidden. "I thought they should be somewhere that wouldn't be destroyed accidentally or by acts of nature. So, maybe they're carved on an old statue or tablet."

"Good thinking, durability is crucial, if we assume that the ancient fathers did not actually know where or when an event that needed containment would occur."

"Then," James continued, "the instructions could not be bound to one place like a statue."

"Unless, of course, if there was a statue or a tablet with instructions in every city on Kaya," Maggie reasoned.

As far as James knew from history and arts classes, there was nothing that had similar markings or paintings located in each city. Also, there was no guarantee that, even carved on stone, anything similar to markings would survive the centuries. Public places would mean that eventually there would be some damage. More than likely, the way to get rid of the Ambit was hidden somewhere.

Again Maggie agreed. "If it is hidden, someone must know about it. Someone who has been around for a long, long time."

"Even though Kayans have what might be called super powers, life expectancy is about one hundred twenty years, not five thousand."

"Maybe, it has been passed on, like an heirloom. Any rich and old families?"

"That's actually a good idea, Maggie. You might finish high school after all."

Maggie punched him in the arm.

James pondered the number of families whose roots reached back millennia. With some poking around in the well-documented archives of the capital, they should be able to narrow the number of ancient families down to a reasonable quantity. After that, persuading people to share their long-kept secret with a bunch of teenagers should be easy. The ordeal would be worth it just to see Leo or Joan arguing with old Aquite ladies who carried pointy walking sticks.

By the time they reached the food bank, the spraying rain had stopped, and their coats were not as wet as previously feared. Still, it was nice to warm up inside and nibble on snacks to tide them over. Coffee and hot chocolate warmed them from the inside. James signed next to the box imprinted with James Knox, and Maggie signed next to Margaret River.

The walk back was much more enjoyable now that there was food in their bellies, and their clothes were dry. James told Maggie about his pacing practice and the dinner conversations about the best way to cook asparagus, or if it was acceptable to use the Waving mark to serve wine. Maggie loved listening to stories about James' life on Kaya. It was a fairy tale for her, and James loved talking her worries away with otherworldly stories. Whatever helped.

Snacks and the following canned beef stew gave them enough energy to make a detour through the downtown to panhandle for a couple of hours. Neither of them enjoyed begging for money from complete strangers, but it was the only way to acquire some cash for the time being. James had started to hate panhandling so much that he considered getting a burger flipping job despite the risk of being discovered by his parents.

Working wasn't an option for Maggie because of her age and the possibility of her being found by social services. She did not want to go back to foster care. For now, bumming was their only way to get by. He remembered reading about some friars living on the money and the goods they begged. Even when they had to travel, they hitchhiked and always relied on other people's hospitality and charity. He could not imagine spending his life like that. It would be the ultimate humbling experience. The only reason he could tolerate their current life was knowing that it was temporary. Hope was what kept them pushing on day in and day out in this depressing life.

Various people of Seattle gave them a little over six dollars that afternoon. It was not bad considering that it was Wednesday, and they were only out about two hours. They headed back to the hidden street that was their neighborhood.

When they got back to their tarp-roofed residence, James and Maggie dumped all of the contents of their food bank baggies on the floor and divided them into three. The biggest pile contained what they would eat for three days including canned meals, chips, protein bars, and dried cereals. Another pile included soup, apple sauce, and the wipes for Mrs. Jackson. She was too old to walk the four miles to the church. Maggie and James could not get an extra bag for her, so they shared.

The last little pile was for the man who slept under a makeshift shelter similar to theirs, but smaller. He suffered from some form of mental condition, but was harmless. His name was John. That was all anyone knew about him. John spent most of his time reading the same comic book over and over again. They would hear him talking to himself about the torn apart book. On the food bank days, Maggie and James usually left him a can of meat, some crackers, and the rest of the protein bars. They didn't know where he got his food from. Every time James left the few pieces of food items in John's shelter, he lifted his head and stared. No words of gratitude or handshakes, only a look that conveyed deep sadness and hurt.

Day 5: Kaya

"You don't look ready for the Seeing class," Claire said as soon as James took his seat with other year-ten students. Every Oneday and Threeday started with double mark classes.

"Am not. Too sleepy," James said. Complete sentences were hard.

Lord Ywi pretended to push the oaken door open as half of his body walked through the door frame. James always wondered if you actually felt anything when you walked through solid matter. T1 level meant that his own Striding ability was non-existent.

First period of double mark classes was devoted to theory and the second one to practice. Seer Theory included learning how the Kayan brain worked, in addition to studying psychology and philosophy that shed light on behavior and body language. Lord Ywi insisted that the more you knew about the brain, the more you would know about the mind.

Kayan brain and psyche were not that much different from humans'. In Aqui, Healers did not have the technology to map the brain like they have been able to do on Earth using MRI, PET, and other devices. Most of their knowledge came from studying cadaver brains and from T7 Healers who specialized in the nervous system. Despite technological limitations, there was quite the accumulation of knowledge regarding the Kayan psyche and behavior.

Today, they were going to learn more about the body's physical reactions to lying. Even though Seeing was associated with being able to tell if a person was lying or not, a properly trained Seer could read other people's anxieties and fears. Then, with the help of their mark, gifted Seers could make a highly-reliable educated guess about a person's next action. It was not mind reading per se, more like weather forecasting. This was the next step of Seeing, which was called discerning. Although a T6 Seer would almost always be able tell if a person was being truthful, discerning required much study and practice. If a Seer wanted to attain T7, they had do put some elbow grease into it.

The first few years, they read about simple ways a low tier can tell about the truthfulness of a person in addition to being able to determine the little changes in the body like tensing up or avoiding eye contact. Some of the things they had to study were even useful in James' human body where he did not have Seeing capabilities.

But now, during more advanced classes, they started to study how a person's heart rate changed or blood pressure increased when lying. The mark of Seeing made it possible to perceive beyond obvious physical manifestations.

After theory, there came practice. As usual, his partner was Claire.

Lord Ywi's practice classes usually took place in the Middle Garden of the Academy. Rows of succulents along the marble walls and outer edge grew wherever they wished. It looked like the plants were trying to invade the whole garden in their slow and steady way. In the middle of creeping succulents, a marble water fountain in the shape of a white lily trickled down water. The contrast between white stones and deep green cacti had a soothing effect. Perfect for concentration as you attempted to invade other minds.

James turned his back to Claire to make things harder:

"I have two brothers."

He knew Claire would be confused, but he took great pleasure in tricking his childhood friend.

"How do you do it? You are the only one ever who can lie so easily, and without any tells. You will be my downfall, James Knox!"

James smiled wickedly, because Claire had no way of knowing about his life on Earth. It was cheating, but he couldn't help it.

Arms folded in frustration, Claire turned her back to lie or less likely tell the truth.

"I've never met my mother."

Well, James couldn't read any of Claire's body language clues from behind. She had mastered them all anyway, so they wouldn't be much help, even if she was looking into his eyes. Try as he might, he couldn't sense her blood pressure rising or heartbeat fastening. She might be telling the truth after all. But he wasn't sure just yet.

He had to use his Seeing, which was a good idea as it was a Seer practice class.

James focused on a spot behind his friend's head as if he was trying to penetrate through the thick wavy curls. Seeing required an extraordinary amount of focus and determination. A person's mind was a strong and dangerous place. One need not dawdle in someone else's mind needlessly.

The strange sensation of putting your face underwater overwhelmed him momentarily, and James knew that she was lying, because the water that was in Claire's mind was an angry red, instead of a calming blue.

"You're lying, Claire Zenger!" James said, perhaps louder than he intended.

"You know I have been an orphan my whole life, James. How could you say that I am lying? I think your Seeing is just getting worse."

"Your mind is as red as tomato paste, Claire. Do you want to tell me what that was about?"

"Not really," she replied, shrugging her shoulders, obviously not happy that James figured out that she was lying.

"Come on, don't be a sour grape. You're just upset that I beat you in your own game."

A little smile spread around Claire's bright blue eyes. James understood why Leo didn't want to leave her side. "You are right. You were just a little Seeling not long ago, and look at you now."

"A Seeling? How dare you! I could See through your wicked lies even if I was a T1 Seer." James defended the honor of his mark and messed up Claire's already fluffy hair.

They kept lying back and forth to each other for another fifteen minutes until it was time to change partners. But James took a mental note to find out what Claire's lie meant and why she would be lying.

When the bell rang to end the mark classes, James caught up with Leo, who always looked a little shaken after his Striding sessions. He wouldn't recover completely until after he gobbled down a hefty lunch, so James didn't want to talk about anything important or serious before they went to work in the fruit orchards that afternoon. There would be plenty of time then to speculate about various unlikely places the instructions might be hidden. It was like, as humans would say, finding a needle in a haystack. Only this time they didn't even know what this particular needle looked like.

Leo walked towards the history class even slower than usual. It must have been an uncommonly-draining Striding session. Since Lord Ywi taught the Seeing classes, philosophy professor Brother Erfyl, who looked like he was always in deep thought, showed his students the secrets of walking through walls. He actually resembled Socrates or Plato. All Brother Erfyl needed was to replace his light gray heavy habit with a breezy toga.

James put down his satchel on the ornate desk next to Leo's. They still had a few minutes before the history professor, Brother Linus, showed up with his utter enthusiasm about anything that was dead or falling apart.

"Did you know Claire actually knew her mother?" James asked.

Leo tilted his head with an inquiring look on his face. James quickly recapped what happened during seeing practice. Talking about Claire brought Leo back to present and cleared the fog in which Striding for two hours had left him.

Many a time, Leo told James, they would have to coach a T4 Strider out of the wall as a weaker Strider would get exhausted and lose the focus that was required to walk through marble columns. James always wanted to see someone half stuck in the wall, but sadly, Striding classes were not open for the public who might show up with popcorn and candies.

Now that James had Leo's full attention, they came up with many unpalatable theories about Claire and her childhood. As far as they knew, when they were still infants, Claire and James both lost their families in the same mining accident. Leo, on the other hand, was raised by his father after his mother had passed away because of an unknown disease even the Theclans could not heal. Then, about four years ago, his father fell from a cliff while rock climbing, leaving Leo an orphan. James and Leo had become good friends when they both had to learn how to braid palm leaves during one of Lord Ywi's detentions in their fourth year. Since then, they had become inseparable.

With wide green eyes, his best friend speculated. "Maybe, her mother is still alive and in hiding for some crime she committed."

"As if anyone can commit a crime nobody knows about in Aqui. Also, where would she hide all these years? The Ambit is only a few hundred miles wide, and unless she has mastered invisibility, somebody would have run into her by now."

Leo was already working on another wild theory when Brother Linus walked in with a sinister smile on his face. They all knew that he had come up with another role-playing lesson, possibly a villain from the history of Kaya.

After devouring three bowls of homemade noodles with beef and almost a whole loaf of bread, Leo was back in action. Stomachs gloriously full, they headed to the fruit orchard to pick more peaches.

James, Leo, and Joan shared the same triangular fruit ladder. Elgar and Claire were working in the coal mines.

"I think we are looking for an heirloom that belongs to a very old and probably very wealthy family," James said.

"Well, since the Dispersal, wealth has become somewhat of a redundant concept, because jewels or money do not have the same meaning in a society with such a small population," Joan reasoned, making things harder as usual. Sometimes, it was annoying to have such a smart and at the same time realistic friend - a talented Healer, but without bed-side manner.

"However," Leo said through a few thick branches, imitating Joan, "people would still keep the things that have been passed down from their ancestors." He took a bite off a ripe, juicy peach. Mouth still full, he added with his regular voice, "That stuff would still retain its value, because of emotional attachment."

"Then we need to talk to every family in Aqui, which might be futile in the end, because we don't even know what we are looking for," Joan said as she brought her already-full bucket down the ladder to empty the fragrant fruits into a nearby crate.

There was a problem with the assumption that the instructions would be passed down in generations. Before James could figure it out, Leo started when Joan returned with an empty bucket.

"I don't think it would be a safe way to preserve anything valuable by trusting it to a family. I mean, families disappear, break apart, or get poor enough to sell everything they own."

"That's true...but where else?"

"With people who have been around a long time, and who do not value or need money," Joan offered as she inspected a peach for ripeness.

"The only people who have no need for money are the crazy rich," Leo said.

But James knew there was another option. "Or people who took vows of poverty."

Both Joan and Leo looked up as they realized that their search had suddenly become much more manageable.

James, Leo, and Joan could not wait until they shared their idea with Claire and Elgar, who walked into the Inn a little after their friends, still covered in coal dust. Digging the stubborn coal out was more strenuous than other works the teenagers were assigned, so everyone had to dig only once a week. They needed the coal and the marble, but people were much more valuable.

After having patiently waited for Elgar and Claire to clean up and eat, Joan told them about their theory.

"Are you saying the monks or the anchorites have the instructions?" Claire asked.

Elgar looked happy that his curiosity had lit a fire in his friends. He swallowed a dumpling whole so that he could put in his two cents.

"That makes wonderful sense! They are the only ones who would not sell or get rid of it. They would treasure it beyond anything else."

"But why wouldn't they use it to save us all?" Claire asked.

"Maybe they don't know what they have." Leo offered, and James added, "Or maybe they don't understand it."

A wave of silence overtook the dinner table. The thought of something that could not be deciphered by the Maelites or the Theclans was overwhelming.

"So," Leo added, "all we need to do is to find who has the instructions, figure out what centuries of the smartest and the best Seers of Aqui could not figure out, and then take the Ambit down...Where should we start?"

They all smiled at the impossibility of their task.

Although James was a little discouraged, he also knew that none of them would be willing to give it up before at least talking to one of the brothers or sisters.

"The monks or the anchorites?" he asked.

"I think the monks. They always have been the ones who were entrusted with acquisition of knowledge, even before the Dispersal," Claire offered.

"They do live in a giant library," Leo added.

James looked around the table and saw that everybody was in agreement. "Let's talk to Brother Linus tomorrow," he said.

Day 6: Earth

Nothing special took place in the life of a homeless teenager on Thursdays. Thursday was a "blah" day.

Thankfully, James had a few things to share with Maggie, who was, as usual, already awake and working on another drawing in her corner. She did not see James wake up, as her colored pencils and the sketch book seemed to have claimed all her attention. James watched her with the affectionate eyes of an older brother.

Thick curly locks framed her round face and spilled onto her shoulders. The smile that was always tucked in at the end of her lips was right there, too. She worked on the drawing with passion, long fingers and small hands moving free. For a moment, James was overcome with how fragile she looked. How could something this delicate endure so much?

James' face suddenly contorted with disgust as he thought about her abusive father and absent mother. Just then, Maggie looked up and saw the expression on his face.

"Is something wrong?"

James dismissed the unpleasant thoughts. "Nope, just morning grouchiness. How long have you been awake?"

"No more than an hour, or at least that's what it feels like. I have been working on a drawing of the Castle of Kaans the way I imagined it."

James was happy that his life on Kaya would bring some enjoyment to Maggie as well. She lifted up her unfinished sketch. It resembled the real castle remarkably well. She captured how the ages-old stones stood the test of time even in the bright sun, how the castle that hosted the kings of Kaya for centuries nestled against the purple ranges of Zita, and how formidable the towers looked from the lower valley. It was truly beautiful.

"You are a rare talent, Maggie. I cannot believe how realistic it looks."

"Buuuuut?" Maggie heard the oncoming addition to James' compliment.

"But," James gave in, "the tower windows are all wrong."

The main building of the castle was positioned in between two cylindrical guard towers that looked like the rook pieces in chess. Even though the lower parts of the towers were solid for easier defense from infantry, a number of windows were scattered along the higher half for archers. James pointed out where the windows were misplaced and corrected the minor errors in Maggie's depiction of the magnificent castle.

"Other than that, I don't think you could have drawn it any better if you had actually seen it." He wanted to finish on a positive note.

"It's all because of how well you described it," Maggie said, pushing a rebellious group of locks behind her ear.

She tentatively made corrections on the drawing to be completed later, and folded the sketchbook closed. Just like James, Maggie always woke up hungry, but she never ate without him.

Goodies they brought from the food bank would feed them today and tomorrow, so they felt free to do as they pleased.

The can of Spam was patiently waiting for their attention, and the hungry teenagers graciously obliged. Sandwiches made of thick slices of canned meat with squirts of mustard that came in the little packages tamed their hunger in silence. The Spam demanded reverence.

They washed down the grease of canned meat and sour taste of mustard with some water, so that Maggie's cookies could find their way down easier. It was a satisfying and delicious way to start the day.

"What did they think about our ideas?" Maggie asked as soon as they settled back to their little corners.

"We think either the monks or the anchorites must have the instructions," James said.

"My mom used to say that those who don't seek money are the ones who find wealth."

She clarified before James could say anything, "I mean, the monks would probably never have considered getting rid of anything so precious just for something as common as money."

At times, her wisdom amazed James.

Maggie seldom talked about her parents. Once in a while, she would mention something her mother said or did, but never a word about her father.

It had been almost four years since the Child and Youth Services took her away in the middle of the night, after one of the neighbors called the police for domestic disturbance. Again.

As long as she could remember, Maggie's father drank. He would start early in the morning and keep drinking until the booze or the money was gone. He never worked at a job more than two weeks; he'd either get fired soon after he started or couldn't wake up to go to work. Most of the day, he kept to himself, but as the dinnertime approached, the monster within would show his ugly face.

An excuse waited around the corner to always make their lives miserable. There wasn't enough meat in the food. The potatoes were too salty. The water was too warm. The power was off. Even though he did nothing to support the family, he always complained about how little they had of everything.

When the shouting did not satisfy or her mother dared to say anything in response, he rose from his chair with the fury of Zeus and started punching her mother as if she was nothing more than a sand bag. He never hit her face, only the places that could conveniently be hidden under clothes.

Maggie would be the recipient of his indiscriminate blows, if she tried to protect her mom with her little body. She remembered the police coming and taking her father away. She also remembered him always coming back, and her mother always letting him back in. Then it would start all over again.

Until one day, there were one too many calls to the police and one too many times her father was given another chance. Maggie was taken to a foster family, then another, and then another. By the time she was eleven, there had been twelve foster families. She decided to stop before the number hit twenty and started to live in the streets.

Not long after she found her way to the dark street in which they lived now, James watched her share her stolen food with Mrs. Jackson. As they slowly became friends, Maggie began to open up and shed the skin of the tentative, scared little girl and became an impossibly cheerful resident in this unlikely place. James loved being her big brother and looking after her. It gave him a purpose. Maggie liked taking care of James. It taught her that not all men preyed on women.

Theirs was a providential friendship that came to rescue both from the darkness that had paralyzed their souls for far too long.

Day 6: Kaya

For some reason, James did not want to get out of the bed that Twoday morning. The sunshine touching his face through the curtains and the warm welcoming presence of the little aloe vera plant on the window sill invited him for another nice day with friends and good food. Unusually, these were not enough. He hauled his body out of the bed and headed to the showers, despite the reluctance.

Even though showers in Aqui did not spray copious amounts of hot water as they would on Earth, the simple mechanism that brought boiling spring waters overhead and poured it out through a tap was more than sufficient to take away the sleepy numbness. One of these days, James planned to make a metal shower head to disperse the water for a more pleasant experience. In spite of his petty complaints about bathroom fixtures, he felt his brain slowly wake up as hot water beat down on his head.

It would have been an unremarkable day, if not for their plans to talk to Brother Linus about meeting with Brother Aelred, the recluse. Philosophy, sciences, and linguistics awaited his scholarly attention in the morning. After that, they would have to find Brother Linus without missing lunch. Sometimes, mornings were too packed. Longer recesses would be great, James thought.

He downed a couple of hard boiled eggs with yesterday's wheat bread and headed to the Academy through the paved road that was becoming more and more colorful as the summer of Kaya approached. Cherries and peaches in the orchard were already ripe, but these trees had just started to blossom. The Aquites might not have the most advanced machinery, but they had mastered the art of agriculture.

With the help of the Reading mark, in the relatively small area within the Ambit, they have been able to grow tens of different kinds of vegetables and fruits, and get at least three harvests for each kind throughout the year. Being a Reader, James could affect the movement of certain plants, but the ways of making things grow better and faster still remained a mystery to him. Animals were much easier and more fun to Read.

As he passed one of the apple trees in full blossom, he focused, tightening his jaw, to make the tree shudder just enough for some of the light pink blossoms to rain down on him. He walked through the fresh-scented petals with a satisfied smile on his face. Reading came the hardest to him, but still he enjoyed this elusive mark.

Leo was ready for the class to begin when James walked in barely a minute before Brother Erfyl. He had to start moving faster in the mornings, since tardiness was not tolerated at the Academy.

After the first hour of philosophy, James and Leo talked about how to persuade Brother Linus to let them see Brother Aelred. After all, they were nothing more than a couple of tenth graders, who have not even mastered their own marks, let alone possess any ability or knowledge to take the Ambit down. As they tried to come up with different approaches, it became obvious that persuading any Maelite to let them talk to their abbot was going to be much more difficult than they had imagined.

Neither James nor Leo paid much attention in any of the classes rest of the morning. Their distracted brains were desperately trying to produce a brilliant idea to no avail.

By the time it was lunch, they lost all hope of persuading their impressive history professor to let them see the legendary recluse. Initially, the plan was to catch the good brother right after lunch, but now that they hadn't been able to conjure up any workable plan, they would have to wait until after work.

Defeated, the two friends looked for the cart that would take them to the farm, where hundreds of cows were tended.

"How about we tell Brother Linus the truth instead of trying to impress him into letting us see Aelred?" Leo asked. They were traveling down dirt roads on the back of a horse cart, their feet dangling over the back.

"Let me see. Are you saying we should tell him that a bunch of us came up with a brilliant plan over dinner at the Inn?" James said.

"Maybe a little more embellished than that, but yes, that's the gist of it," Leo replied.

"Even I don't know, Leo. Why would he even take us seriously? I don't take us seriously."

"Well, we don't have any other ideas. I say, let's give it a shot."

James gave a sigh of surrender. "Alright, truth it is then."

They remained quiet the rest of the way, half enjoying the beautiful view, half feeling like their genius quest had come to a premature end.

The day's chore at the farms was not his favorite even though he was a Reader. Working with animals was one of the best things about James' life on Kaya, but shoveling cow manure was a smelly, labor-intensive business that needed to be done, but no one wanted to do no matter where you were in the universe. Sadly, there was no picking and choosing.

By the end of their shift, every breath smelled like it came from the back end of a cow. James' arms and back were achy. Leo, on the other hand, reaped the benefits of being a Riser, only complaining of the smell.

The horse cart awaited them at the gate to take the workers out of the green meadow where black and white cows lazily hung out all day. The ride was quiet again, but this time because of exhaustion. It seemed as if their more than likely brief conversation with the history professor would have to take place tomorrow. Neither of them had the energy nor the cleanliness for such an encounter.

Slowly, the horse pulled the cart back to the Academy on the hardened dirt road. James and Leo stared at the orange sun disappearing beyond the forest. The fruit orchards ran for miles along the road, making the view even more stunning.

One of the Maelites also enjoyed the beautiful sunset under the cherry trees. James studied the wearer of the gray habit, and his head jerked towards his friend as soon as he saw who reclined merely a few yards away from the road. Leo must have seen him as well.

As if they had arranged it previously, both of them jumped out of the cart onto the packed dirt road, landing not too far from Brother Linus. It would be inconceivable to let this opportunity go.

The brother who was overly animate concerning things about history was uncharacteristically still. James knew that many Maelites preferred to meditate in nature, and wondered if it was a bad time to disturb Brother Linus. But before he could express his concern, the monk looked their way with a genuine and rich smile that dissipated James' concerns.

Leo, walking a little faster than James, greeted the middle-aged history teacher.

"Excuse us for bothering you, professor. Do you have a few minutes for us?"

With the warm smile still on his face, Brother Linus replied.

"My good boy, I have a few hours for you. Come sit with me, the grass is soft, and the sun is still warming on the face."

James and Leo sat on the fresh grass, legs folded.

"What can I do for you on this fine day?"

Leo looked at James, making his friend shift uncomfortably, not knowing where or how to start. Since Leo was a little more at ease when it came to talking to professors and girls, he took up explaining the situation.

As their ideas about the Ambit and how to get rid of it were summarized, Brother Linus listened carefully, without giving any hint that he was excited or impressed. James thought that he was merely being a polite and considerate educator.

When Leo was done, Linus took a deep breath.

"I am going to be absolutely frank. You are not the only ones who have ever thought about taking the Ambit down. All those who tried failed miserably. Even the most gifted minds of the Maelite order could not put a crack on the shimmering face of our cage. It cannot be done."

"Can we at least talk to Brother Aelred about the existence of instructions for directions?"

"I cannot possibly bother the head of our order, a recluse, to satisfy your curiosity. I am sorry boys, but my answer is no."

He said it in such a serious and final way, which was not at all his style, that James and Leo knew further insistence would be absolutely futile. They rose from their grassy cushions, bowed slightly to show respect, and headed back to the dirt road. On top of rejection, now they had to walk all the way to the Inn.

A nagging voice in James' head kept poking his brain, reminding him what Leo told him earlier - "We will tell him the truth."

They had told him the truth, but not all of it. As the road swallowed their footsteps, the word "truth" kept bugging James. He stopped dead in the middle of the road, falling behind Leo, hesitated for a moment, and then turned around to tell one more thing to Brother Linus.

James' soft leather sandals made shuffling sounds on the hard road, making Brother Linus look up one more time, with a curious expression on his face.

Without introduction, James whispered so Leo did not hear.

"I am from another world."

He didn't know what else to say, and he didn't know how to explain.

"We wanted to tell you the truth, and that is the whole truth."

Brother Linus' fatherly smile froze on his face, and his eyes widened. Was it shock or disbelief?

Not being able to handle the silence, without another word or gesture, James started back to where Leo waited.

"What did you tell him?" Leo asked as they started to walk.

"Nothing," James shrugged.

They hadn't taken five steps before Brother Linus yelled.

"Come to my cell in the tower, tomorrow after work."

They turned around to answer, but the Maelite had already gone back to his contemplation.

Since James was supposed to cook that evening, he had to clean up fast. They had already lost an hour because of having to walk back. At least he knew what he was going to cook.

He successfully passed off meatloaf as his own invention on Kaya. For the last six months, he cooked the same thing without one complaint. Actually, everyone looked forward to Twodays to taste James' amazing culinary creation one more time. His mother on Earth had taught him this recipe. It was easy and delicious, especially served over roast potatoes and carrots. James was the master of meatloaves, and he had to deliver every week.

After getting rid of the unpleasant odor of the day, James headed toward the kitchen to start dinner. Leo and Claire were already in deep conversation when he arrived. As he put on the stained apron, in walked Elgar and Joan. It was a good time to tell them about Brother Linus' invitation, but James did not know how to explain the stubborn Maelite's sudden change of heart.

Leo must have read his reluctance, because in his version of the story, the part of James' going back to Linus was conveniently deleted. He was thankful for this unburdening kindness, but he also knew that the subject would come up again when the two of them were alone.

Everyone was excited over the prospect of them meeting Brother Aelred. The man was a legend. No one actually spoke to him for years other than select few monks, but tomorrow, James and Leo might get to talk to him.

"Do you think he'll come to the Academy?" Elgar asked.

"Brother Linus wasn't exactly forthcoming about the meeting. We don't even know if we're going to see Aelred or just Linus," Leo answered.

"I think you should think about what you're going to tell him, in case he's there. We wouldn't want Leo to make a fool of himself," Joan added.

"I'll charm the man in a matter of seconds with my finesses and sophistication," Leo replied, his right hand in the air, his eyes on the horizon.

"I really don't think we'll meet the Abbot, but we'll prepare just in case. Everything we thought about sounds a little childish and silly now," James said.

"Speak for yourself, peasant!" Leo said with a fake deep voice and took a giant bite from an apple.

"Don't be silly. Can you imagine him leaving the Castle just to talk to a few school students?" Claire said. She had been in a bad mood since the Seeing class.

"You're right," Elgar said, trying to ease the tension Claire created, "we're only a few students, but Brother Linus would have told them if there was no possibility of seeing Brother Aelred."

Claire must have noticed the negativity she instilled, because she softened her tone a little bit, "True, but I don't think we should get our hopes up just yet."

She was right. After all, James did not know why Brother Linus wanted to see them. Maybe, it was going to be a counseling session for the insane teenager. It could be that he was going to ask more questions about the meaning of "being from another world."

As he chopped carrots and potatoes, he realized that Leo would be there when Brother Linus asked him about this other world. He turned his gaze to his best friend momentarily, and with a piercing thought wondered if today was going to be the last day of their friendship. The secret he had kept all these years had the potential to lead to two unappetizing paths. Leo would either be upset that James never told him, or he would declare that his friend had lost his mind. Both were rational reactions. Was it worth it to lose his friend to take the Ambit down? James didn't know the answer to that question.

That night's meatloaf did not taste as good as usual, although even the last little bite of the loaf and every scraping of potatoes were gone. Nothing would taste the same if he lost his best friend.

For the first time during his life on Kaya, James did not look forward to tomorrow.

Day 7: Earth

James rolled over in his hard bed as soon as he woke up. He wanted to stay in bed all day and just be. He wasn't even hungry, which was a miracle in and of itself.

"Are you alright?" Maggie asked, knowing exactly what time he woke up every day. He wasn't alright.

"I told one of the teachers that I was from another world," James said, still facing the cardboard wall. This would be a good occasion to cry, if he had ever cried. Tears had deserted him since Jake's accident. Alas, the only emotional tool he had was moping.

"What?" Maggie exclaimed. She knew that he had always been very afraid of people's reactions on Kaya. When he didn't say anything, she pressed, "But why?"

James shook his head.

"I don't know why, but I know it was the right thing to do. When I told Brother Linus that I was from a different world, he agreed to talk to us and maybe let us meet with Brother Aelred."

"Well, that's good news. Why are you so upset then?"

"Leo and the others will probably find out about Earth when we go to the tower to meet the monks. Everything was perfect on Kaya, and now I messed it all up. I don't even know if it's worth it."

"Oh, stop it!" Maggie raised her voice, sounding a little too much like his mother. "You know it was not for nothing. Even if nothing happens in the end, it is a good thing that you got rid of this secret."

"What if I lose my friends?" James asked, sounding more like a scared five-year-old boy than a young man of sixteen.

"Then they weren't really your friends,"

"But, I have been lying to them, especially Leo, for all these years."

"Yes, and you shouldn't have, but true friendships endure fierce storms. I'm sure all will be well," Maggie said.

How was it that more often than not Maggie was the more mature one? James was grateful for her wisdom, patience, and cool-headedness, especially when he possessed none of those virtues. After Maggie's stern but kind words, he felt like some of his worries dissipated enough to remind him that his stomach did not care about his problems in another world. Shaking off the sleepiness and some of the pessimism, he straightened himself up and looked at Maggie expectantly. She knew that expression well enough to hand him a protein bar and a few cheese crackers.

"That's all for breakfast," she said, ripping the wrapper off another bar for herself.

During their less than satisfactory breakfast, James retold Maggie about the happenings of the day before.

"It was your conscience," Maggie said when he was done with telling her about their unlikely meeting on the side of the road.

"My conscience?"

"Yep, I think you have been wanting to relieve yourself from this crazy secret of yours for a while now. You took the first opportunity when Leo hinted at the importance of truth. It shows character, actually," Maggie explained her point, since the cracker-crunching James was not sure what his conscience had to do with anything that had happened yesterday.

"Well then, I wish my annoying conscience would learn to shut up!" James said, smiling for the first time since he woke up.

"I don't think your conscience will ever shut up, James, and I am very happy for that." Maggie returned his reluctant smile.

"If you have me, you want to share me. If you share me, you haven't got me. What am I?"

"A secret," James said.

His secret had been begging to be shared, and the time had finally come. He didn't want to do it, but he was ready to unburden himself.

"What should we do today?" Maggie asked after giving James a few moments to shake off the remnant feelings from his life on Kaya. Food was not a worry because there were still leftovers from the food bank goodies. That meant this Friday was relatively free.

"Do you wanna go see your mom?" James offered.

Every once in a while, James and Maggie took the long bus trip to get a glimpse of Maggie's mother. It was a sad and awkward affair, but he would not let Maggie sever the only tether she had to her family, just like she would not stop making wagers that would require James to call home if he lost. It was their way of keeping hope alive for each other. Not all was lost. Yet.

Maggie nodded reluctantly at his offer, foregoing her bright smile in favor of the deep sadness that lurked behind her eyes. "It's been a while, hasn't it?" she asked. "I wonder if she is still with him."

Every time they hid behind the trees across Maggie's house, James hoped against hope that they would only see her father. Maybe this time Maggie's mother would have finally had enough. Maybe this time Maggie's mother would have decided to start a new life. Maybe this time Maggie's mother would have wanted her daughter back.

But after months of seeing both of her miserable parents either sitting behind the kitchen table or vegging in front of the television, James knew that the possibility of Maggie having a life with her mother without the fear of becoming a punching bag was small to none. He wanted the door to stay open for Maggie, but he was not too optimistic about her prospects. The business of realism was a hard one to learn and a harder one to practice.

Once the dullness of sleep left its seat to a more energetic wakefulness, Jake and Maggie rose from their paper abode to begin their journey to the dilapidated house Maggie grew up in. Since their traveling funds were limited, they would walk as far as their legs or the weather let them through the city, and then ride the bus for about thirty minutes to get off at least three stops before Maggie's house.

Until now, only one person who happened to be one of Maggie's former teachers had recognized her, but they did not want to push their luck. Once they got off the bus, walking through the alleys, woods, and quieter roads was easy enough.

The rain started drizzling again a few minutes after James and Maggie alighted the city bus. They kept walking in the rain, because Maggie hated to dawdle any more than was absolutely necessary to accomplish their simple task. There were rare occasions that she would become withdrawn and lose all the words that normally could not wait to get out. Instead of the wise young woman who advised a mopey teenage boy a few hours ago, a frightened little girl walked these streets. If James wasn't sure that returning to her home every once in a while was for her own good, he would never put her through this ordeal.

In a manner, these visits were akin to purging. Every time they came back, Maggie saw that her mother was trapped in a way that most abused women were. It was also important for her to see that her father was not the all-powerful man she remembered him to be. She began to feel more compassion for her mother, and in time, the fear her father instilled in the depths of her heart started to diminish. It was a long way to healing and reconciliation, but James could see that these one-sided encounters were painfully helpful. All he could do for his little sister was to be present. Under the rain he walked next to her without a word.

Thick tree trunks and lush bushes provided an excellent cover for them to watch the happenings of Maggie's small, battered home. After all the hours they spent watching the light pink house with old wooden shutters, James could not help but find a resemblance between the human and the dwelling. They both were neglected, but not beyond repair yet, remaining strong despite all the beating they had taken literally and figuratively. They both refused to give up on those who had treated them so badly for so long. The silent strength of the little pink house and the frightened young girl made James' eyes well up. Good thing it was raining.

Hiding behind the bushes, an hour passed before they spotted any movement in pink house Her mother brought a big, white plastic bag out on the back porch to put in the green trash can that had a gaping hole near the bottom. She was in her forties, but looked much older. Her long ponytail had more gray than black. Wrinkles and unsightly bags framed eyes that looked like Maggie's. The mother who was not able to protect her daughter took a pack of cigarettes out of the pocket of her jeans and lit one with shaky hands. She looked past the woods into the horizon in a dream state, having no awareness that her only child was watching her. James saw tears trickle down Maggie's cheeks like tiny waterfalls. He hugged her shoulders.

"She is still here," Maggie whispered in between her silent sobs. "She looks older, too," she added after a few moments. "Do you think she misses me?" the little girl asked, breaking James' already broken heart.

"I know she misses you," he said.

Maggie's mother was lost in her own thoughts, not able to pull herself out of the misery she suffered every day. Pain and longing branded her tired face, but James was sure Maggie's mother did not want her little girl back in that house no matter how much she missed her baby.

The sad woman went back in the little pink house. The tearful girl wiped her cheeks and blew her nose, ready to return to the cold dark streets. James glanced one more time to the broken shutters and thought of his own parents.

Did his mother miss him when the oblivion of alcohol left her?

Did his father?

Day 7: Kaya

James entered the kitchen, where the air was stained with the smell of meatloaf through the night. Despite having lived a whole day on Earth, the uneasy feeling in his stomach about his day on Kaya remained more persistent than ever. A breakfast of buttered and jellied scones did nothing to erase his anxiety, but at least the ever-present hunger was evaded for the time being. He gulped down his sweet chay and headed to the Academy. No tardiness today.

Following the math class with Sister Ita, there was the Reading class with Sister Lea, who once a week commuted between the Academy and the island where the Theclans lived. The trip was arduous for a non-Pacer, but as far as James knew she never once missed a class.

The Readers' Garden was composed of the biggest greenhouse James had ever seen and a spacious outdoor area that was home to countless herbs, bushes, and trees. The eclectic residents of the gardens looked like they jumped out of a Monet painting. It was the busiest, but also the most peaceful place James had ever been.

On one end of the gardens, the gray marble barn stood steadfast with its door ajar for the animals roaming about the meadow. It wouldn't be surprising to run into a thoughtful chicken, an over-friendly goose, or a playful cat chasing various fowls around the shrubbery. Most of the animals in this rather unusual environment were trained by the Readers over the years not to kill or hurt each other.

Even the rabbits had learned not to destroy the cabbage or carrots growing in the gardens.

Admittedly, as peaceful as it was, the gardens were also strange. If, as a Reader, James found the behavior of these animals curious, he couldn't even imagine what Maggie would think if she saw a fox calmly enjoying the sun without even stealing a glance towards the nearby chicken coop.

When he entered, Sister Lea was already in deep conversation with a rosemary bush. Even though Readers could talk to plants no more than your ordinary human beings on Earth could, Sister Lea was regularly found discussing philosophy or detailing intricacies of her latest carpentry with a fragrant fig tree or a squishy succulent. James thought it was probably a saner version of talking to yourself, especially if you are as gifted a Reader as Sister Lea.

Did the plants talk back? He didn't know.

James put his brown satchel down and leaned against a particularly thick bamboo. More students trickled into the green house where the rosemary bush was possibly contemplating the benefits of using a mortise chisel instead of a paring chisel. Their professor was into sculpting nowadays.

Zoe Rose, who was one of the best Readers in the Academy, walked in with an iguana's tail visible over her shoulder. She brought that animal along wherever she went. Basil the iguana was nearly as famous as his almost T7 Reader owner. Once Zoe passed her mark test next month, which everyone was sure was going to happen, she would become one of the youngest T7 Readers in Aquite history. James would have been jealous if his heart rate did not go a little berserk every time he saw Zoe. Besides, Pacing was his thing, not Reading, or even Seeing.

Only a handful of Readers —seven to be exact—attended Sister Lea's class, since, for some reason, there were fewer and fewer students who were born with the Reading mark. James wondered if eventually all the marks would disappear as long as the Ambit stayed up.

Their eccentric professor took a sip of who-knows-what from her unadorned clay mug, wiped her hands on her forever stained apron, and brought out a cage covered with white fabric. It was going to be an animal Reading day. James wished that his mind was not preoccupied with Linus, Aelred, Leo, or the Ambit. Performing Reading on an animal needed focus and patience, neither of which was in his possession currently.

Sister Lea was not much for introductions, but she was a wonderful teacher. Even though most mark classes required some kind of theory, the traveling anchorite insisted on two hours of practice and assigned the theory part for the students to read when they were not among animals and plants. Without ceremony, she yanked off the cover and revealed one of the rarest animals on Kaya: a dragon.

Unlike the tales on Earth, dragons on Kaya were no bigger than lizards, but they were incredibly fast and almost impossible to Read. This little dragon had scales of orange red glowing under the bright sunlight as if on fire. Its wings seemed as delicate as lace but in fact were strong enough to carry the dragon for hours without any rest. Despite its size, the magnificent animal still looked vicious. Its intelligent eyes scanned all of the students as if to challenge them to force their will on its tiny, yet mighty being.

As a T5 Reader, James did not have a chance to get this defiant animal to do anything. Sister Lea went through the basics of Reading briefly and asked them to form a line so that they could all have a turn to get the dragon to open the cage by flipping the latch.

It was going to be a long class.

James waited his turn as three other Readers stared at the glowing dragon without any success. When he stepped in front of the cage, he took a deep breath and looked into the dragon's clever eerie eyes. Just like Sister Lea had been telling them for years, he tried to put himself in the dragon's place, see through its eyes and smell with its nose. When James tried the same thing with a cat or a fox, usually after about thirty seconds, the animal would slowly do what it was asked to do. Nothing too complex like getting out of a cage, more in the line of walking through a maze or drinking from the blue bowl instead of red. But with this dragon, James felt like he was banging his head on a wall. A few minutes later, a headache started to form on his temples, drops of sweat rolling down to his cheeks. He broke eye contact with the stubborn animal and looked at the sister. There was not a trace of disappointment in her eyes as she handed him some cloves to chew on. The tiny aromatic flower buds helped the Reader to clear off the mind from the strain of unsuccessful reading.

Zoe was at the back of the line, petting Basil absentmindedly, which made James glad that she wasn't watching his failure. Another half an hour passed as they all took turns to force the dragon into freedom. The little reptile would not budge. Once everyone gave up on the endeavor, Sister Lea called to the back of the green house,

"Zoe, would you care to give it a try?"

Zoe walked towards the dragon cage, her pet friend still visible on her shoulder. She sat on the mossy ground, long brown hair flowing down almost to her waist as straight strands formed a striking contrast with her peach muslin gown. The dragon turned its head as Zoe whispered inaudible words to the animal. The headstrong beast reacted to her differently. She focused her gaze into the creature's eyes as if it was a friend, not an animal to be dominated. The contempt emanating from the cage slowly disappeared. Not a minute had passed before the dragon started towards the small gate. The dragon stuck its right claw out through the bronze bars, hesitated for a moment, unhooked the latch, and then twisted the little nub that kept the unlatched gate in place.

All that was needed was a nudge, and the gate would swing wide open. The captive was free. As soon as Zoe broke eye contact, the animal shook its head as if to get rid of the other mind. The dragon spread its delicate wings and took off with a speed that would be the envy of many a Pacer. James now knew why dragons were so hard to capture.

Zoe pushed herself off the ground, straightened her robes, and took her place at the back of the green house without a hint of pride on her beautiful face.

When the bell chimed five times after long and arduous hours in the coal mines, marking the end to their work hours, both James and Leo were more than ready to get back to the daylight. The sun was about to hide behind the mountains as they emerged from the mines. Since there was no time to get back to the Inn, the showers at the mine would have to ensure that the young miners would not have to travel covered in coal dust.

Squeaky clean and dressed in the best clothes they owned, James and Leo headed to the West Tower reserved for the Maelite cells.

In the years James had been a student at the Academy, he had never seen the inside of one of the Maelite cells. Each professor occupied an office in the main building, and that was where the students would have their meetings with the brothers. Unless you were invited by a Maelite, the West Tower was out-of-bounds. To make sure that students with their adolescent hormones overcoming good judgment did not wander into their private quarters, there was always a brother guarding the entrance to the tower.

The brother on duty that day put his book aside and stood up as James and Leo approached.

"Leo Pyle and James Knox," Leo announced, when the monk moved to position himself between the entrance and the visitors.

"Oh, you are the ones Brother Linus is expecting." The guard brother relaxed his posture. "You are the only ones he has ever invited to the tower."

James didn't know if he should feel worried or proud.

The architecture of the West Tower was legendary. Elegance of the carvings along the outer walls and the unique dome that could be seen from miles away were described in classic Kayan literature as well as by travelers and historians. Despite living and studying so close to such a wonder, very few students have had the privilege of seeing the inside of the beautiful building.

Just like the rest of the Academy, the floors and inner walls of the tower were made from white marble that had shades of grey swirling in no discernible pattern. Spiraling marble steps with cast iron railings stood in the middle of the ground floor. To prevent visitors or bare-footed monks from slipping, the middle of the stairs was covered with worn-out gray carpet trampled by countless Maelites over the years.

James and Leo slowly climbed the marble stairs as they admired the art that accompanied them. The outside walls of the Academy told the story of Kaya, and the inside of the West Tower depicted the most famous myths of Aqui. The half-elk, half-man hero who was supposed to have led the Aquites out of the mountains during a vicious winter ran ahead of tired travelers. The mermaids that aided the sailors who got lost in the White Sea sunbathed on rocks. The elegant reliefs possessed the whimsical cheer of fairy tales, in contrast to the sharp seriousness of history. West Tower was a visual feast.

Brother Linus lived on the sixth floor of the tower. Once they finished climbing the ancient stairs, both had to shake off the trance the beautiful walls had put them in. Leo knocked on the old oaken door with a lion's head brass knocker. James was glad that Leo had always been the talker of their duo, and even their group. He took a step back as they waited to hear Brother Linus' footsteps.

But the door opened unexpectedly, as just like the Theclans, the Maelite order declined to don any footwear, allowing them to tread silently. Brother Linus beckoned them in with a hand motion. James and Leo stepped into the small room.

Despite the rich wall and ceiling carvings, the cell clearly belonged to a person with few possessions. The furnishings were beyond scarce, close to non-existent. To the right of the heavy wooden door lay a thin mattress on the hard floor, without a bed frame. A pillow and a gray woolen blanket were the only friends of this humble bed. A thick wooden slab functioned as a night stand. Books were neatly placed on top of each other next to a candle holder, which was almost invisible in the middle of a solidified candle wax puddle.

There were no dressers, no wardrobes, or anything that could remotely be called bedroom furniture. Two pieces of clothing, folded perfectly in squares, were placed on the floor without much attention to interior design.

Behind the door, there stood a rickety table that looked luxurious since it was the closest thing to furniture in the room. Still, considering the heavy school desks that were painstakingly carved by master carpenters, this table was nothing more than a piece of rectangular wood settled on four sticks. It did not belong to one of the most beautiful buildings in the whole planet. Next to the wobbly table, hundreds of books were piled on top of each other, threatening to topple over at any moment. James' room in the Inn looked like an extravagant five-star hotel compared to the monk's accommodations.

Brother Linus walked behind his plain desk to settle on a stool and invited his guests to occupy the two similar stools that were possibly brought from other rooms.

"Tell me more about your plan," the historian monk demanded.

James and Leo had practiced how to explain their plan that was not much of a plan.

"We were all talking about the Ambit merely being a method to contain a disease or a disaster, and not a magical boundary to punish us." Yes, Leo had memorized that whole sentence. "Actually, it was James' idea."

Both men looked at James briefly, forcing him to smile in acknowledgment.

"Then, we thought," Leo continued, "if this is indeed a scientific contraption, there must be a way to take it down. Those who came up with such an amazing method to prevent contagions from spreading must have also comprised a way to take it down when the threat was eliminated." He sounded like Elgar. James would have laughed if his heart was not beating too fast.

Brother Linus listened intently and nodded every now and then to urge Leo to keep talking.

"If there is a way to take it down, they would have to be sure that it was safe. Only the people inside the quarantine would be able to tell if it were safe or not."

"So, what you are suggesting is that the Ambit can only be taken down from the inside, by us?" their professor asked.

James finally gathered enough courage to speak. "That's what we think. Also, there should be some sort of instructions detailing how to proceed."

"Who is this *we*, by the way?"

"It's us, Claire, Elgar, and Joan," James replied, happy to mention their names as well.

"I'm not surprised that you would invent such incredible tales during the long evenings at the Inn," Brother Linus said without a smile. The cruelty was unlike him.

James and Leo were taken aback by the sudden change of attitude, and neither of them appreciated being treated like children. However, as respectful Academy students, they held their tongues and continued to explain.

"It was Elgar who insisted in reading and researching about the Ambit and the possibility of living beyond the boundary," James said, getting irritated.

"You think you are the first teenagers who thought about taking the Ambit down and freeing Aqui? Any self-respecting Aquite imagines being free of this golden cage at one time or another. What makes you so special?"

"We don't think we are special!" James said, his volume higher than he intended.

"But," Leo put his hand on his friend's knee before James got more upset, "except Elgar, we all thought like you. Until one day James came up with the idea that the Ambit was simply a technological device and, therefore, there would have to be a failsafe. Unless you think it's magical." It was clever to provoke the professor with talk of magic.

The moody monk waved his hand, shooing the idea of magic away. "Come on, Leo, you know the Maelites do not believe in magic. Some might call walking through the walls or lifting hundreds of pounds magical, but we always believed that the Ambit was an unexplainable side effect of Haydar's disastrous experiment."

He stopped talking and stared at James for a moment. "How did you think of the Ambit being a containment field, so to speak?"

James shifted his weight, not knowing where to put his hands. "Is it related to what you told me yesterday?" the monk further questioned.

The moment of truth had come, and all James wanted to do was to jump out of the window and hope to land on a bush. He could feel the piercing gazes of Leo and Brother Linus.

"Yes," he said finally and exhaled a sigh of surrender.

"Would you care to elaborate on that?"

"Every day I go to bed on Kaya, and wake up in a different world called Earth," James said in one breath like pulling off a Band-Aid. As soon as he said it, a feeling of relief and lightness overcame him. It was all out in the open now, and there was no going back.

"What do you mean 'another world?'" Leo asked, his body twisting to face him with a suspicious and worried look on his face.

"Well, I am pretty sure it's a planet far from our sun, because the two night skies have different constellations and there is only one moon."

James wanted to be able to actually read what went through Leo's and Brother Linus' minds at that moment. Sadly, that would be impossible, even if he was a T7 Seer, so he resolved to waiting for further questions.

"How long have you been living on that other planet?" Leo asked.

"Almost four years. One day, I woke up here and there. It was a little confusing at first, being flooded with new memories, as if two minds were combining together. I haven't a clue how it happened, but since that day, I live a day here and then a day there."

"Why didn't you ever mention this before?" Leo asked, betrayal and hurt hidden behind his question.

"I didn't know how anyone would react. I was afraid that you'd think I was crazy. Also, there is almost nothing happy about my life on Earth. I like it here on Kaya," James tried to explain, and hoped against hope that he had not just lost his friend.

"What changed yesterday?" Brother Linus interrupted.

"Actually, it was Leo. Before we saw you in the fields, he was adamant that we should tell you the truth without omitting or embellishing. After you said no, the word truth kept echoing in my head, and I knew that you needed to hear that I lived in two worlds."

Before he finished talking, James felt the presence of someone else in the room. Before he could turn around, a fourth voice joined the conversation. "Yes, he did need to hear," said an older man in his sixties with a shaven head, wearing the monk's charcoal habit. As the man approached the table, Brother Linus stood up.

"James, Leo...This is Brother Aelred, the head of our order."

The shocked students hastily stood up, pushing their wobbly stools back so that there would be more room for the legendary Waver to approach. As far as they knew, the fabled recluse had not left the Castle for thirty years since he had announced a desire for solitude. The decision came a mere two years after his election as the youngest abbot. Aelred had been conducting all the affairs of the monastery from his cell in the castle for decades without any major problems. Now he had made the trip to the Academy, just to see a couple of teenagers.

Nobody had to tell James and Leo that something was seriously wrong. Two other monks waited outside the door, arms folded, feet apart. It was disconcerting to see peaceful and soft-spoken Maelites act as bodyguards.

"We need more privacy," Brother Aelred said, pointing to the top of the tower. As they followed the quiet and calloused bare feet of the monks, James and Leo did not dare utter a word.

At the top of the tower, spiraling steps came to an end at a small room with a sky window. In the company of four monks, James and Leo climbed the pull-down attic ladders. The silence and secrecy were making them more uncomfortable by the minute.

The guard monks checked all around the walls and the floors for the next fifteen minutes, touching every piece of carving and connection. Once they were satisfied, each gave a nod to Brother Aelred, who finally relaxed his shoulders and sat on the cold floor, his legs folded. Not knowing what else to do, James and Leo followed suit.

"You and your friends have come to the right conclusion," Brother Aelred started. "There is indeed a way to take the Ambit down. Also, as you say, the invisible boundary is not magical per se, but we still don't know how it works. Regardless of its nature, there is a set of instructions that was entrusted to the Maelites thousands of years ago. We call it the Manual. Any questions?"

James and Leo looked at each other as if they did not know which question they wanted to ask first.

"Why haven't you used the instructions to take the Ambit down then?" James asked.

Aelred exhaled with exasperation. "It's a little complicated. When the Manual was left with us, there was also a harbinger about the person who would be able to decipher these instructions. During the centuries when the Manual was still in our possession, despite out best efforts, we could not unravel the mystery within."

"What do you mean 'when the Manual was in your possession?'" Leo asked.

"Let me finish. The harbinger that was left with the Maelites claimed that only one who is from another world can elucidate the secret of the Manual and make the world anew."

"Well, where is this Manual?" Leo asked again, more agitated.

"Again, let me finish," Brother Aelred said, still calm. "For a long time, the monks thought the person from another world meant an alien who would visit Kaya from beyond the stars. But since the Ambit is as impenetrable from the outside as it is from the inside, we were resolved that Aqui would remain captive forever."

The abbot's eyes became glazed as if he remembered a painful memory.

"Then, a little over thirty years ago, I met a young man who showed much promise in sciences and philosophy. He was a rare talent with his intelligence and his marks. As he grew in knowledge and age, he also became interested in the Ambit and the Manual. One day, he came to me asking about the ways to take down the Ambit, not unlike yourselves. I had just been elected abbot and was more than happy to share all my knowledge with someone who was such a wonderful gift to Aqui. As we talked more and more about the mystery that traps us in this beautiful part of Kaya, he gained my trust. One day, just like you did, he told me that he was from another world. Even though I had trusted him, I had never told him about the harbinger. When he told me that he was from another world and explained to me how that world functioned and how advanced it was, I knew he was the one in the harbinger. Fooled by his insincere friendship and blinded with hope, we decided to show him the Manual."

"But he betrayed our trust and escaped from the Castle with the instructions. When we finally cornered him, he told us the parchment that held the way to our freedom was destroyed, and he did not have it any more. All was lost. We failed in our duty to safeguard the Manual. After we found out that the Manual was lost forever, I decided to become a recluse and devote myself to scribing and contemplation."

All the hope they had felt mere moments ago drained.

"Who is this man?" Leo asked. James, too, was curious about the person who was able to fool so many accomplished Seers.

"After our confrontation, he used his intelligence, his marks, and no doubt his knowledge about that other world to become a very wealthy and influential man in Aqui. The reason for our vigilance today is that he remains to be a very powerful and cunning man." Aelred took a deep breath and finished his sentence. "He is the Rex."

Leo unfolded his legs in a hurry and stood up, towering over everyone else who remained seated.

"Are you saying the only thing that explains how to take the Ambit down is in the hands of the most powerful man in Aqui? Not only the most powerful but a T7 Riser and Seer?"

James watched his best friend sit back down, defeat weighing on his shoulders. "Why didn't you make copies or memorize the instructions during all those years you had it?"

"The reason the prophesy mentions the Outsider is that Kayans cannot read the Manual at all. For us, it is nothing more than a blank parchment. Nevertheless, we know and trust that the instructions are detailed in there, and the Outsider would be able to decipher the way to freedom. Until today, there has been only one who could read it. Now there are two."

"Then," James continued, "our only hope is to talk to the Rex?"

"I am afraid so," Brother Aelred said without confidence, "but we need to be prepared for the possibility that the Manual might be lost forever."

A few moments of silence dominated the room, hope and defeat hand-in-hand.

"Still, we must try. Meet me again at the top of the West Tower tomorrow following work and keep everything I told you secret," Brother Aelred said and adjourned their meeting.

James and Leo walked through the serene pathway to the Inn in deafening silence. Something was broken in their friendship. When they arrived, Leo headed straight to his room, without a word.

James' worst nightmare had come true.

He had lost his best friend.

Day 8: Earth

The air smelled of humidity mixed with a healthy dose of gloom, another cloudy day in Seattle. He would have thought the weather was miserable even if it was an extra scorching sunny day in Florida. For all these years, happiness and contentment of his Kayan life sustained him through his hard days on Earth. When Kaya became less than perfect, overnight James turned back into the scared boy who listened to his parents from behind the couch as they yelled at each other. That little boy wanted to hide in that narrow dark tunnel between the couch and the wall, just like this big boy wanted to stay in the dark cardboard shelter for as long as possible.

"Everything OK?" Maggie asked. She knew that James would have told Leo and Brother Linus about his life on Earth.

Not a trace was left from yesterday's hopefulness. Thanks to Murphy's law, which also functioned perfectly on a different planet, everything that could go wrong had gone wrong.

"I spilled my secret for nothing and lost my best friend," James said, hoping that talking might ease the pressure on his rib cage.

"What happened?" she asked softly, crawling over to his side just to put a hand on his shoulder.

Reading class with the dragon or torturous work hours in the mines were not worth mentioning in the light of what took place in the West Tower. Even the breathtaking carvings went without mention, despite the fact that Maggie would have loved to hear what the legendary tower looked like from the inside.

While James recited their conversation in the highest room, Maggie refrained from asking questions.

"When I told everyone about my life on Earth, the monks didn't think I was crazy," James said.

"Well, that's good."

"Yes, but, Leo didn't say a word after the meeting."

"You living in a different world is a hard pill to swallow. Believe me, I should know. He will come around. He needs to process the crazies."

Her words were less than sufficient to ease James' pain.

"I don't think he will. I lost his trust," he said.

"This thing all things devours;
Birds, beasts, trees, flowers;
Gnaws iron, bites steel;
Grinds hard stones to meal;
Slays king, ruins town,
And beats mountain down." Maggie recited a riddle from memory.

"Time? You think he needs time?" James asked.

"Yes," Maggie said, "a friendship like yours will not be easily broken. Just give him some time."

Either that was all James needed to hear or the call of his stomach had temporarily eased the pain, because suddenly all he could think about was where their next meal would come from. He gave Maggie a smile that did not spread to his eyes. Knowing him all too well, she brought out the last can from the food bank packages and offered him a silver spoon. Spicy chili was on the menu for breakfast that morning. James was more than happy to indulge in the bean and meat mixture, even though it was not nearly as appetizing as his mom's chili.

With Leo occupying his thoughts, James was bound to spend a grouchy day. He was sorry to subject Maggie to it, but life looked nothing but gray at the moment. Normally, this was the day of the week, weather permitting, when they went to watch the street performances. It was one of the best parts of city-life. Other than that Maggie would be perfectly happy living in a house in the middle of nowhere.

Hoping that exercise would help him shake off the numbness, but mostly because he did not want Maggie to wallow in his self-pity all day, James agreed to take a walk towards downtown, where exciting people like saxophone players or jugglers shared their talents. They needed to bum some change anyway, now that they had eaten the last of the food bank goodies.

The sad, teenage boy wandered around aimlessly, people-watching, cheering for the performers, and panhandling. There wasn't much talk or chatter. James was grateful for Maggie's understanding.

Minutes went by slowly, but the day went by fast. People must have been feeling extra happy, because they collected almost twenty dollars in change despite James' sullen stature.

Maggie splurged and bought some pecan cluster ice cream for them to enjoy after dinner. But even the rare treat did not lift James' spirit up. He went to sleep with the taste of ice cream in his mouth and the bitterness of dread on his mind.

Day 8: Kaya

One of the most dreaded days of his life on Kaya arrived with lightning speed. For most of his childhood and since he moved into the Inn, Leo had always been there for him. Theirs was a friendship forged in the loneliness of being orphans, but could that bond could ride through the current storm? James hoped.

Just like every morning, he was the only one in the kitchen and the only one walking down the path to the school. But unlike every morning, he felt alone. The feeling was disturbingly similar to the one he had right after leaving his family to live in the streets on Earth. Beauty of the spring blossoms vanished in the shadow of losing something as precious as a lifelong friendship.

The classroom door swung open on its creaky hinges. Leo was at his usual spot, but every time James tried to catch his gaze, he pretended to be preoccupied with a book or a blank parchment.

Lord Ywi's happy voice and Sister Eata's stern instructions washed over him as the day's classes came and went. James was positive that he would not remember a word from that day at the time of the final exams. He didn't care. School was the least of his worries at the moment.

Lunch had no taste, and work in the fields was nowhere near as enjoyable as usual. All in all, the day was turning out to be terrible. He couldn't even conjure up any enthusiasm to meet Brother Aelred, but since one did not ignore an invitation from the head of the Maelite order, James headed back to the Academy after an arduous day at the fields. All the muscles in his body ached as he approached West Tower. It was hard to decide if the day's work was taking a toll on him or the heavy silence between him and Leo was making life more exhausting than ever.

Whatever the cause, the spiraling steps of the tower were looming in front of him in the company of white marble reliefs. James did not find them as pleasing as yesterday.

He was the last one to arrive to the meeting. Brother Aelred and the other monks were at the same spots they sat yesterday, as if they had not moved at all through the night. Actually, he wouldn't be surprised if they hadn't. Life of monks either enticed respect or a strong desire to run in the opposite direction.

James muttered an apology under his breath with a string of excuses ranging from the field being far to the shower being cold. When Brother Aelred pointed next to Leo, he stopped his almost inaudible mutterings and joined the meeting of these serious people.

Apparently, the Abbot was not one for introductions or ice breaking, because he did not waste a moment talking about serious topics.

"Until you told Brother Linus that you were from a different world, I had thought all hope was lost. But now, we can begin anew and decipher the Manual to reach the instructions. After that, it's a matter of time to follow the steps that lead to freedom."

As James listened to the older man's calm but determined voice, he realized that trusting Brother Aelred came easily. He didn't know why, especially because suspicion and distrust had become tools of his trade since he had left his family behind on Earth. Memories of people stealing the little food you had or kicking you in your sleep flooded into his Kayan mind from who-knows-how-many light years away. Even though his life in Aqui had never been as hard and full of pain as his life in Seattle, James couldn't help but carry the emotions from each world back and forth, often bringing hope to Earth and sometimes infecting Kaya with despair. Now, as Brother Aelred talked about the Manual and the instructions within, both sides of James trusted him implicitly. With this trust came the sense that all would be well. His tense shoulders relaxed a little, and his mind started to actually pay attention to the Abbot's words.

"Why would Rex Cathan meet with us, since he claims to have destroyed the Manual?" Leo asked.

James thought of that the previous night. According to the Maelites, Rex would do anything in his power to prevent them from taking the Ambit down. The man wanted to be the king of this tiny kingdom. It was the same wherever you were - the allure of power was irresistible.

"The government of Aqui is somewhat unique because of our special circumstances. Different bodies of the administration perform separate government functions, and since technically the head of the Maelite Order is also one of the ministers of state, the Rex cannot refuse to meet with a member of his cabinet, and in this case with you as well," the Abbot answered.

James was glad they would at least get to talk to the man who had stolen the only hope the Aquites had to see beyond the Ambit. "When will we be able to meet Rex Cathan?"

"Tomorrow. I arranged for you to skip work after school, and meet me at the lower gates of the Academy after lunch. We'll talk more on the way. Goodnight."

That was all. He leaped to his feet with an agility that was unexpected from a man of his age and swiftly exited the top room of the West Tower. The monks who came with him followed their abbot with equally soundless footsteps.

James and Leo were left alone with one of the most breath-taking views in Aqui and with one of the most awkward situations in both their lives. All of a sudden, Leo started to talk so quietly that James was almost sure that he was addressing the marble walls.

"Sorry, did you say something?"

Leo straightened his back and assumed the confident posture James always envied and appreciated at the same time. "I said, I am sorry I have been so full of myself since yesterday."

A wave of relief wash over James, and suddenly the sunset felt warmer.

"The thing is..." Leo continued without eye contact. "At first, I couldn't believe that you would hide such a big part of your life from me. I felt betrayed, but also I was mad that I never really knew you. Then, as I thought about it through the day, I realized how crazy living in another world sounded. I believed you because it was you and because Brother Aelred believed you. Anyway, sorry for the silent treatment. It takes a while for me to catch up sometimes."

He got on his feet and approached James, who was having a hard time believing his ears. Once he was close enough to look at James, he asked, "Friends?"

A smile spread from east to west on James' face as he hugged his friend and patted him on the back. He could not have been more thankful. "I'm sorry, too."

"Well, the crazies are hard to confess," Leo said with a half-smile. That was that. All was well. James was more grateful than ever before for the simplicity and clarity of Leo's mind.

They headed out, talking animatedly about Brother Aelred, Rex Cathan, and the elusive Manual. Recapping the day's events put everything into perspective and made the foggy parts clearer in James' mind. He realized as they walked back to the Inn that the peacefulness and serenity of Aqui had returned once more, leaving the gloom back in Seattle.

Once they entered the old, white building that had been their home for years now, James and Leo went their separate ways to fetch Claire, Joan, and Elgar.

In twenty minutes, all five were gathered in a far corner of the garden stretching towards the mountains behind the Inn. Even though they were willing to share everything with the others, James and Leo wanted to be sure that nobody was eavesdropping.

"I brought some goodies for our super-secret, open-door meeting," Joan said, the lover of picnics. "I thought some bread, cheese, and apples to nibble on might be good as we talked about saving the world."

"Don't mind if I do," Leo said, stuffing half a loaf in his mouth.

James took a deep breath. It was like pulling off a Band-Aid, or more like a long piece of duct tape.

"The reason we were able to meet with Brother Aelred is that I live in two worlds. Here on Kaya and in another planet called Earth."

All three of them stopped eating, Elgar's hand suspended in the air, halfway to his mouth. Leo didn't skip a beat as he polished off the remainder of the aged cheddar.

"What do you mean 'another world?'" Joan asked. "You mean like an alien? Do you have a spaceship or something?"

"No, no, no...I don't know how it works, but when I go to bed here, I wake up there."

"So you don't have a sleeping disorder?" Elgar asked.

"Nope."

"How does it relate to the Ambit and Brother Aelred?" Claire asked.

James and Leo tried to ward off the question storm. The picnic and emerging stars had become nothing more than distractions as each one took turns of posing question after question. Confusion was getting a little overwhelming for everyone.

"Ha! That's why I could never See you during the mark classes! You were telling the truth! That's cheating, James!" Claire yelled with a triumphant tone.

Joan had a little over a thousand questions about Earth and his life in Seattle. Did he look different? Did they have peaches over there? How many suns and moons did Earth have? Did he have a family? On and on and on. James decided to briefly summarize life on Earth without showing emotion. Even though being homeless was not part of his account, when he was done, there was silence.

"I thought we had it bad here in Aqui stuck behind the Ambit," Elgar said as he played with a piece of bread, not looking James in the eye.

"At least you have parents there," Claire said. "Things might get better."

"I really don't think so," James shrugged his shoulders. "But at least I have you here."

It must have been getting too serious for Joan, because she decided to change the subject.

"So, do you think Rex Cathan will have a sudden change of heart once he sees five teenagers and an old Maelite?" she asked.

"We don't know," Leo said, "but we need to find out if the Manual is still intact."

After that, they finished their meager dinner that was sweetened with camaraderie and washed the two-day-old bread and cheese down with some sour cherry juice. For a little while, James didn't worry about being trapped inside the invisible cage. The fear of losing friends or being ostracized were blown into the evening breeze. He was safe, and his secret was safe.

Day 9: Earth

Yes, yes, it was time to wake up and give Maggie a hug she dearly deserved. He sat upright as soon as consciousness hit his head on Earth, traveling thousands of light-years from Kaya. Maggie was startled at his sudden movements.

"Are you alright?" she asked, furrowing her eyebrows in such a characteristic way that her future children would one day love.

"You were right!" he exclaimed, reaching to give her a big hug that was possibly a little too tight, because she was struggling to breathe. It was a good idea not to kill her on such a happy day.

"Right about what?" Maggie asked.

"You were right about Leo needing some time to process things. Everything's back to normal, better than normal!" James explained as he folded his legs on the cardboard, which once contained a swing set.

"I'll tell you everything on the way to the church; I'm starving."

It was Sunday, which meant that the warm meal the Catholic ladies served awaited their forever empty teenage stomachs.

Maggie was more than happy to oblige. She listened to James with a smile on her face while he recounted the events of his previous day on Kaya with great enthusiasm. After yesterday's daylong gloom, she looked pleased to listen to his non-stop excited talk under the partially-cloudy sky.

It was one of those days when his life on Kaya made his life on Earth much more bearable. The threatening face of dark rain clouds in the East could not take away the merry bubbles exuding from him. By the time they arrived at the

129

church a little too early, James had had time to tell Maggie about every single unnecessary detail of his previous day and even the stuff he did not feel like talking about the day before.

Finally, he stopped to take a breath. Maggie walked towards one of the empty wooden benches across the street. They had to wait around a while before lunch was served.

"A few questions." She sat down on the slightly wet bench with hands still in her pocket. There was an urgent need to catch one's breath after talking for a long period of time, but still, James answered equally peppy. "Fire away!"

"When are you gonna ask Zoe out?"

"What? Is that the first question you ask after all the information I just vomited?"

"Why, yes, it is. Because I already knew that Leo would forgive you, so no surprises there. Sometimes, others see our situation more clearly than we do. Nothing new on the Brother Aelred and the Manual front either. But when you talk about Zoe, you're a little bit different." That unbearable mischievous smile appeared on her face again.

"What do you mean 'different?'" James asked, curious about what gave him away, wishing that his Seeing skills would transfer to Earth.

"Well, you act like you are uninterested and cool when you talk about her, which tells me that you are interested and uncool. It's kind of cute, actually." She nudged him with her shoulder.

"I don't know what you're talking about," James said. "I was merely impressed with her Reading skills."

"I am sure that was *all* you were impressed with," Maggie said.

"Anyway," he continued, desperate to change the subject as his body shot a dollop of red through his cheeks, "I was more curious about your thoughts on the Manual."

"You're like a little boy when it comes to girls, you know that?"

"Enough with the girls, Maggie River! We have more important issues to talk about."

"With or without the Ambit, you will need a girlfriend eventually, James Knox. So, I think it is rather important," she pressed, enjoying James' discomfort a little too much.

"I tell you what, I'll ask her out when we take the Ambit down."

"When the fish climb the tree. Nice compromise," Maggie said. She did not neglect to put air quotes of the word compromise.

"Well, that's all you get," he smiled and thought about taking a long walk in the forest with Zoe, talking about animals and plants as he watched her long hair sway. He shook his head and decided to get back to other topics that he had just deemed more important.

"I don't have anything new to say about the Manual. We'll have to wait until after your meeting with this Rex," Maggie added.

She was right. Not every day was full of revelations. As they watched the increasing number of people who jogged or walked their dogs in the relatively mild weather, the next few hours flew by despite the call of their empty stomachs. Time was a lot less formidable when you were happy.

The lunch line was longer than usual. When he first started going to different soup kitchens around the city, he had felt out of place. After all, he had a home and people who would take care of him, even though his dinners consisted of corndogs and potato chips. He felt guilty about taking the little food truly homeless people so desperately needed. But the more he got to know others in his situation, the more he realized that his situation was not necessarily unique. Many of the young homeless kids came from broken or dysfunctional families. There was abuse in all its terrible ugly forms imaginable, and there was neglect. His family, even after Jake's death, looked like a model of success compared to some of the stories he heard.

Now after a few years of having to depend on others for sustenance, James had become used to being a part of this crowd. Most of his fellow soup kitcheners had glazed stares and vacant expressions. They have been in the streets too long. They have been without families too long. He thought about Kaya, and how everyone took care of each other. Being an orphan in Aqui was infinitely preferable to being a homeless teenager in Seattle.

James got lost in thought looking at a man in his sixties who held onto a battered green backpack as if it contained the crown jewels. His white hair was disheveled and greasy, showing clear signs of not having been washed for a while. He was there for the food, but it was easy to see that he did not trust anyone. James thought about the lonely life the old man must have led. He heard Maggie's voice as if it was coming behind a thick glass door and yanked himself back to the present.

"James! Grab a tray!" Maggie nudged him in between the shoulder blades. He was at the top of the line already. The sadness that had enveloped him eased up, as he picked up one of the brown plastic trays. As plates of lasagna, garlic bread, and fruit salad filled the empty tray, James found himself wanting to look at the old man who was trying to serve his food one-handed while clutching the dirty bag with his other hand. For some reason, James could not get rid of the feeling that he was looking into a mirror that showed what would come to pass.

As the red sauce and hearty meat of lasagna filled his belly, he regained his pep. Maggie had picked up another children's book and she was looking through the pages that depicted a mother and a child playing in a cabbage patch. Because they had been talking since seven in the morning, a quiet lunch in the hum of activities did not bother them. Soon the food was eaten, and the coffee with cookies were gone. They both leaned back in their chairs for a while to celebrate a properly fed body. It was one of the best feelings on Earth.

One lived for simple pleasures when one had so little.

Day 9: Kaya

When he walked into the kitchen, Joan and Claire were in the middle of a discussion with the animated hand motions of two Italian grandmothers. As soon as they heard someone enter the kitchen, the animation and the chatter stopped. James bid good morning to the ladies who were almost as late as he was and went to the pantry for some bread and a jar of Ebru's homemade pepper jam.

Joan looked towards the door to make sure there were no more people coming in and approached, eyes darting around with conspiracy. James chuckled with amusement. Despite her ever-present sarcasm, Joan was one of those people who got excited about the simplest of things. Even though she was a strong Healer, when the two edges of broken skin slowly weaved together to heal a cut, she was still amazed. Everything was a wonder. She experienced the same exhilaration every time she Paced through the woods.

James brought the bread and the jam to the table and started treating a fine slice of bread with butter and red pepper goodness.

"What were you two whispering about when I walked in?"

"Claire and I were wondering if you are married in that other world?" she asked, lowering her voice even more when she said the words "other world" as if anyone would know what she was talking about.

James laughed so hard that he almost spat out the food in his mouth. "Married? I am still sixteen...Also life is not very good over there." He had omitted the homeless runaway troubled youth part of his life on Earth, even though he knew it would come up sooner or later.

"Life's too good to waste on a girl, anyway."

"How dare you? You should be happy if any girl would be willing to be seen with you, let alone marry you!" Joan said with mock indignation.

"So your life on Earth is not much different from here?" Claire asked.

"It is and it's not. People on Earth don't have marks like Kayans, so I have to walk everywhere. But they have coffee." James replied, still not wanting to talk about the downsides of sleeping in a make-shift cardboard box during a rainy night.

"What's coffee?" Joan asked.

"Coffee is a drink that wakes your brain up when you're late to school, like we are."

Claire and Joan both jumped to their feet, since unlike James, both girls hated being late. By the time he put his plate in the sink, the only thing that was left of his curious friends was the hem of Claire's dress disappearing behind the door.

He grabbed his satchel off the floor and followed after them. Even though it was Fiveday, they had decided to meet in the study hall to work on their marks and use each other as test subjects. The mark test of the following month was looming over them.

Suddenly, the oncoming day weighed on his shoulders, taking away the joy of being surrounded with loved ones last night and this morning. He did not look forward to their meeting with Rex Cathan.

To begin with, he never liked the capital city Xavi. Since the Dispersal, even after four centuries, the damage Haydar's experiment caused was visible in quite a few areas. Many of the government buildings were restored or rebuilt depending on the level of destruction, but the majority of university structures and residential areas remained uninhabited, covered in black scars of fire, chemicals or magic that even the monks and the anchorites could not erase. Xavi was an ancient city half in ruins and half in development. The only people who wanted to travel into the center were those who worked there. James did not want to be surrounded by the melancholy that emanated from annihilation.

Leo, who was rocking back and forth on his chair next to the window, looked considerably happier than James. At the sight of his smiling friend (and the fact that Leo was still his friend), the rain clouds in James' head separated a little for him to get through the morning without wanting to pull the dark curtains and listen to loud metal music all day.

The five of them met for lunch. Now that the time was near, they all felt the dread and anxiety of going against Brother Aelred's wishes. Lunch was a silent and tasteless affair and ended all too quickly.

Satchels slung over their shoulders, dressed in the best clothes they owned, James, Leo, Claire, Joan, and Elgar walked down the windy path that led out of the Academy grounds into the wilderness first and then eventually to the destroyed city of Xavi.

Unadorned horse carts of the Maelites lingered at the bottom of the hill where the stone wall of the Academy yielded to the swirling and spiraling cast iron kissing gates. Other than Brother Aelred and Brother Linus, there were four more monks.

When Brother Aelred saw that five students instead of two were strolling down the hill, he got out of the cart and with deliberate steps stomped through the gate to meet them.

"I thought I told you not share what we have talked about with anyone."

"Yes, you did," James said, feeling unusually brave and defiant.

"But Claire, Joan, and Elgar have been with us from the beginning and their input have been and will be valuable." Leo added, a little less defiantly and a little more convincingly.

"Do you trust them?" Brother Aelred asked, looking at James, Leo, and Brother Linus.

James and Leo said, "Absolutely," at the same time, and then they turned to Brother Linus who nodded once.

"We will keep the secrets," Joan said.

Brother Aelred smiled and shook his head. "Well, you already know too much."

Then, he turned around and took his seat in one of the carts once more. They all followed his example without a word. Soon, all eleven of them were seated and ready to undertake the ride to see the most powerful man in Aqui. Monks and orphans against rexes and rulers. It was going to be an interesting day indeed.

After three hours of watching breathtaking Kayan wilderness and fruit orchards pass by, the city of Xavi appeared in front of them following a sharp bend of the packed dirt road. The capital of Aqui was hidden behind green rolling hills covered in pink and white wild flowers. Scars of the city were invisible from this distance, and tall ornate government buildings looked serene in the afternoon sun.

Distance was deceptive. When horses pulled the carts through the outer city, the burn marks that were covered with ivy tentacles and the half-demolished, half-intact houses became apparent, urging silent reverence in everyone. Ghostly structures bore witness to the consequences of one man's greed and hunger for power.

In half a mile, depressing scenery gave way to a cleaner and more organized center where most of the inhabited buildings were located. In many parts, almost all taint of the dispersal was eliminated. The desire for a new beginning had scrubbed the blood stains and painted over the burn marks through the centuries. The dead remained dead, and the living lingered on.

When the carts stopped in front of the City Hall where the offices of the Rex, the ministers, and the dukes looked over the city, there was no one to greet them or check for concealed weapons. In contrast to the governments on Earth, the small intimate community of Aqui had thus far failed to breed assassins. Surely there was crime, thievery, robbery, and even occasionally murder, but the evils that increased with multitudes of people living in close quarters without actually connecting were non-existent in Aqui. The lack of regular threats to politicians made the City Hall a much more welcoming place.

The unlikely entourage climbed up the marble stairs. White stones reflected the sunlight so fiercely that heat radiated to their legs. James followed Leo as all of them entered the building through a gate in the middle of which hung a golden anchor, representing the government's dependency on the people.

Two aids from the Rex's office met them as they walked down the corridor where the floor was partially covered in dark blue carpet, adorned with silver flowers. The ceiling was so high that one would mistake being outside if it weren't for the walls holding numerous paintings that depicted famous scenes from Kayan and Aquite history. James recognized some of the scenes and people from his history classes, but most of the faces remained strangers to these sixteen-year-olds. No doubt, Brothers Aelred and Linus would be able to recall every little detail of each painting and every tiny person that was watching the events unfold. James had never been good at memorizing and remembering. Leo was the historian.

The faint smell of ink and fresh parchment travelled with the visitors. The long, wide corridor finally led through a set of dark wooden doors with carvings of dragons and sea serpents. It was impossible not to be intimidated when an eight-foot-long serpent stared down at you, real or carving. They walked through the door into a circular room that could easily hold hundreds of people. Sculptures under every window accompanied the life size paintings of former rexes. The place looked like a throne room of a monarchy, rather than the work place of an elected official. Just as he thought about this, Brother Linus leaned over and whispered.

"This room looked much different before Rex Cathan. After assuming office, he himself designed the chair and redecorated the entire room."

A throne room, it was.

A dark oval table stood in the middle of the otherwise empty hall. Twenty chairs formed a half circle around the table, facing the throne. Twenty was for the number of ministers, some elected and some appointed, like Brother Aelred, because of the merit of their position. At the beckoning of the aids, they all picked one of the long-backed chairs, near the Rex's throne-like seat, which was much bigger and much more ornate with a taller back. Cathan's seat was placed on a platform, further ensuring that all the ministers would be looked down upon. There was something eerie when one exalted oneself rather than being exalted by others. How can the king crown himself? It appeared that Cathan did.

Ten minutes after they took their seats, a door to the side of the throne opened and two other aids entered, then a man in his late fifties. The monks stood up and folded hands on their chests as the Rex entered the room and waited for him to be seated. Once the blue corduroy cushion of the bigger and taller chair was flattened by the Rex's almost royal bottom, James and his friends could get back to their humble seats.

Cathan looked tall and intimidating in his black satin robe even when seated.

James didn't think he actually needed the platform. But he could also see the effect since he felt a little smaller looking up into the deep black eyes of the face, framed in salt and pepper beard and shoulder-length hair. The wrinkles around the Rex's eyes gave him the air of a stern and wise grandfather.

As soon as he sat down, Rex Cathan turned to Brother Aelred, who occupied the furthest chair from the throne:

"What a pleasure to see you once again, Aelred. We surely have missed your counsel over the years."

Brother Aelred bowed his head almost imperceptibly.

"Thank you, your grace, accept my apologies if my attempts to remain part of the governance fell short. The knowledge that your grace is counseled by perceptive and intelligent ministers lightens my burden."

James looked across the table and saw that Joan was rolling her eyes at the formalities and fake gestures of concern. At least the rest of the group was tactful enough to wear the neutral faces of professional poker players. After a few more lines of pleasantries, Rex Cathan waved his hand to dismiss all the aids and got up from his throne. When he turned to Brother Aelred again, the fake smile was replaced by a look of disdain and displeasure. With the silver embroideries of his robes shining in the sunlight, the rex headed towards the opposite direction from where he had entered the room, and pushed something under one of the torches. A door that was concealed a moment ago opened to reveal a flight of stairs to a lower level. Without a word, he disappeared. Brother Aelred was already at his heels.

James was sure that they were not going down to the wine cellar for a glass of properly aged red or to put the wet laundry in the dryer. At least, the stereotype of having secret passages in high profile rooms was justified. What did the one in the Oval Office look like? Surely the President would need a route that offered a timely getaway once in a while.

The torches along the walls barely gave enough light for them to see the next few steps. James turned around to look at Elgar who shrugged his shoulders to make the I-don't-know motion. Good to know that everyone was equally clueless.

The stairs came to a sudden end when he saw Leo's back enter into a small, dark room through an ancient door. The table here was much simpler than the one above. A thick layer of dust had settled on the simple furnishings of the underground meeting room. Obviously, Rex Cathan had not had to carry any secret conversations for a long time. Once again, they all settled on the chairs. This time there were no tall backs nor cushions for their comfort. Nobody, including the Rex with his fine silken robe, seemed to care about the dust.

"Why are you here, Aelred?" The Rex demanded with the authority of a man who was used to people obeying his every command.

"You know why I am here," Brother Aelred said, not intimidated by Rex's commanding posture.

"Then you have broken your recluse for no reason. As I have told you before, the Manual is destroyed." A venomous hatred oozed with his every word. "Besides, even if it weren't, I wouldn't give it to you. What would you do with it anyway?"

"Are you so arrogant to think that you are the only the harbinger mentioned? Passing years have not been able to teach you humility, I see." Brother Aelred answered with an expression that was unbecoming for a monk who was selfless enough to devote his life to solitude and contemplation. Clearly, forgiving Cathan, his friend and student, had been much harder than the Abbot had expected.

"Don't be delusional! I have not yet met another like me all this time. Are you saying there is one now?"

"Yes, there is." Brother Linus joined the conversation of former friends and new enemies.

Rex Cathan's eyes searched for a clue about this new one as he looked at everyone around the table, but could not find one. "I assume it's one of the students?" he asked finally.

"Yes," Aelred said, not taking the bait, "You know that we need the Manual to progress. You have had your chance at saving Aqui and did not use it. Over the decades, you have accumulated wealth and influence. Please give us the Manual so that we can end this captivity. No one knows when we will again get another Outsider."

"You make it sound like I am a selfish, power hungry villain!" The Rex smacked his palm on the old table, making a cloud of dust rise into the air in order to escape his fury. "I did not follow the Manual, because Aqui was and *is* Paradise. I knew from my other world how awful things would become eventually. Nevertheless, today, even after centuries, the tight-knit community and technology-free life of Aqui are nothing less than heavenly. Yes, we can't travel all around Kaya, but that is a small price to pay in exchange of living in Paradise."

"How about our diminishing numbers?" Elgar spoke from the far end of the table. It was uncharacteristic of him to speak up. "If we cannot take the Ambit down, there will be no one to enjoy your perfect world."

The Rex studied Elgar with his piercing dark gaze. The man was not used to being addressed by a minor so disrespectfully.

"It's an issue we have been working on," he said when Elgar did not waver.

"You are young and you don't understand the evil and the greed of the outside world. The other planet I live in is full of murderers, thieves, dictators, and torturers. We don't have that in Aqui. As soon as that Ambit comes down, all that poison will creep in. You should ask the Outsider among you about the wonders that await."

Falling into Cathan's trap, instinctively, every one of his friends looked at James. The brothers were a little more alert at not giving away the identity of the Outsider.

Rex Cathan's gaze found James' eyes. "So, it's you," he said with a triumphant smile. "Where are you from?"

James would not be intimidated. "Nowhere you would know."

"Are you sure? I am from Toledo, Ohio. Sound familiar?"

"You are from Earth, too. What are the odds of that happening?" James asked, taken aback by the knowledge that the Rex of Aqui was from a town in the Midwest. He couldn't even say the world was small.

"I don't know how it is at all possible to live in two different planets, but after all these years, one of the things I reasoned was that there is a connection between Earth and Kaya. Obviously, one crucial aspect of this connection is the similarities of the human and Kayan biology. Except for the marks, of course. Because the odds of any extraterrestrial bodies sharing this much commonality are almost none, any Outsider you might meet on Kaya would most likely be from Earth."

James had not put that much thought into it, let alone forming a coherent conclusion about any connection between the two worlds. He adjusted his face from the mild admiration to the disdain that was on all the brothers' faces. When James could not come up with an objection, the Rex asked him the question he dreaded.

"What is your world like, boy? Where do you live?"

Even though his friends did not want to put him on the spot, he knew that the same question was burning in all their minds. James realized curiosity had triumphed over being considerate or polite, since they all looked at him, waiting for an answer.

"Tell them how wonderful life on Earth is," the Rex egged on.

"I can't," James said, almost with a whisper. He looked up to see Leo's shocked eyes. But there would be no lies, nor secrets, anymore. He took a deep breath and continued,

"Earth is a miserable place. I live in a big city with millions of others. There are no Ambits. If you have the means, you can travel anywhere. Despite this freedom, I live in the streets. I steal to feed myself and beg for money. My family is broken beyond repair, and I haven't seen my parents or my brother for years."

The confession was like being in one of those dreams where he was naked, not able to wake up. When he finally swallowed the rising tide of tears and looked at his friends, he saw sadness rather than disgust or disbelief. At that moment, once again, he realized what wonderful friends they were. Instead of cursing Earth, they wanted to take away the loneliness and pain James suffered daily. He felt grateful and ashamed all at the same time. Grateful for their silent embraces, and ashamed that in just a few sentences he had confirmed Rex Cathan's theory of doom.

A shroud of silence fell over the occupants of the dusty room. The Rex did not want to speak in order to reap the benefits of James' life on Earth. Clearly, it was much worse than what he had expected.

"That is..." The Rex savored the moment of shock. "This *is* what you would find beyond the Ambit, a life of despair, poverty, and loneliness, not the freedom, love, and happiness you dream. Kayans are just like humans from Earth. I guarantee you that Kaya outside of the Ambit is not much different. In exchange of false freedom, corruption, and decadence of the rest of the world will taint your lives forever. You are all sorely mistaken if you think Haydar was the only Kayan who could leave disasters in his wake. I will not be part of the plan that would leave this Paradise in ruins."

No one spoke a word. Not even Brother Aelred. It wasn't hard to see that he had not anticipated that James would be coming from such a painful background.

"At least, then, we will have the option to choose whether to live in heaven or in hell. A golden cage is a cage nonetheless," the Abbot said, standing up.

Defeated, he headed for the stairs. Right before he exited, he turned around and addressed the Rex one more time. "Thank you for seeing us on such short notice, your grace."

"It was a pleasure to see you again, Aelred," said Cathan, with a faint hint of sorrow in his eyes.

Quietly, they all followed the barefoot abbot. Thwarted and tired, tonight, there would not be conversations about where to travel when the Ambit came down.

Day 10: Earth

James woke up to the unintelligible sounds of an argument or a fight outside. As far as homeless areas went, their small neighborhood on this secluded corner had been nothing but peaceful over the years. Surely, there had been a few fights and thefts, but for the most part, thugs and drug pushers had left them alone. James never knew why they had enjoyed such peace, but he did not care.

He jumped to his feet to make sure that Maggie was alright. But she was not in the safety of their fragile cardboard haven. Then, he heard her yell at someone, "I said leave her alone! She has nothing!"

James shot out of the shelter to see what was upsetting Maggie so much so early in the morning.

The unusually bright sunlight blinded him momentarily before he could gauge what all the commotion was about. Once his pupils contracted enough to function in the morning light, he saw Maggie trying to stand between two youth and Mrs. Jackson's shelter.

"What's going on here?" James yelled, instinctively placing himself between Maggie and the other guys. Even though he did not have the build of a Pacer on Earth, he was still taller than most guys around his age. Having been well-fed and participating in various sports for a long time, James had a presence that would not be easily overlooked. The aggressors took a step back to size up the new nuisance.

"They're trying to steal Mrs. Jackson's stuff!" Maggie explained the situation, holding the fragile old woman around the shoulders.

"What does she have to steal?" James asked, trying to ease the tension as he came up with a plan that did not include him being plastered by two thugs.

"Get out of the way," the thug on the left said and shoved James in the chest. He was probably in his early twenties, almost as tall as James but not built as well. His dark hair was cut short and spiked up with an inordinate amount of product. He must be requiring the possessions of an old homeless woman in order to support his cosmetic needs.

James recovered from the push, and once again planted his feet firmly in front of Maggie. "I'm afraid I can't let you do that," he said, sounding much more confident than he felt.

The other thug was not pleased with this unexpected resistance. He was shorter than his partner-in-crime, but sported strong shoulders under a well-worn black leather jacket. James could not help but smirk at the classic bad-guy look this guy employed. The leather jacket guy walked past the spiky hair guy and pushed James aside, nearly making him topple over Mrs. Jackson. As soon as James regained his balance, he threw himself at the leather jacket guy and knocked the bully on the ground. Before he knew it, there were punches and kicks. Despite not knowing what he was doing, James was able to subdue the leather jacket guy with a well-placed uppercut to the jaw.

Spiky hair guy, on the other hand, was not willing to engage in hand-to-hand combat that morning.

"Com'on, Bobby, we'll stop by later," he said.

The leather jacket guy quickly got up and straightened his clothes that were carefully coordinated for the needs of a life of crime. "We'll be back," he said.

All three of them stared at the thugs as they turned around the corner and got lost in the shadow of nearby buildings.

"I can't believe you fought that guy!" Maggie said, letting go of Mrs. Jackson to check up on James.

"I can't believe it either," James said. "I thought I was bluffing." He smiled. It hurt to smile. He must have taken a few punches.

"I'm sorry," Mrs. Jackson said and fished a small glass bottle out of her purse.

"No need to apologize," James replied while Mrs. Jackson dabbed the contents of the bottle on her hand and applied the mystery substance on James' bruises. It smelled like soap.

"Lavender oil," she explained. "It will help with the pain and the bruising."

James thanked her for the unconventional first aid. He was not going to the ER for a few bruises, but a bit of help would not hurt. The oil seemed to have worked quickly as the discomfort of smiling had already eased.

"Thank you very much," Mrs. Jackson said again, turning to Maggie this time. "You're my beautiful guardian angel." Not knowing how to answer the old woman's compliment, she smiled.

Mrs. Jackson assumed her usual thoughtful composure and went into her tiny shelter that did not contain anything worth stealing.

"Jerks!" Maggie said under her breath and checked the bruises and cuts on James' face once more. "Thankfully, his punches are as lousy as his sense of fashion; you don't need any stitches."

"I am sure Mrs. Jackson's magic oil will heal me in no time," James said. It was good to feel useful for a change.

"So, how did it go?" Maggie asked. The fact that thugs and drug dealers visited their peaceful neighborhood once in a while did not bother her any longer than needed. It was the reality of homeless life. Actually, they had always wondered why things like this did not happen more often. Usually, thieves came when no one was around and took whatever they found inside wobbly shelters. Pickings were slim. You needed to be either desperately in need or utterly cruel to rob the homeless. Sad to say, it was usually the latter.

"Oh, you mean the meeting with the Rex?" James asked.

The retelling of the events of yesterday did not take long. Trying to describe the sadness James saw in his friends' eyes when he told them about his life in Seattle made his voice tremble. Since they were all orphans, James had never felt a hint of pity from them before. Once in a while, he could see signs of sorrow in the eyes of a monk or an anchorite when he explained how his Kayan parents died, but witnessing a similar look from his friends was much harder, for some reason.

"I wouldn't believe anything this self-appointed king says. Also, Toledo, Ohio? Isn't that in a John Denver song?"

James stood up and started to sing the only lyrics he remembered,

"Here's to the dogs of Toledo, Ohio
Ladies, we bid you goodbye!"

He took a deep bow. As he rose, a feeling of lightness embraced him.

"My dad loved this song, but I only remember the last bit."

Maggie clapped for the overdramatic performance.

"You know, you're right. Why should I trust the word of a man who used all his gifts to become the most powerful person in Aqui? So, you don't think he destroyed it?"

"Nah," she shook her head, "if I were a power-crazy man who betrayed a bunch of monks, umm, no I would not have destroyed something that might give me leverage over them sometime in the future."

"You have a point," James said, "but where would he hide it? He probably had dozens of hiding places. How can we even narrow it down?"

"Well, we need to know the man," Maggie jumped to her feet. "So you need to gather some intelligence, Mr. Bond."

"I shall!" James stood up, grateful for Maggie's spiritedness that made him shake off the blues.

The rest of the day passed unremarkably. The excitement of the morning coupled with the emotional weight of the previous day was more than enough to beg for a smooth afternoon. Maggie seemed to have forgotten the unpleasantness with the thugs, since all she did was come up with one crazy idea after another about the Manual. Even panhandling and the lack of food after a bad day did not dampen their spirits.

On the way back, they picked up some wipes and saltine crackers for Mrs. Jackson. The remainder of the money went to a dinner of almost expired canned food that was on sale.

When it was bedtime, James was content, Maggie was content, and Mrs. Jackson was content, because the cruelty of the world had not erased all kindness.

Yet.

Day 10: Kaya

The memory of his smiling friends during the picnic behind the Inn flooded his mind, the friends whose hopes got crushed under the weight of his miserable life. Good thing it was still Sixday, as none of his muscles wanted to move even an inch. He rolled over and stared at the tiny little plant living happily in its humble clay pot, oblivious to the troubles of others. James concentrated hard on its dark green, spiky leaves. The plant shuddered in its pot, not having an idea or sense that something strange had invaded its body. Even the clueless plant in his room did not like being manipulated.

He picked up a book from the pile on his cluttered night stand, pushed himself on the heels of his hands to sit upright, and started reading. He stopped after a few pages since not one word about the contents had reached his mind. The book fell off his hands on to the bunched-up white sheets. There was not going to be any reading that morning. A nice warm shower might clear his foggy brain.

As he thought about what happened yesterday, the queasy feeling in his stomach returned. What Rex Cathan had said about life in Aqui was true. He could not imagine a better place to spend his life. That was the reason for so many years the Ambit did not bother him, especially having lived another and much more disagreeable life for a long time. Why would he want to bring down the only thing that had been holding the inevitable darkness at bay?

Showering was not enough to take the gloom away. Maybe Pacing practice would give him a different perspective. He wanted, no, needed to get out of this fog. Otherwise, life in Aqui would be as poisoned as life on Earth.

He changed into shorts and did his stretches. Again, without ceremony, he took off. Destination did not matter, neither did time. James ran faster and faster, pushing his Pacer muscles to their limit. The sun was rising in the blue sky, and the trees greeted him in full bloom. He refused to feel this depressed when nature sang such a glorious song. Bright green branches adorned with white and pink blossoms flew past his face in the beautiful countryside, defying dark thoughts.

At first, he did not have a destination in mind, but his legs must have had a different idea, because soon James found himself running the stone cobble road that meandered up to the Castle of Kaans.

He was going to see Aelred.

James was sure that people did not casually drop by the residence of the Maelites, but he also knew that the library was open to the public.

The bookshelves of the Castle held thousands of books, the intellectual treasure of Aqui. James wandered among aisles, breathing in the old parchment smell. When his class was here last month, the guide monk had warned them of the forbidden areas. The living quarters of the Maelites were not to be disturbed without an invitation. James was not invited.

In the huge library of the castle, he walked around nonchalantly checking if any of the doors that led to the eastern side of the castle were open. No luck on the first and second floors, but on the third floor, a monk headed out, lost in the pages of a book. Thank you, Brother Distracted. James slipped through before the young monk came back to correct his mistake of leaving the door wide open.

The dark stone-walled corridor that lay beyond the library was deserted. He walked quickly, paying close attention to landmarks. A dozen open doors led into other rooms that were covered in books wall to wall. Apparently, the brothers did not want to part with their precious tomes even when they slept or ate. Elgar would approve.

At the end of the corridor, another flight of stairs went up to one of the archer towers. It was reasonable to assume that the highest room of the furthest tower would be the best place for a recluse to spend his days. No one was coming down or going up. Good thing he was a Pacer, which prevented climbing hundreds of steps to the top of the tower from being a time-consuming endeavor leading to discovery. The steps disappeared under his feet, and before long the end of the stairway approached.

In his haste of avoiding discovery from anybody below, he almost run over a monk who was slowly and quietly climbing down the steps. Inertia was not kind to those who stop abruptly. He lost his balance, grabbed for the railing and instead of feeling cold iron in his hands, his fingers wrapped around the rough fabric of the monk's habit. James could not imagine a more awkward introduction. The Maelite was lost for words and simply stared at the youth who had the audacity to invade the privacy of the brothers and their abbot, in addition to trying to disrobe him.

James regained his composure and pointed up the stairs as if there was nothing wrong with the current scene.

"I was going to visit Brother Aelred. He is here, isn't he?"

The good brother shook off the shock and straightened his habit.

"One does not simply visit the Abbot. Did you not know public is not allowed in our quarters? You should not have used your Pacing to sneak in."

Being scolded never sat well with James.

"I just Paced up the stairs. One of the brothers left a door open, so I *simply* walked in."

"Which brother?" The old monk raised his voice all too suddenly. James realized he was about to get someone in trouble.

"It wasn't his fault. I slipped in before he could see me."

"No matter. You may not see the Abbot. He is a recluse."

"Since he was willing to see me the last two days, I am sure he will make an exception for me," James said with confidence he did not necessarily feel.

"You don't know what you're talking about, boy. Now, please leave this part of the castle immediately before I call the Riser brothers."

Just as the monk finished his threat, the door at the top of the stairs opened. Brother Aelred stood at the threshold, his hands folded, looking down.

"It's alright, Brother Cadoc. James can visit me any time he wishes. Thank you for your concern."

Brother Cadoc bowed his head and started down the stairs once more without a word.

James climbed without Pacing and walked through the threshold where Brother Aelred stood moments ago.

The Abbot's cell in the Castle was not any better furnished than Brother Linus' in the West Tower. There was a neatly made bed on the floor. Next to it stood a simple nightstand, covered in candle wax. The Abbot was considerably messier than their history professor, as books were scattered all over the room. There might be an order in the chaos, but from where James looked, disorder seemed to reign. A wide, elegant wooden desk was almost invisible under old parchments, books, and maps. The only visible parts, the legs, indicated masterful workmanship as the intricate designs of animals criss-crossed along all four. Instead of facing the room, the desk and chair looked towards the window that displayed a magnificent panorama of the lower valley hosting the Academy and the Inn. The view was stunning.

In an ancient stone hearth, a small fire crackled on the other side of the room. Brother Aelred invited him to sit on one of the old cushions, haphazardly thrown on the floor in front of the fire. The aged monk sat across James on the floor, closer to the heat.

"What can I do for you, dear James?"

James heard a tone that was much softer than their previous encounters. A hint of defeat was hidden behind his words.

"Well, first, thank you for seeing me without an invitation," James mumbled.

"Of course. You wouldn't invade our privacy without a good reason. What troubles you?"

James wasn't sure if he had a good reason to roam the Castle of Kaans uninvited.

"All of my friends seemed to have lost hope after learning about my life on Earth. Even you look defeated. I don't know what to do. I thought you might be able to help me, but I am not so sure anymore."

Brother Aelred took his piercing gaze away from James and got lost in the disappearing flames of the almost dead fire. Soon there would be nothing but crimson coals.

"I don't have any wisdom to offer. In my selfishness and eagerness, I rushed to see you and then I rushed all of us to see Cathan. I should have foreseen that his years on Kaya and on Earth must have prepared him for the eventuality of another Outsider. I apologize for my impatience."

James had not come for an apology, but the abbot's remorse released some of the tightness around his chest. It felt good to share the guilt.

"I am also sorry that your life on Earth has been less than pleasant, especially combined with growing up an orphan in Aqui."

"I love my life here," James said, feeling defensive about Kaya. "It's infinitely better than Earth."

"Which is possibly why you tend to agree with Cathan," Aelred added without any judgment in his voice.

"That is why I'm here...I'm confused. Life with my human family was wonderful until my brother Jake was killed. There is so much selfishness, crime, and misery there. Now, after talking to Rex, I am afraid it's the same on Kaya beyond the Ambit."

"What makes you think that all is well in Aqui?"

"Well, there are no serial killers, mass murderers, or merciless tyrants."

"Yes, but that doesn't mean there isn't crime or hopelessness. Even though our prison is not full, there are people who spend their days behind bars in Aqui just like any other place on Kaya. I am sure you have witnessed the hopelessness and despair the Ambit generates in your own life."

"Are you talking about the Goners?" James asked.

"Yes, but they are the extreme examples. At one point or another, every Aquite deals with depression that comes with captivity. Some move on, trying to pretend that the invisible cage is actually not there. We convince ourselves that we live our days in Aqui with consent, not by force."

James was still not convinced. "Does it matter?"

"I believe it does...a great deal. What is the difference between a prisoner's life and my life in this cell?"

"You are here voluntarily, but a prisoner is a captive against his own will."

"Do you think it matters that I can leave whenever I want, even though I never do?"

James saw where he was going. "Yes, of course."

"What I have is freedom. My living in these quarters year after year, much longer than most prison sentences in Aqui, is bearable because it is a matter of choice." The Abbot sighed with exhaustion, not from the current conversation, but from defeat. "Look James, I cannot tell you that taking down the Ambit will be the best thing for everyone. I cannot tell you that Cathan is an evil liar. I cannot even tell you this is worth fighting for. All I can tell you is that I like being able to leave this castle, even if it is only once every two decades."

James heard the tone of frustration mixed with years of struggle in the Abbot's voice.

He thought about how Maggie came to be homeless, how despicable actions of her father and passive surrender of her mother pushed Maggie away, just to survive. She truly had no choice. Despite all the darkness in her life, she had more life in one of her intrigued smiles than James had in all his being. Freedom came in all different shapes. James had some and not the others, and Maggie had some and not the others. But in Aqui, freedom was a scarcity.

"You know, I am voluntarily homeless on Earth. I just couldn't handle living in a home where everyone is either depressed or an addict. In a way, I had the freedom to stay or leave. Not everyone has that choice, but I did, and I am grateful for it."

He didn't know why he was telling all this to a man he had just met and knew nothing about. Something about this monk with his shaven head and salt and pepper beard exuded trustfulness and peace. James stood up and headed for the door, "Thank you for listening, Brother Aelred."

"Any time, James. If you need me again, send a message with an animal. I know you are a strong Reader. I prefer cats."

The older man repositioned himself on the antique chair instead of the cold floor and started reading one of the parchments that was unraveled on the ornate desk. The conversation was over. James left without another word.

Once outside the castle, he started Pacing again, his feet feeling lighter with the confidence and reassurance of knowing what to do. Being at a crossroad, at the brink of a decision and not being able to take the next step was exhausting, but now he had at least picked his path, even though he did not know where it would lead.

He Paced the heavily-traveled dirt roads and footpaths under the burning noon sun. Heat did not bother him. The world was warm and light.

At one point, his agile legs slowed down to make a sharp turn so as not to fall off the cliff. The presence of someone else in the middle of the forest shocked his Seer senses. He came to a sudden halt and squinted his eyes in the direction of the movement. The bushes among the high trees tousled again, revealing the presence of some big animal or a person. James quickly hid behind a tree and watched. To his surprise, Claire appeared from behind one of the dead tree trunks, looked back as if to make sure that she was not being followed and ran deep into the forest. Even though James did not know what she could possibly be doing in the deep of the woods on a Sixday, his desire to talk to Leo and the others trumped his curiosity. Claire was probably looking for heavy stuff to practice her Rising, and the forest was the perfect place for that. James shrugged, winked at one of the inquisitive squirrels on a high branch, and resumed Pacing.

He found Leo, Joan, and Elgar lazily reclining in front of the fireplace when he got back to the Inn after over an hour. The Pace had made him feel exhilarated and a bit out of breath, but wonderful. He busted the door open and gulped down water right out of the pitcher. All three looked up at him with inquiring eyes. Once he was done hydrating his over-worked body and got his breath back, James sat on the divan and broke into the speech that had been forming in his mind.

"I am sorry for yesterday and for not having told you more about my life on Earth. I didn't want you to feel sorry for me. To be honest, Cathan convinced me yesterday that it was better to live in paradise as prisoners than to be free in a cruel world. But I came to my senses today....with a little help. I believe it's important to have a choice even when it leads to failure and misery sometimes. I think the risk is worth it to see the rest of Kaya. Who knows, maybe they have flying cars!"

"What is a car?" Leo asked. Joan elbowed him in the ribcage.

Elgar started talking without acknowledging Leo's ice-breaking attempts.

"First of all, I have never heard you speak this much, James. I hope it is a good omen. Second of all, I am not sure if I want to live in a miserable world. My parents died a few months apart from each other, and nobody in my extended family wanted the responsibility of raising a child. Then I moved to the Inn. Life has never been this good. I am not sure if I want to give that up yet."

Elgar had been much older than everyone else when he lost his parents. His mother died of a persistent fever that did not come down despite the Healers' best efforts, and his father died of an aggressive brain tumor, while his only child watched helplessly. James knew his friend's pain all too well.

Joan leapt up off the chair. "But Elgar, *you* were the one who had the vision, *you* were the one who persuaded all of us to find a way to get rid of the Ambit. How could you give up now?"

"I had always imagined that everything would be better once we could travel anywhere we wanted, experienced different cultures, and learned more languages. I had never thought that there could be so much evil and despair. It's not like we can go back. Once the Ambit is down, it's down."

James thought about the *Anne of Green Gables* movies his mom watched who knows how many times. Thinking about his mom when she was a happy mother of three, uncontrollable boys made him smile.

"My mom used to read these books," he said, adjusting his story since technology in Aqui was still far away from television. "The main character, Anne, always dreamt of traveling out of the little island they lived in. She was not content until she met new people and experienced life beyond the charming island. In the end, she came back to her hometown, married her childhood friend, and lived happily ever after."

"That's exactly what I am saying," Elgar said, throwing his hands in the air.

"But, she would never have been content if she did not have the choice to see the world," James replied.

Leo was unusually quiet. As the free-spirit natural leader of the group, everyone always appreciated his input, and often expected it, even mixed with silliness and jokes. "What do you think, Leo?" Joan asked finally.

"I don't want to have regrets," Leo said, "I don't want to look back twenty years from now and wish that we had tried a little harder."

"But in twenty years we all will be living in a village, with a job we like and possibly married. Why would you regret a happy life?" Elgar stood his ground.

"What if I have a child and he becomes a Goner?"

"What do you mean?" Joan furrowed her brows, confused by the change of direction.

"I mean, we could have been just like the Goners, depressed and in despair. They seek thrill and excitement because they can't handle being prisoners. I don't know why we're not more like them. But what if I have a child who becomes a Goner, because he could not bear the thought of living his years within the few square miles of Aqui? How could I tell them that I could have helped to create a better world, but I didn't?"

"This is bigger than us," Joan said, looking at Elgar.

"I am just afraid to lose the only good thing I have." Elgar said, staring into the dying fire.

"I don't think you are ever getting rid of us, Elgar," Leo reassured his friend.

Their thoughtful, intelligent friend took his eyes off of the disappearing flames and nodded. He had changed his mind, or rather had decided not to give in to fear.

Everyone was on the same page finally.

"So, what's the next the move?" Joan asked, then looked around. "Wait...Where is Claire?"

"I saw her walking into the forest about an hour ago," James answered.

Joan shrugged her shoulders and asked again. "What's the next move?"

What indeed?

Day 11: Earth

Letting hot water run over his matted hair during his weekly shower at Sarah's place was just what James needed that morning. His short, dark, straight hair still managed to catch all manner of dust, pollen, and even food through the week. He wished there were two Tuesdays. Maggie was gracious enough to let him go first even though her own long hair needed some attention from the shampoo-conditioner duo.

He left the bathroom, drying his now food-free hair. A pleasant peach shower gel aroma filled the small apartment. No shame in smelling girly; any scent was better than week-long body odor. As soon as he entered the kitchen, the sweet smell of French toast greeted his ever-hungry stomach. Yes, eggy bread slices drowned in maple syrup would quiet the rumblings.

He grabbed a plate, piled up eight already-buttered toasts, and carefully poured syrup in between the layers. Life was good. Luckily, Maggie never underestimated his appetite, because otherwise she herself would go hungry. Together, they devoured the rare treat that was cooked breakfast.

"Sarah left all the ingredients on the counter," she said, explaining their good luck.

"It's definitely an improvement on cereal, but even then, I can't complain," he said in between gigantic bites of sticky yumminess.

James could tell then that Maggie had something brewing in her head. The apprehensive look and quick glances towards his general direction were telling, but she waited for him to finish his food before saying anything. It did not take long for him to polish off the plain white plate and lick the remaining syrup for good measure.

Maggie rolled her eyes in disbelief at such blatant ignorance of manners, but it must not have been time for sarcastic comments. Instead, she dropped a Post-it note on the table in front of James, as she took away the literally licked-clean empty plate.

"Sarah left this next to the maple syrup," she said.

James picked up the yellow paper, swallowed the last of his juice, and read the note written in Sarah's delicate hand writing:

> *Your mom wants to meet. She is sorry.*
> *If you want to see her, give me a call.*
> *love, Sarah*

Once more, he read the note, this time aloud, just to overcome his disbelief. How was it that his mom was able to sober up long enough to talk to Sarah? Also, he was disappointed that Sarah had betrayed their confidence.

James stared at the note for a while, then crumbled it in his hands and threw it in the open trash can from a distance. He did not miss.

"What? You're not gonna see her?" Maggie asked.

"Nope," he said and pulled a banana off of the fruit basket.

"Are you telling me that you are gonna completely ignore the chance to get back to your family?"

"Yep!" he said still chewing the banana. Maggie raised one eyebrow, which meant that she would like an answer of more than 'yep.'

James sighed and swallowed.

"Look, she feels guilty now for a little bit, possibly has been sober a few weeks. But once I get back home, I am sure that she would resume her drinking, and everything will fall apart once again. I am not going to torture myself like that." He hoped Maggie's eyebrow was satisfied.

"How can you be so sure that she would start again?" The eyebrow was relentless.

"Well, she quit drinking four times before I left home, each lasting no more than a couple of weeks. I got hopeful every time, and I got burned every time."

"But you haven't seen her for years, and you don't even know how long she's been sober. I think you should at least talk to her," Maggie said leaning back against her chair, arms crossed.

"Why would I subject myself to another disappointment?"

"You have nothing to lose and everything to gain!"

"Nope!"

She swore under her breath and stormed off to the bathroom to clean off her own hair from the funk of the week. James eyed the crumbled-up yellow piece of paper in the garbage but started to clean up the dishes instead of retrieving it. As he washed the remnants of the French toast breakfast, memories of his mother and his family rushed into his mind. He missed them all, but much had changed in such a long time. Even if his mother had come to her senses, James didn't know if he could go back to the way things were. His life was broken into a thousand pieces, and there was no way to put Humpty Dumpty together again.

That day was not as fun as James had hoped a Tuesday would be. Usually, their time at Sarah's apartment resulted not only in showers, clean clothes, and bagged lunches, but also an uplifting day of knowing that someone cared enough for them to put peanut butter and jelly on bread slices. Today, he had to endure Maggie's dignified silence when another three attempts to persuade James to see his mother failed miserably.

They walked around in unusual silence. If she wanted, Maggie could be extremely stubborn. It appeared that she wanted it very much that day.

By the time they sat down on a bench next to a man-made lake to enjoy their bagged lunches, they might have exchanged ten words. Maybe.

James opened his brown bag and saw his usual sandwich and apple. How could one be so grateful for such a simple meal? But there he was, with a smile on his face, munching on Sarah's kindness. When he picked up the bright red apple, another yellow piece of paper lined the bottom of the bag. He rolled his eyes and picked it up.

Give her a chance, she's been trying very hard to stay sober for the last four months.

He could feel Maggie's annoying gaze over his shoulder. He could also feel the restraint she tried to show, because an "I told you so" would be warranted under the circumstances.

The skeptic in him couldn't believe that his mother had made it without a bottle as long as four months. That was indeed much longer than he had ever seen her sober. But still he could not imagine facing her. What would he tell her anyway? If there ever was an awkward situation, a conversation with an estranged, alcoholic mother would qualify as one. It did not help that something in the pit of his stomach bothered him. The little voice whispered that he was not as guiltless as he had come to believe.

He crumpled the yellow note just like the previous one, put it in the brown bag, and threw them all in the trash can.

Maggie didn't say a word.

Not then, nor for the rest of the day.

Day 11: Kaya

Leo had agreed to tell Claire about their emotion-laden conversation from the night before, since she was still gone by the time everyone slowly shuffled to their bedrooms.

Onedays on Kaya were greeted in a similar fashion to Mondays on Earth. Everyone woke up a little cranky, and the first few hours of the day were spent grunting and complaining. James joined the crowd of whiny students, even though he was more than happy to wake up in the Inn and start chasing after the Manual again. Today, he was a man with a mission.

The classes went by with minimal attention, which might lead to a series of disastrous final exams, but he concluded that tomorrow's worries would have to wait until next month. When Leo and James dragged their satchels into the dining hall for lunch, Joan and Elgar were already talking in a manner suggesting that nobody else was welcome to their conversation. Obviously, James and Leo were exceptions. Claire was nowhere to be seen. Again. Her regular disappearances were starting to worry everyone. They decided to look for her after having nourished their teenage bodies, which required a significant amount of fuel, particularly when they were trying to save the world.

Joan and Elgar stopped their conversation as James and Leo approached with trays heaping with roast meat, mashed potatoes, and eggplant salad. They would have to go back for fruit and dessert.

James and Leo started to shovel food down their throats in an efficient manner.

"Here is what we came up with so far," Joan said and leaned forward, lowering her voice to a whisper. Everyone watching was aware that they were talking about something secret or planning something mischievous. Possibly both.

"Even if Cathan destroyed you-know-what, he still would have looked at it, right? Obviously he never intended to use you-know-what, but I cannot imagine that he at least did not take a look at you-know-what," she said.

Leo swallowed a big dollop of mashed potatoes. "You don't have to call it you-know-what; nobody knows that it exists. You can call it the Manual. You shouldn't use Rex's name, though, you might explode into tiny pieces or turn into a platypus, which would be an improvement, by the way."

Joan poured a glass of cold water over Leo's head for that. "You never know what anyone knows."

"Wiser words have never been uttered," Elgar mocked her, siphoning off the water from Leo's wet hair.

Joan was content with elbowing Elgar in the ribs for now.

"Aaannnyyyway," Joan continued, "all we need to do is to persuade the Rex to tell us what he saw." She folded her arms with satisfaction. Checkmate.

"How do you propose we 'persuade' the man to spill the secrets he has so faithfully kept for three decades?" Leo asked.

"Well, I am the idea girl, not the execution girl. But there must be something he wants in life. I don't know, maybe the Maelites will help us."

"We couldn't think of anything else," Elgar said.

If the Manual was indeed destroyed, their only chance was to get the Rex tell them about the instructions. But none of them had the slightest idea how to change the man's mind, or even how to talk to the Rex of Aqui without Aelred's help. The Rex and the Abbot plainly disliked each other, and James was sure that another meeting any time soon would be a stretch, especially now that Cathan knew what they were after.

Leo put his two cents in as if he had read James' mind.

"I don't think Cathan would want to see us again. He is required to see every minister when there is need. But Brother Aelred would not be able to convince anyone that there is actual need, especially when he was the one who decided to conduct the state affairs through writing. Rex's time is precious."

"So, there is no way of talking to him again? I thought living in a relatively small community made the leaders more reachable. But I guess royalty is royalty anywhere," Joan said. "By the way, has anyone seen Claire since yesterday?"

"I saw her this morning and told her what we talked about last night. She seemed distracted. I don't know where she is now," Leo replied.

"She should be brainstorming with us. She has the best practical mind among us," Joan said as she looked around the dining hall to catch a glimpse of their elusive friend.

"I need to head to the mines," Elgar said, picking up his tray and satchel off the table. "Let's think about a solution this afternoon and regroup at the Inn tonight."

The afternoon in the cabbage fields was unremarkable. Neither James nor Leo could come up with a workable idea that did not include kidnapping or threatening the most powerful man in Aqui. The pickings for plans might have been slim, but there were plenty of cabbages that awaited the attention of their hands. So they labored more quietly than usual, compelling their brains to work overtime.

By the time Risers pulled the carts loaded with baskets of cabbage to the sheds where the vegetables would be sent off to different villages or preserved for the winter, both of them were ready for a nice dinner and a cold drink.

Godric had made one of his delicious stews, and Ebru had baked fresh honey bread. The dinner was nothing less than glorious, especially after the addition of lemonade made with ice cold water that trickled down from the mountains. James and Leo carried their cups to the common room to meet with the others. Most of the remaining residents of the Inn were out on the porch in this warm spring evening, but James and his friends needed the privacy marble walls offered.

Shortly after they put their feet up on one of the stools, Joan and Elgar entered, also carrying cups filled with lemonade. From their tired faces and lack of Joan's customary pep, James gathered that the night would end without a revelation concerning the current whereabouts of the Manual. He was so sleepy that he didn't care.

They talked about Brother Aelred and whether his shaved head ever got itchy or sunburnt, and about Rex Cathan and if he had servants who picked his nose. It was not the passionate, idea-filled night James had hoped, but it was relaxing and warm. He began to drift into sleep, still holding his cup.

No one had any ideas about where to start looking for the Manual, if it was not destroyed. Without paying much attention, he started listening to the others arguing about if Rex Cathan was evil and selfish enough to destroy the only thing that might free Aqui.

"He did not destroy it," Claire said out of nowhere. Nobody had heard her come in.

A deafening silence followed the short sentence. For a few seconds, they all stared at her, trying to understand what she meant.

"How do you know that?" Leo asked.

"Because I read the Rex while he was talking about the Manual yesterday. When he mentioned its destruction, his mind was blazing red, which means that he was not truthful. But the rest of the time, as he was talking about the evil of the world, his mind was a calm blue. He truly believes that he is doing the best for Aqui," Claire explained.

"Well that's good news," Elgar said, having recently gained his former enthusiasm for the destruction of invisible barriers.

"Where is it?" Joan asked.

"Well, I might know someone who knows where it is. She is willing to meet with us tomorrow," Claire replied.

By the end of that sentence, they were all at the edge of their seats, eyes wide open. The sleepiness of moments ago was replaced with a hundred questions, but the answers would have to wait, because once she was done talking, Claire, the bearer of curious news, turned around and went to bed, leaving behind a room full of bewildered teenagers.

Day 12: Earth

Was he moving?

As soon as his consciousness returned to his body, James realized that he was not in the stillness of his hard but dry bed. He *was* moving. More accurately, he was being moved. In a wave of panic, his eyes shot wide open. It was not good news. Leather jacket guy and spiky hair guy had brought in a rather large friend of theirs. The big dude and spiky hair were pulling James by the legs as the leather jacket guy kept a yelling and threatening Maggie at bay. Even quiet Mrs. Jackson contributed to the string of threats at the sight of James' limp body being dragged.

When the realization of being pummeled to paste by three thugs hit, James started to kick and thrash with all his might. Catching the kidnappers off-guard, he was able to free one leg, which gave him more room to maneuver. But the big dude was much stronger than spiky hair guy, so he would not let James' helpless left leg go. Trying to kick or get up was futile. James felt like a turtle on his back. Actually a turtle would have had a better chance of freeing himself.

He tried to kick the big dude's legs with no luck. He attempted to hold on to the sidewalk, again with no success. How was it possible that bad guys seemed to have an unlimited supply of overgrown thugs? He felt defenseless.

While James struggled to free himself from the large hands of the big dude, in his peripheral vision, he saw someone march towards the commotion in haste. Next thing he knew, his trapped leg was once more his. James stood up as soon as the big dude let him go and braced for the inevitable attack to prevent his escape.

He was not wrong. The spiky hair guy swung a vicious uppercut that was unexpectedly strong coming from a man who spent too much time applying hair gel. The impact clouded his vision. He tried to regain his composure in order the stave off the next swing. Ducking the next uppercut finely manicured hands wanted to deliver was difficult, but manageable. Finally, James' right hook found its target and knocked his opponent down. He stood over the spiky hair dude and delivered another heavy punch to the head, knocking him out cold.

Breathless, he turned around to deal with the big dude, only to find the man fighting with someone he could not see. The leather jacket guy was also about to assist the big dude, because whoever had the audacity to help James was about to overpower his formidable opponent. But, despite being the brains of the operation, the leather jacket guy had made the mistake of underestimating Maggie and Mrs. Jackson. Maggie took advantage of the diversion and kicked the leather jacket guy in the privates. As soon as he bent over to protect his manhood, Mrs. Jackson kneed him in the face. James was glad that the ladies were on his side.

Since Maggie and Mrs. Jackson seemed to be able to take care of themselves, James walked towards the big dude to help the mystery stranger. He reached up and grabbed the thug on his biceps to turn him around. Then, he delivered another timely hook on the taller man's right cheek, making him swagger. Another blow came to thug's stomach and another to his face. In a matter of ten-seconds, the big dude joined the spiky hair guy on the pavement, unconscious and bleeding. James looked on without compassion at the shaven pudgy face that would certainly live to bully another day.

When he turned to see the identity of his savior, John was putting his jacket back on calmly as if nothing out of the ordinary had happened. Right before John, the ever-quiet comic book reader, put his left arm in the sleeve of his once brown coat, a tattoo on his arm caught James' attention. A globe, an anchor and an eagle. He could not believe that John was a Marine, but it explained his expertly delivered strikes as opposed to James' haphazard attempts.

"Thank you very much," said a surprised but grateful James as he picked up John's comic book off the side walk and handed it back.

"I didn't know you were a Marine."

John was not willing to accept any gratitude for helping or praise for his fighting skills, so he grunted. Maybe it was a sign of humility. After zipping up his fluffy coat, the hero of the day grabbed the treasured comic book from James, nodded briefly, and headed back to his shelter.

"Wow! Did you see that?" James asked Maggie and Mrs. Jackson.

"Are you alright?" Maggie checked his face for bruises and cuts for the second time in a week. Today was worse than the day before, but he was not about to admit that.

"I am OK, a little banged up, but alive." He smiled and turned to Mrs. Jackson. "That was one butt-kicking kick, Ma'm."

"Not the first time I've had to defend myself," Mrs. Jackson said with a smile that brightened her wrinkled, gentle face. James knew from his own handful of encounters that she was all too right. If it was not thieves, it was drug pushers. Then there were turf wars for the best spot to sleep. It was a jungle out on the streets, and one needed to learn to fend for oneself quickly. James and Maggie had been relatively lucky the last couple of years for not having had much trouble. Now that he thought about it, most likely, they owed their good fortune to John. The Marine comic book reader who was never seen hurting a fly had just driven off three thugs almost single-handedly. It didn't take a genius to know that they were not afraid of a couple of teenagers and an old woman. A wave of gratitude overwhelmed him for their mute guardian. He did not know how to thank the ever-quiet man.

Maggie came over with some disinfectant wipes she borrowed from Mrs. Jackson and started to clean up James' face. He could feel a nice shiner coming on. It could have been worse, much worse actually, if the big dude was able to drag him off to a more secluded area for a thorough beating for standing up for others. He was happy to have escaped with only a shiner and a few cuts and bruises.

She cleaned him up as much as disinfectant wipes allowed and headed to John's shelter without a word.

James could tell she was still upset with him for not wanting to see his mother.

"Was he alright?" he asked when she returned a few minutes later.

"Not a single bruise," she said, a little surprised.

"He is a Marine," James said.

Maggie was eager to get back to her silent treatment. Before she entered the now-safe cardboard house, she turned to James once more. "You know this would not have happened if you were living with your family."

He rolled his eyes to her disappearing back. She was not going to let this go.

Despite the exciting morning that almost broke Maggie's stubbornness, the rest of the day remained quiet. Once it became clear that James would not die of his battle wounds, she returned to the punishment befitting his crime.

They managed to communicate through simple motions. Also, their monotonous lives and the routine of panhandling helped them through the day.

Finally, as the afternoon yielded to evening, Maggie sighed and turned to James, who was fed up with the situation a while ago.

"Look, I will stop the silent treatment, but I want to tell you that you are making a mistake. You need to forgive your mother and move forward. You can't hold onto the past forever." James could see that she was genuinely upset and more than a little mad that her best friend would not attempt to make things right.

He waited until she stopped talking, and replied with cheerless voice, "I am not ready yet."

"OK," Maggie said, and that was that. She did not bring up his mother again.

Day 12: Kaya

Since no one would be able to see the mystery lady until after work hours ended and the miners got cleaned up, this Twoday was on its way to being the longest day James had ever experienced on Kaya. It might even surpass the day when Leo refused to talk to him. All day, James and Leo speculated about the identity of the enigma woman. They even went as far as exchanging notes during the philosophy class. It would be embarrassing and detention-worthy to be caught doing something only fourth graders in the Academy did, but the temptation was too strong to resist. Thankfully, they came to their senses before Brother Erfyl noticed one of the notes changing hands.

Fruit picking had brought some quiet to their incessant conversation as some ninth graders had come to share their ladder. James was preoccupied with another picker anyway. Zoe Rose, as an excellent Reader, enjoyed being among the trees as much as she enjoyed setting captive dragons free. James appreciated the view, to the detriment of his apple-picking abilities. Thanks to Zoe, the four hours of work went faster than anticipated. Before they knew it, Leo and Claire were helping other Risers to take apple-filled baskets to the shed.

All day, Claire avoided answering any and all questions. She was not a talkative one on the best of days, but since they started debating about taking the Ambit down, she had become even more introverted. Her behavior was disconcerting for everyone, especially for Leo, who had a much closer relationship with Claire than anyone else. James could see that his best friend was troubled by this change, but both were helpless until the meeting with this mystery woman was over.

The three of them walked back to the Inn for a bite to eat while waiting for Joan and Elgar to wash off the soot of the mines. By the time they left, with Claire in the lead, the sun was descending towards the mountains.

It was eerie to observe Claire's silence spreading to the whole group. But tired from the day's work and belly happily full, James did not mind hiking through the mountains that he Paced too quickly to enjoy a few days before. It was not hard to conclude that they would leave the trail where he saw Claire disappearing in the woods. When their sullen leader took a left turn behind an exceptionally spherical boulder, James was not surprised.

Soon, they were in the thick of the forest. Even though the area inside the Ambit had only a radius of a few hundred miles, the woods along Zita Mountains were left untouched by the Readers and the need for arable lands. Some of the trees had grown so high over the centuries that James wondered if there were creatures like Tolkien's Ents on Kaya, tending ancient plants day and night.

They must have walked more than five miles into the shadow of cascading willows and sky-hiding oaks. The setting sun, combined with arches formed by sturdy branches, made the hikers feel uneasy. Soon, it would be dark, and for some reason, all of them, including Claire, had come unprepared to spend the night outdoors. It was good to have at least one Reader among them, but James was not sure if he would be able to persuade any predator to go against its primal instincts when hungry. Live and learn, he thought.

After another quarter of an hour of hiking, an area rockier than their path unfolded before them as the trees became sparser. In a few minutes, they were standing at the bottom of a giant boulder which appeared to be sticking out of the mountain side like Pinocchio's truthful nose. Claire walked towards the dark and uninviting corner where the boulder and the mountain met. She beckoned Leo with a hand motion. When the others approached, the two Risers were moving a boulder that would be impossible for a non-Riser to shift. Once the boulder rolled aside, only darkness laid beyond.

Without hesitation, Claire entered the cave and disappeared into the blackness. With much hesitation, the rest of them followed.

The cave was so dark that James instinctively lifted his arms up to feel his way. Almost at the same time, he felt Joan's hands touching him on the shoulder, compelled by the same instinct to protect one's head. As he followed Leo's lead, who was right behind Claire, he wished that there was a fire or a night vision mark. Unfortunately, running fast or telling if someone was being truthful was utterly useless at the moment. Simple lack of light humbled all their marks.

An eternity and two minutes later, a glimmer of light appeared fifty yards away from them. Torch flame became brighter as it came closer. Everyone let their hands drop to their sides when surroundings became once again visible. They were walking through a tunnel whose walls were too smooth to have been formed naturally. At the end of the long passageway stood a woman in her early twenties, holding a torch up high to shed light to their path.

Still without a word, the woman turned around and walked away. The tunnel reached an end soon after, leading the narrow path to an opening as big as their common room at the Inn. Candles along the walls and on small wooden tables cast an eerie but warm light. The circular room with walls of rock looked like the living quarters of the woman who led them into this hidden cave.

The fireplace on the far left corner of the chamber was alive with flames pouring out from big logs. Tattered old rugs thrown all over the rock floor and battered cushions invited the hikers to take a rest. Next to the fireplace, a small row of shelves held a frying pan, a pot, and a handful of bowls. Wooden utensils rested inside a big ceramic cup on top of the shelves. An iron cauldron sat on a stand between the dishes and the fire, emanating the pleasant and appetizing smell of stewed meat and thyme. Everyone was hungry again.

James studied their hostess as she placed the torch in a high holder. "Come...sit," said the mystery woman and showed them to the scattered cushions in front of the hearth. Everyone, even the Pacer James and Joan, were happy to stretch their legs out before the calming fire, and hopefully gulp down some of that stew. The woman ladled the fragrant dish into wooden bowls and divided a loaf of dark bread into five. As she handed James his share, he noticed that her eyes were the exact same shade of blue as Claire's.

Other than slurping and gentle clanking of wooden spoons, there was no sound. They gratefully munched on delicious venison stew with beets and parsnip.

Leo put down his empty bowl on the floor and wiped his hands on his shirt. "Thank you very much for the food, ma'm. It was much needed. Now, could you please tell us why Claire dragged us all here?"

The woman was more than ready to oblige their curiosity.

"Thank you for coming all this way, and more importantly for holding your tongues about our meeting. It's crucial that my identity and whereabouts remain secret. I am counting on your reticence from now on as well."

"Of course," Joan said.

"Well then," the woman continued, "My name is Kea. I have been living in this cave, hidden from everyone else in Aqui, for a little over thirteen years. Up until tonight, only a handful of people knew where I lived or *that* I lived."

"Why do you live here? Did you do something wrong?" Joan pressed further.

Claire glared at her, but didn't say anything.

"Yes and no," Kea answered. "Depends on who you talk to."

Leo never liked riddles. "Assume you are talking to us."

"No, then," Kea replied, seeing that her pushy guests wanted nothing more than simple answers.

"We're all ears," Elgar said, reclining on a battered cushion in front of the fire.

"Twenty years ago, a woman married a wonderful man who was intelligent, caring, and handsome. He had strong marks, too. She could not have asked for a better husband. She was happy, and happily blinded. The man had a good relationship with a gifted monk, and they spent hours discussing history, philosophy, and science. One day, he returned with a memento this monk had given him. Together, husband and wife hid this memento because the man wanted to keep it safe. The woman realized that the man changed after the arrival of the mysterious gift. He was not as truthful as before. Whenever she tried to See him, his mind was always a reddish shade of purple, telling her that he was in distress because of something he was hiding or something he did. She did not know what to do, but soon they found out that they were expecting a baby. The woman forgot her worries and waited for her baby to arrive. The baby girl brought them back together, and the woman stopped using her mark on her husband. Denial gave her peace. But a false peace it was."

"One day, she received a sealed letter informing her that her husband possessed the knowledge to take the Ambit down, but refused to do it because of his selfish desires. Those two sentences dissolved the fake peace the woman had bought with her denial. She knew that the man she loved had been lying to her. She also knew that the memento they hid together held the answers. The time had come to reveal all the secrets."

"But when the woman went to the hiding place of the memento, it was gone. She did not tell her husband about the anonymous letter or that she went to look for the little box that had caused much trouble. Without making the man suspicious, she tried to See its location."

"One night, as the man slept she Saw where the memento was hidden. It was a map she couldn't read, with a riddle she couldn't solve. Now that her husband's secrets were revealed, it became clear that he was not who she believed him to be. There was no way that the woman would let her daughter grow up with such a man."

"The following day, the woman took her baby girl, faked their death as part of another mining explosion, and disappeared."

"The woman and the girl started to live in a cave."

Kea stopped talking and looked around the room to see if her words had made any effect on her confused guests. Nobody said a word.

Finally, James broke the heavy silence.

"You are the girl?"

"Yes," Kea replied.

"What happened to your mother?"

"She died a few months ago."

"I am sorry," mumbled a few of them.

"Where does Claire come into this picture?" Leo inquired further.

"What the woman did not know was that she was pregnant for the second time when she left the man. Needless to say, getting pregnant twice was and is very rare after the Dispersal. But, in less than a year, she had another baby girl."

Kea's features relaxed as relief brightened her eyes. She let the third person narrative go. It was time to own her story.

"I don't know if she would have left my father if she knew about her pregnancy. The baby stayed with Mom and I for a little over a year. But after that, mom did not want to inflict the same fate on her second child, so she left the baby at the orphanage."

"Claire is your sister?" Joan yelled, her hands over her mouth.

"Yes," Kea said, still obliging Leo's desire for simple answers, but the night was getting more and more complicated by the minute.

Elgar decided to sit up straight after hearing the news that Claire was not an orphan after all, and had a sister, which was in itself a miracle.

"Are you saying the Rex is your father?" he asked.

"Yes."

"And you know where the Manual is?" James asked this time.

"I think so," Kea said.

"What do you mean, 'I think so?'" Leo pressed.

"I have a map of sorts and a riddle. I need your help to solve it."

"You have been hiding this information for years. Why tell us now?" James asked.

"Because Claire told me that you are an Outsider like my father."

The awkward silence once more ensued.

Elgar stood up, towering over everyone else.

"Let's get to work then, shall we?"

Kea turned to Claire. "Are you sure we can trust them?"

Claire nodded.

James could not even imagine finding out what Claire had discovered over the last couple of weeks. She was not an orphan, she had a sister and a mother that lived not far from the Inn, and her father was the Rex. It explained all of her strange behavior. The secrecy and the shock of it must have been overwhelming. James wished that she had confided in them. Secrets could be dreadfully heavy at times. He knew.

Kea crossed the room towards a tower of books to produce an ink pen and blank parchment. As curious eyes watched, she started to draw circles on the page.

"There is a map or rather a collection of circles and a very short riddle. This is what my mother saw in my father's mind as he slept. Knowing that he was married to a Seer, he concealed the location of the Manual in his thoughts. If we can decipher this, we will find the instructions and take the Ambit down."

Everyone gathered around Kea as she worked on the circles. When she was done, the blankness of the parchment had not improved much. It was a cluster of twenty-five circles that had formed a diamond shape, each edge consisting of five circles and the rest of them in rows. At the very top there was one circle, then the second row had two circles, third, row three circles and so on and so forth. Each circle that formed the edges of the diamond was divided into two with a horizontal line. Then the circle in the middle was divided into four quarters. That was it.

It did not look like anything James had ever seen. He looked to his friends and saw nothing but confusion.

"Is there more?" Claire asked, breaking her vow of silence.

"There is also a short riddle," Kea said as she wrote below the circles.

James fell asleep.

Day 13: Earth

James bolted upright in his cardboard home.

"No!" he screamed, making Maggie jump in her place. After yesterday's events, it must have been hard to catch her off-guard, but James seemed to manage making her choke on the water she was drinking. As compulsive coughs tried to get rid of the foreign substance in her lungs, Maggie covered her mouth and gave James a disapproving look. As soon as her breathing capabilities were restored, she yelled with indignation, "What's wrong with you? I almost drowned in a sip of water!"

Ah, nothing like good old hyperbole, but James had more important things in mind than the exaggerations of a teenager.

"You won't believe what happened!"

Seeing James' expression, Maggie forgot her near-death experience and was all ears to hear his unbelievable day on Kaya. By the time the long tale of Claire, the cave, her sister, and the puzzle had been told, both of them were sitting on the cardboard floor, their knees pulled to their chests.

"I can't believe you fell asleep right then! It's like a cliffhanger at the end of an episode. At least, we won't have to wait a week," she said while stretching her legs to move the blood around her muscles.

"Also, how come you let time get away from you? That's never happened before."

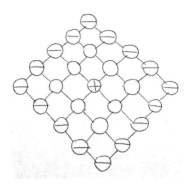

"I know," James said, a little self-conscious but mostly worried. "I need to be more careful; it could be very dangerous during the current state of things."

"Right. It would be awful if something happened to you while sleeping. Also, I am pretty sure your friends wouldn't like to drag your unconscious body around," she smiled.

"Well, they probably just left me on the cave floor until the morning. It's not like I care."

"Never mind that," Maggie said. "Draw this puzzle for me, would you?"

Thankfully, it wasn't hard to remember the map, or as Maggie called it, the puzzle, so James drew the simple combination of circles and lines on the sketch book that contained various scenes from Aqui. When he turned the finished product for Maggie to see, he had hoped that she would brighten up with recognition, but her furrowing eyebrows filled him with disappointment. For some reason, he thought Maggie would surely know what that map was, and he would return to Kaya triumphant. However, as it was in life, things were not that easy.

"You've never seen anything like this?" he asked. She shook her head, "No, but I am sure we can figure it out. What are libraries and the Internet for?"

Was there anything that would faze her? Her ever-present optimism was worthy of admiration.

Once the excitement of his Kayan day wore off, a loud grumbling from his stomach reminded him that they had not eaten anything for almost a day. James was grateful that he did not have to remember sleeping hungry. It must be agonizing to wake up to the call of your body in need of sustenance, but not be able to satisfy it in the darkness of the night. He felt sorry for Maggie. He also felt bad for not remembering that she must be starving.

Unfortunately, on Thursdays, they did not have a regular place to get food, especially early in the morning. Still, there would definitely not be anything to eat as long as they stayed within the confines of the shelter.

Their feet brought them to the public library. It was almost nine o'clock. Mothers of little children slowly trickled through the main entrance as James and Maggie tried to do research about the puzzle despite their hunger. The screaming and giggling youngsters provided enough distraction and commotion to forget about their own woes for a moment and wonder from where three-year-olds got their endless supply of energy.

The noise of toddlers calmed down for fifteen minutes as a firefighter bunny from a colorful book came alive in awe-struck imaginations. Little faces looked up at the librarian with wondrous twinkles in their eyes. After those passing moments of peace, toys and board books were all fair game along with rows of shelves and tables. The world was a wonder to be destroyed, licked, and spat on.

The best part of the toddler mornings were when two people showed up with pizza, apples, and cartons of chocolate milk. Maggie and James looked at each other with wide open eyes after roughly counting the number of children and the number of pizza boxes. By lunch time, they both enjoyed a few slices of pizza along with whatever fruit and drinks were left over. They were both happy that toddler hours during the summer had started, because it meant that homeless library dwellers would not go hungry on Thursdays for a while.

After they enjoyed their cold, cheesy slices and ample amount of apples, Maggie opened her sketchbook to stare at the circles and lines James had drawn earlier.

Most of the afternoon passed as they typed circles and lines on search engines. Clicking on pictures remotely resembling what Kea drew on the cave floor ate up their hours. Nothing useful came up.

"Maybe the riddle will help us decipher it. Also, it wouldn't hurt if we knew more about this Cathan person," Maggie said after having read through another dead-end article.

"Yes, maybe," James agreed, feeling pessimistic, with a headache pounding on his temples. "Let's come back tomorrow. My eyes are killing me. Also, we still need to figure out dinner. The pizza and apples are long gone."

Maggie nodded, still scrolling down the web pages that consisted of circles. A lot of circles. No revelations.

Day 13: Kaya

His Kayan consciousness returned to him on the floor of Kea's cave, covered in a woolen blanket next to a long dead fire. His friends slept soundly, forming a protective circle around him during the deep slumber from which he could not wake. Up until now, him falling asleep at midnight had not been a problem in Aqui, but last night he had not noticed how fast the time had passed as they discussed Claire's mom, Kea, the Rex, and of course the Manual.

Kea walked in, carrying a tray full of cucumbers and tomatoes for breakfast. He wondered how she could tell day from night in this pitch-black cave. The only reason he was awake was his ever-precise biological clock that woke him up in a different world at seven in the morning every day.

"We were very worried about you," Kea said as she peeled and chopped the fresh vegetables. Springy cucumber smell enveloped the cave. "It almost looked as if you were dead."

"Nope, still alive," James said, feeling uncomfortable. "It happens like that every night. Normally I'm very much aware of the time, but last night was a little bit too exciting."

"You could say that again." Leo rolled over to face James and Kea. "I now know why you never wanted to sleep outside or go camping. I never bought you being afraid of the dark, the lamest excuse ever!"

"Sorry," James said, a little ashamed that he had lied to his friends for years.

"We did talk about stuffing your body into a chest or shaving your head clean." Joan was awake.

"Even you wouldn't be that cruel, Joan!" James pulled her ponytail.

"You need to give us a heads-up next time." Elgar sat up on his makeshift bed. "We're gonna be in trouble with Ebru and Arin when we get back to the Inn."

James had not thought about that. There were no rules against spending the night out as long the family was informed beforehand. Now, all five of them were gone all night without notice because of James. They would also miss at least the first part of school. Truancy was not tolerated. They would have to endure one of Lord Ywi's all too creative detentions.

"Sorry," James apologized again.

"It wasn't your fault. Besides there are more important things than Ebru's wrath and Ywi's crazy punishments," Elgar said, placing an old copper kettle over the fire.

Kea passed everyone a wooden bowl, filled with sliced tomatoes, cucumbers, soft cheese, and leftover dark bread. They nibbled on their breakfast sipping mint tea. James could not tame his curiosity about the riddle any longer. Maggie was upset that he had fallen asleep without having heard it.

"It was as unhelpful as the symbol. We worked on them most of the night trying to make sense," Joan said in between bites.

"Maggie and I spent the whole day looking at ancient symbols and anything that could resemble what Kea drew on the parchment, but didn't find anything useful. She thinks if we have the whole picture it might be more helpful." James said.

"Fathers counsel at the heart of the triads," Claire said.

"Is that all? Or is there more?"

"That's it," Kea replied, sounding let down. Surely she had expected more from the Outsider whom the prophecies talked about. Her disappointment hung in the air.

James sipped the last of his mint tea and shook off the heaviness. "Also, we need to find out everything we can about Cathan. The more we know about him, the narrower our research on Earth will get."

To their luck, the Rex's life had been successful, which meant that the monks had chronicled all that was known about him for the sake of posterity. Thus, a long afternoon at the library was scheduled. Everyone was responsible of researching a certain period of the Rex's life. Kea was going to write anything and everything she could remember from their family life and what she had learnt from her mother. They agreed to meet again at the cave that night.

The two Pacers, James and Joan, took off at the entrance of the cave. It would attract too much attention if all five of them were late.

Pacing the miles between the cave and the Academy raised his adrenaline levels and cleared his mind for the task ahead.

After grabbing some bread and fruits from the dining hall, lunchtime went by in the vast library of the Academy. James and Leo scribbled down everything they could find on Cathan. Unfortunately, it was their turn to mine coal, which indicated a long afternoon with little conversation. James worked in the twilight of the mines, sometimes even using

Pacing, which was not advised because mining required painstaking precision. One was not as accurate as one should or could be while Pacing. When the supervisor rang the bell marking the end of their work day, James and Leo could not have gotten out any faster.

A quick shower and a light dinner later, all five of them were once again lost behind various politics, history, or science books.

Having dabbled in technology, research, and elections, the Rex was a jack of all trades. James was surprised to read that their power-hungry Rex was the one who "invented" the concept of showerheads and saved much water and time by converting many of Aqui's baths into showers. He wrote a master's thesis on the history of Aqui's political structure and was at one time a partner to an apothecary.

Rex Cathan's passion or occupation on Earth might be the key to solving the puzzle and the riddle. Since Maggie's online research had come up empty, their best luck was to find a clue as to who he was on Earth from his life on Kaya.

As they scribbled anything and everything that could be useful, the hours melted away. They still had to hike up to the cave, so the research session came to a premature end. The books were put away, and the parchments were folded. Their walk back to Kea's humble abode was rather quiet, since no one could uncover any revealing information. The puzzle remained as puzzling, and the riddle stayed as riddling.

Yesterday, Ebru and Arin had given them a long-winded lecture about being responsible and considerate. Today, they made sure to tell the Inn parents that all five of them would be camping out again tonight. They knew Ebru was still upset when she refused to make some of her delicious pastries in the morning.

Life was sometimes very hard in Aqui.

The tired five arrived at the cave a little after ten and found Kea reading a large leather-bound book, with a scroll of parchment and a quill lying next her. It must have been her part of the assignment.

Again, she was thoughtful enough to have something delicious boiling in the cauldron, giving off the savory, earthy smell of chicken and fresh basil. There was another loaf of bread sitting on the shelf as well. James wondered where she baked her bread. After exchanging pleasantries, everyone served themselves a bowl of chicken soup along with a torn piece of bread. Only one night and they already felt at home in Kea's strange but cozy place. Their hostess sat in her corner, quietly watching everyone with a smile in her eyes. James realized for the first time how welcome their presence was to her, and his heart ached for Claire's lost sister.

In the background noise of slurps and paper shuffles, one by one, they shared the fruits of their research. The Rex was an upstanding citizen who had done much for the improvement of life in Aqui. Claire was right – the man always believed that he was doing the best for the people. James would have preferred a villain like Hitler or Stalin on Earth. Cathan had never hurt anyone, to their knowledge, and contributed to the advancement of technology and medicine as much as he could without revealing his second life. James could not help but feel a little impressed.

It was obvious that Claire and Kea did not share his feelings. After all, he had been a father who pushed their mother into exile, forced Claire to grow up an orphan, and Kea to be disconnected from everyone else. Did all his attempts to better life in Aqui stem from a desire to do penance for not taking the Ambit down or for driving his wife away with his child? After all, he had never married again. James did not like complicated things or people, but this entire situation, along with almost everyone involved, was nothing but complicated. The only simple person so far was Brother Aelred, and he had spent most of his time in isolation.

"Brother Aelred!" He yelled at the thought. "We need to talk to him!"

"He probably knows much more about the Rex's life on Earth than anyone else," Leo agreed.

The rest of them stopped discussing various accomplishments of Cathan and paid attention to James and Leo's conversation. It was soon decided that they would send a message to the Castle of Kaans to talk to the Abbot.

They needed an animal.

"Do you happen to have a pet?" James asked.

"I wouldn't call her a pet, but there is a wombat that answers my call. I sometimes hang out with her when I go hunting before dawn," Kea answered.

"Perfect," James said, but also chuckled a little when he imagined Brother Aelred finding a wombat in his cell. Strange times called for strange measures.

It was getting close to midnight. James hoped the wombat would show up fast. Kea stepped out into the open and looked at Claire hesitantly, whistling an eerie call a few times, then starting to softly speak into the darkness.

"Claire! Come here, little girl! Claire, where are you?"

Nobody could hold their laughter as Kea called her sister wombat, but no one dared to look at Claire either. When the stifled laughter died away, James gathered the courage to glance at Claire. Tears rolled down her cheeks under the cover of the night. Kea had named her best friend after her lost sister. The heartache got stronger.

The small, chubby body of Wombat Claire waddled over towards the cave next to her two-legged friend. It was unusual for a wild wombat to befriend Kayans, but Kea probably had enough time over the years to defy some of the rules of the wilderness, even though she was not a Reader.

As the only Reader in the group, James approached the chubby animal whose eyes gleamed in Leo's torch light. He sat on the moist ground cross-legged and stared into the animal's eyes. Ten seconds later Wombat Claire was almost sitting on her hind legs, awaiting instructions. James tied the message around the animal's neck and gave her the mental image of where she needed to go. Wombat Claire tapped on James' knee twice with her claw and disappeared into the darkness. James knew that Kea's animal friend was reliable and would deliver the note into the hands of Brother Aelred.

Midnight was fast approaching, and James did not want to be caught outside. While he told Kea that the time for his sleep was near, Leo and Claire walked a little distance away, engaged in a conversation that was not meant for the rest of them to hear. It was good for Claire to talk to somebody, James thought.

The four of them walked back to the cave, while Kea talked about her other animal friends who were diurnal and often accompanied her during daily wanderings. James enjoyed the sound of a stress-free conversation that did not involve freeing Aqui.

He fell asleep in the tunnel a few yards outside of the cave room.

Somebody would have to carry him.

Day 14: Earth

"Fathers counsel at the heart of the triads," James said as soon as he took his first breath on Earth.

"Good morning to you too," replied a confused Maggie.

That look of confusion had been frequenting her face often nowadays. James was not sure if that was a good thing or a bad thing.

"That's the riddle. Fathers counsel at the heart of the triads," came the explanation.

"That's it? That's nothing. I should know, I am the riddle master," Maggie said, flexing her biceps to demonstrate her mastership of riddles.

"I know. We spent all day looking for answers yesterday. Nada." He laid back down, hands folded under his head, inspecting the flimsy ceiling. "There must be something."

"What did you learn about the man?" Maggie asked, refreshed from the sleep and ready for another day of clicking on pictures of circles and lines. For the first time in years, James' mind did not feel rejuvenated from the sleep he did not remember getting every night. Maybe carrying the troubles of one world to the other this intensively was taking a toll on his brain, even when he technically had two brains to carry the load.

"I'll tell you everything useless we found out about his life on Kaya, but I desperately need some food and coffee. What day is it?"

"It's Friday," Maggie said. "I don't know where we can get coffee. Did you wanna walk to that youth shelter?"

"Sure, it's not like we have any urgent business. We can brainstorm on the way," James replied and reluctantly rolled out of his bed. By Friday, the clean scent of the shower he took on Tuesday was replaced with a pungent body odor. It was getting bad when you could not handle your own smell.

Their hungry and thirsty state of mind was not conducive to a fruitful walk when it came to freeing people from some other world. Humid and stuffy Seattle weather did not provide clarity of mind either. Still, James told Maggie everything they had learnt concerning Rex Cathan's life on Kaya. Nothing rang a bell or provided an "Aha!" moment.

To their pleasure, James and Maggie arrived at the youth shelter early enough to get some coffee and donuts. A sugar rush from deep-fried, chocolate-covered rings of dough lifted their spirits. Even though there were a bunch of open seats along the narrow, white plastic tables that Frank, the youth shelter guy, provided for homeless and wayward teenagers, they preferred to stay away from other people. If someone eavesdropped on their conversation, it would be awkward to try to explain everything.

"I wish there was a way to take one coffee bean to Kaya. There is nothing like it," James said after having taken a sip from his black-with-one-sugar coffee. Maggie preferred hers with lots of sugar and lots of half and half, definitely no powdered creamer.

"Well, it's not like inventing the shower, is it?" Maggie said with smug satisfaction.

"I know! I'd rather have coffee than showers," agreed James. "Any ideas about the puzzle or the riddle?"

Maggie took another huge bite out of her donut and kept talking, her mouth still stuffed.

"I'm positive it's something related to Earth, or something he learned here," she swallowed the pastry, "so that even if somebody discovered the puzzle and the riddle, they wouldn't be able to solve it."

"You are absolutely right. That's why, I hope, back in the day, when Cathan still trusted Brother Aelred, he shared some of his secrets with his friar friend," James said, then reached for his fifth donut.

"How many can you possibly eat?" Maggie asked, a little distracted and a little disgusted.

"I'm a growing boy," he smiled.

"Anyway," she continued, "I don't think we're gonna find anything until we know more about him. But we should still go back to the library and do more clicking."

"Yep, that's what I was afraid of. Should you always be so reasonable?"

"One of us has to be," she smiled. Coffee and donuts made life much more enjoyable.

To the library they went.

The typing and clicking were endless. The Internet was an ocean of information, and they were looking for one little fish. Without any direction, their chances were infinitesimally small, but it was better than doing nothing. So, article after article and picture after picture, Maggie and James tried to crack the code of the Rex's puzzle and riddle, to no avail.

Day 14: Kaya

Again he woke up, tucked in warmly with one of Kea's blankets, his back to the dead fire. Unlike yesterday, Kea's home was deserted this morning. Worried, he shook the blanket off and sat up. There was a bowl of still warm oatmeal near the hearth and a folded piece of parchment under it. James moved the bowl to read the message.

"We all went to school. Being tardy two days in a row would attract too much attention. Pace back and try to make it on time. Leo."

It made sense. James quickly ate the sweet apple oatmeal spiced with nutmeg and drank the milk Kea had left him. She had been a wonderful hostess.

He got up, found the brown satchel, and started Pacing as soon as the morning sun hit his face outside the tunnel. It was a good idea to slow down once the Inn came in sight, so he Paced as fast as possible to make it on time.

Still, James entered the classroom as Brother Linus wrote today's key words on the blackboard. He slipped in quietly and took his seat next to Leo. Brother Linus turned around, gave a slightly disapproving look, but didn't say anything. Leo nodded. James was happy to have made it without getting in trouble. The last thing they needed was to lose more time in detention. Especially now, after yesterday's tardiness, they all had to write an essay about the necessity of order and authority in a society, while standing on one foot, with one hand behind their back.

Brother Linus' voice slowly drifted into the background as flashes of pictures and articles about the puzzle flooded his mind. James was not sure how he was going to pass the final exams with the amount of attention (or lack thereof) he had been paying to classes, but it was impossible to not stare at the twenty-five circles drawn on his notebook. Leo's concentration did not seem to fare any better, since twirling a charcoal pencil on his thumb and staring at a similar set of circles were not part of today's lesson plan. They were going to need Godric's notes.

James tried to return his attention to the subject matter Brother Linus, Sister Eata, and other professors discussed through the morning, but soon the teachers' voices became a lullaby to his disoriented thoughts.

Lunchtime came with the headache of focusing on the same thing too hard and not getting anywhere. It was frustrating. The Rex knew how to hide the Manual. Despair threatened to show its smirking, self-satisfied head.

James and Leo exchanged some fruitless ideas as they ate and listened to other similarly fruitless ideas from Joan, Claire, and Elgar. They all decided to take a walk and get some fresh air into their slightly-frazzled brains. Maybe something would inspire them suddenly. Though, short of a lightning bolt, James didn't know what could help them.

A stone cobbled path led to the carts that pulled them to their works station. James and Leo walked as slow as possible in the warmth of the sun. No one was in a hurry. As they walked passed, a blueberry bush tussled and a familiar wombat peaked at them from behind newly formed berries. Leo looked around to check if anyone was watching, and leaned over, "Claire! Come here, girl." The wombat took a step back. "It's sad that both Claires treat me the same way," Leo said, making sure that the other Claire wasn't in earshot.

James approached the bush. A few moments later, Wombat Claire stretched her neck out for her Reader friend to remove the small scroll dangling at the end of a twine string. Once unburdened, she gave James a pat on the foot as a sign of approval and disappeared behind the shrubbery. Her mission was accomplished.

Two sentences were scribbled by an artful hand on the rolled paper.

Let's meet for dinner where you slept last night.
P.S.: The wombat bit Cadoc.

James and Leo let out a snort when they pictured poor old Brother Cadoc trying to shoo away a persistent wombat in the middle of the night. Thankfully, there were more than a few talented Healers among the monks. Otherwise, James might have felt guilt instead of amusement.

They both were relieved at the news that Brother Aelred would be joining them that night. A fresh perspective, from the head of the Maelites least of all, might be just what this quest needed. Toiling away at the barn, building a new chicken coop complete with hatcheries and different levels of perches to ensure the happiness of the egg-rich fowls, made the time fly by.

Once they washed up and packed some food for dinner to be eaten at Kea's cave home, James and Leo headed out. Joan, Claire, and Elgar had already left.

Ebru and Arin were waiting for them on the porch with folded arms and raised eyebrows.

"Another night out?" Ebru asked. She already knew the answer.

"Yes," Leo said hesitantly, "I thought Claire had told you that we were camping again tonight."

"Yes, she did," Arin said, trying to sound unconcerned but failed. "We were wondering where your sudden love of the great outdoors came from."

"Well, it's spring and the weather is nice. We thought it would be good to spend more time together before mark tests and final exams overwhelmed us," lied Leo. He was not convincing at all. James was glad that neither Arin nor Ebru was a Seer.

Still, it did not take a truth-seer to know that Leo was lying, but they didn't pry. After a short pause, "You have one more night. After today, we'll have to talk to the regents," Ebru said with finality in her voice.

James and Leo nodded and left. None of them wanted to hide anything from their beloved Inn family, but they could not risk sharing the secret of the Manual with anyone else.

The twin moons were already high in the sky by the time they made it to the cave. Leo pushed the boulder aside for them to enter the tunnel. Merry chatter poured out as they approached the cave room. The ominous air of the tunnel was gone, and the long darkness became nothing more than a prelude to an evening of friendship.

Brother Aelred had already arrived and was stirring something in the cauldron as he talked. The other four were watching the Abbot intently from a distance as if they did not know how to act around one of the most powerful and famous men in Aqui.

"Ah, James and Leo! Just in time to taste my extra-special clam chowder. Until today, I only cooked for the monks, so I am excited to have more victims for my culinary adventures."

James was surprised that years of recluse had not taken away anything from the Abbot's social skills. He peeked inside the cauldron and saw the hodgepodge of vegetables and clams floating around in creamy sauce. It didn't look particularly appetizing, but he would rather get poisoned than declare that the head of the Maelites was a lousy cook.

The Abbot ladled the chowder into familiar wooden bowls. James looked at his friends, all of whom appeared as hesitant as he felt. His nose was pleasantly surprised with a waft of fish and herbs. He stirred clams around, trying to delay the inevitable. Hesitantly, he ate a half spoonful. Surprised and relieved by the delicious blend of onions, carrots, cream and clams, James polished off his bowl with almost rude speed. Once swallowed, he said to an appalled Joan and Claire, "We built a chicken coop today." There were no more explanations necessary.

Pleased that his cooking was well received, Brother Aelred settled on one of Kea's cushions. "So, what can I do for you other than filling your bellies?"

"How did you know we were here?" Leo asked, a little abruptly, but the Abbot didn't seem to care.

"I was one of the confidants of Kea's mother. When I found out about James' life on Earth, I encouraged Kea to get in touch with Claire, so that you can all share your intelligence." He added after a pause, "Both meanings of the word."

"We haven't been able to figure out the puzzle or the riddle Kea showed us. If you could tell us everything you know about Cathan, maybe it will be helpful," Claire said.

"Especially anything about his life on Earth, because we think we know enough about his life on Kaya," James added.

"To be honest, Cathan was always secretive about his life on Earth. He was a little like you on that account, James. Because he, too, had some rather unpleasant experiences that led him to believe that life in Aqui within the Ambit was the best it could ever be."

James shifted in his place uncomfortably. Leo must have sensed his friend's reluctance to talk at the moment, because he pressed the Abbot for more details. "Do you know what he did for a living on Earth?"

"He taught chemistry and math in a middle school."

"That explains why he was interested in so many different things here," Elgar said.

"Yes. He was passionate about both subjects. He tried to explain to me some of the many achievements of humans on Earth, but most of it was too much for me to understand without collective knowledge."

"Do you remember anything in particular he talked about?" James asked, having shaken the awkwardness off.

"The only things I remember were how humans harnessed the power of atoms, and how mathematics was mysterious and beautiful."

Neither information jogged anything in James' memory, but his occupation might be useful when he woke up in Seattle.

"Cathan chose to be single on Earth because he was already married on Kaya and wanted to remain faithful to his wife. I also remember him traveling around the world when he was younger. It was then he saw much hunger and suffering. What he saw during those years sowed the seeds for his obsession of making Aqui perfect and keeping it that way."

James listened to the dual life of another, understanding what the Rex had felt all those years ago. James' broken life on Earth had affected his life on Kaya as well. The more he had lost on Earth, the more he clung to the little he had on Kaya. The more introverted he became as a homeless teenager, the shier and less talkative he became on Kaya. The two lives were inseparable, as hard as he tried to pry them apart.

As Brother Aelred finished his account of the Rex's life on Earth, they heard movement in the tunnel. They all jumped to their feet to hide Kea, but the intruder was none other than Claire the Wombat, who directly went to her best friend and started to claw at her feet. A little embarrassed, Kea explained, "Sorry, sometimes she insists that I see her nightly hunt. I'll take her out and be right back."

Ten minutes later, sounds of hurried shuffling and whispers came from the tunnel again. This time it was obvious that it was not the quiet scuffles of a wombat. Was it possible that Kea was a little too loud?

When a group of lexers, strong Risers that functioned as the police in Aqui, instead of Kea entered the cave room, James understood why Wombat Claire was so persistent at getting her friend out of the cave.

"You are all under arrest," declared a blond and rather large Lexer.

"With what charge?" Brother Aelred inquired, stepping in front of the kids.

"I am sorry, minister, but the Rex ordered your arrest and everyone with you," explained the captain lexer.

"With what charge?" insisted the Abbott with an authoritative tone James had not heard from him before.

"Conspiracy and treason," explained the lexer. "I am sorry, Brother Aelred, but I must carry out my orders," he continued, clearly not comfortable with arresting the Abbot. Aquites of all ages still deeply respected the monks.

The Risers chained James, Leo, and Elgar together. Joan and Claire shared another heavy chain so that escaping would not be an option. The four lexers, who had not said a word, led them out of the cave, each holding one end of a chain. Another lexer stepped in front of them holding Servus shackles, which would make sure that none of the prisoners would be able to use their marks to harm the lexers or escape their prisons. The Servuses were only used for the most violent of criminals. How times had changed!

Restrained without an escape route, their marks taken away, James and his friends were not prepared for the direction their night was taking.

The captain escorted the Abbot, who was shackled but unchained for now.

They exchanged incredulous looks as the well-traveled path through the forest disappeared under their feet, the chains clinging in the night. When they reached the Inn, three carts were waiting for them, along with everyone who lived in the House of Sevgi. As lexers loaded them in carts, Ebru watched them, eyes wide with disbelief. The ominous insignia of the capital with two dragons entwined gleamed on the side of their prison transports. James could not even look up because of the weight of the humiliation, even though he wanted to scream that their only crime was to try to bring the Ambit down.

Before they reached the lexer command in Xavi, James fell asleep.

Day 15: Earth

As soon as his eyes shot open, James sat up, sweating and breathing hard, as if waking from a nightmare. When did his perfect life on Kaya become frightful? Maggie was at his side in no time, waiting for him to come back to Earth, but not expecting the terror she saw on his face.

"We were arrested," he whispered once his lungs were able to suck some air in.

"Arrested? For what?"

"For treason," he lowered his voice even more. All his life, even as a homeless teenager who had to shoplift now and then, James had managed stay out of trouble with the authorities. His parents had instilled a healthy fear and respect when it came the men in uniform, not because they were vicious, but because they were the faces of the law. He had always felt the same way towards the lexers on Kaya. Not because they tend to be at least T6 Risers, but because they helped in keeping order. Until today, he had never had any reason to question this thinking. However, for the first time in his life, he found himself at odds with the authorities and innocent at the same time. He did not know what to think nor what to do.

As his breathing regulated and the drops of sweat he had imported from Kaya slowly dried out, James told Maggie about his strange day. She quietly listened to the limited, but still valuable revelations about Cathan's life in Ohio. Even trying to picture a middle school teacher as a selfish tyrant in a different planet sounded like they had wandered into the set of the next Star Wars movie.

"We have to figure that puzzle out," James said with resolve, recalling the embarrassment of being dragged in chains through the Inn grounds for all his friends to see.

"At least we know what he does here on Earth. That will narrow down our research significantly. Let's go and talk to Uncle Google again," Maggie encouraged James to shake off the nightmare.

The walk to the library was somewhat quieter than usual, since James was still in shock at having been arrested and fallen asleep in the lexer cart on top of that. He wondered who had to drag his limp body to the holding cell. Hopefully, the lexers still held the Abbot in high enough regard to treat his friends with some respect.

This early in the morning, there was no one other than the librarians among long rows of book shelves. One of the librarians, an older lady called Judy, waved at them. She had a genuine love for books and all book lovers.

Maggie and James started to type keywords that popped into their heads about chemists and mathematicians. It was going to be a long day. They were barely into the second page of the search results when Judy brought them two apples and a scone with two cups of black coffee. James could not have been more grateful. The older woman smelled of vanilla cookies, a silver crucifix dangling from her neck. She did not say anything but patted their shoulders affectionately before leaving.

"I love her!" Maggie whispered loudly as she took a bite off the cranberry scone before handing the rest of the pastry to James.

The food and the caffeine brought some life to their research while chemical and mathematical theories that might have inspired the Rex appeared on the screen. Again, they spent hours in front of the computer or flipping through various books. By the time it was one in the afternoon, it felt like Wiley Coyote had dropped one of his anvils on top of James' head. Words and pictures became blurs. He desperately needed a break.

Maggie did not seem to fare any better than him. She was absentmindedly turning the pages of a rather large volume about noted chemists.

"Let's take a walk," he said, pushing the books away as if they carried something deadly and contagious.

"Good idea. Maybe we can find something to eat."

The bright sun outside blinded their eyes momentarily, since they were sitting at one of the windowless corners of the library.

"It burns," Maggie said with mock pain.

James smiled and took a deep breath. They both needed some fresh air, so a stroll among lush trees and fragrant blossoms would help them clear their minds.

Giggles and screams of children greeted them as they entered the picnic area around the small playground. Parents had taken advantage of the sunny day and brought their little ones to spend their limitless energy outdoors.

Maggie and James sprawled on the dry grass close to a mother and her elementary school age daughter. The tired teenagers laid down on their backs and closed their eyes enjoying the warmth of the sun, the happy sounds of children. A mother patiently explained shapes and numbers to her daughter. Maggie drifted off to sleep.

When she opened her eyes, she would have looked refreshed if it was not for the nagging hunger. James got back to watching two little boys chase each other.

"That's a diamond," the mother said to the little girl, who was playing with a plastic set of colorful shapes. Maggie turned to watch her teach the little girl.

"Think of it as two triangles stuck at the bottom." The mother picked up two blue triangles and combined them at the bottom to make a diamond to demonstrate.

Maggie jumped to a stand.

"Two triangles," she whispered to herself and shook James violently, as if waking him up from a deep, peaceful slumber.

By the time they rushed back to the library and settled in front of the glowing screen once again, James still had no idea what epiphany Maggie had at the park. She kept talking to herself incoherently, leaving others no way of following her train of thought. James knew better than to try to get any answers when she was like this, so he waited patiently.

The excited girl finally organized her thoughts in a pattern that regular mortals could comprehend.

"It's two identical triangles, not one diamond," she said.

"And?" James urged her to continue, because her revelation was insistent on escaping him.

Maggie typed the phrase "number triangles" in the little rectangle of the search engine.

"I think those lines in the circles are numbers, like the Chinese numbers."

She clicked on a picture and a page titled "Pascal's triangle" popped up.

"Do you see it?" she asked.

"Ummmm" James' brain was a bowl of noodles.

Maggie exhaled a loud sigh and pointed at a pyramid on the right side of the page.

```
        1
       1 1
      1 2 1
     1 3 3 1
    1 4 6 4 1
   1 5 10 10 5 1
```

The sketchbook that contained James' clumsy drawing of the puzzle lazily rested in Maggie's bag. She ripped out the page and folded the picture into two, revealing identical triangles that formed a pyramid. Then she clicked on a picture subtitled "Pascal's triangle depicted by using Chinese rod numerals."

James could not believe his eyes. It was Cathan's puzzle with some minor differences. Maggie had solved it. The lines within the circles were numbers, the lines connecting the circles were there just for decoration. She picked up a pen and filled in the rest of the empty areas with Chinese numerals for 2, 3, and 4. Cathan had tried to hide Pascal's triangle by using its Chinese form and doubling the triangles. After Maggie's intervention, it was as clear as the day.

He hugged Maggie, lifted her off the chair, and planted a big, squishy kiss on her cheek.

"Margaret River, you are a genius!"

Day 15: Kaya

The marble wall stole the warmth from his cheek, and his left arm was numb and tingly. The stone floor of Kea's cave was much more welcoming than the holding cell at the lexer command. Elgar and Leo were dozing off in similarly uncomfortable positions. The holding cell was no bigger than a kitchen, since crime rates in Aqui were low. Across the corridor in another cell, Claire and Joan huddled together on a wooden bench, whispering in excitement. James approached the cast iron bars. When they saw James awake, both girls came to the front to talk to him.

"What happened?" he asked.

"You fell asleep in the cart," Joan rolled her eyes for having to state the obvious.

"I know that, thank you. I mean, what happened after that? Where is Brother Aelred?"

"You didn't miss much. Once we arrived, they put us in these cells, gave us some water, and we haven't seen anyone since. We assume Brother Aelred was taken to a better cell to wait. This area, I think, is for common criminals," Claire answered.

How had they become common criminals overnight?

"Do you think they are listening?" James asked with a whisper. He could not wait until he shared the news with them. For once, his long day in Seattle had paid off.

"I'd assume so," said Claire.

Then the news would have to wait, because James could not risk someone else overhearing that they had solved the puzzle, and that only the riddle remained.

"We have news for you, too," Joan said with a bright gleam in her eyes. James hoped that they had cracked at least some part of the riddle.

However, since they were all incarcerated within impenetrable marble walls with Servus shackles, various news they were dying to share would have to wait. James wished the Aquites had invented bailing out. Then again, he did not know who would pay the bail for a bunch rebellious orphans. All they could do was to wait, and spend this wonderful Fiveday behind cold and unyielding bars.

James sat back down on the hard floor and braced for the waiting game. He was not good at it.

Hour after hour passed. There was nothing to do. The idleness was driving James and Leo crazy. Elgar was the only one who handled captivity relatively well. He repeated the contents of their history curriculum over and over until even James memorized every tiny detail about various Kayan leaders and events. Maybe Elgar's annoying calm would prove to be helpful during the finals. Once everyone was fully versed in history and even learned about the lives of some important philosophers, Elgar attempted to practice his waving with some of the drinking water. The metal Servus around his wrist prevented him from making the liquid even stir, but he did not give up. James wished he had some of his friend's presence of mind.

Leo, on the other hand, was on the opposite end of the calm/agitated spectrum. From the moment he shook off his sleepiness, his Riser-Strider friend had been irritable and impulsive. For a while, he kept talking to their invisible captors, as if they were standing right beyond the cells. When he realized there was going to be no answer coming from behind the wall, he started talking to himself. For a period, Elgar's talk about some of the philosophers distracted him, as he enjoyed Brother Erfyl's class, but that diversion was short lived as well. James had never seen his best friend like this before. Leo had always been the leader and talker of the group. Maybe he just did not like it when there was no one and nowhere to lead. James had a feeling that both situations would be remedied soon.

Joan and Claire were composed almost the entire time, mostly because they had bouts of whispery discussions to which the male side of the holding cells were not privy. From the desire to keep their voices down, James knew that they were working on the riddle, but that was the extent of his knowledge. To discover the rest, all three of them would have to wait when they got out of this Riser-proof prison.

If they did get out.

It must have been afternoon, James guessed, because none of them had a way to know what hour it was. On Kaya, they measured time with vertical sun dials that were placed at various locations around buildings. A colossal elevated sundial in the Academy garden that was visible from almost all the classrooms, and even from the Inn, instructed the students about the slow passage of time. But clearly the lexers were not thoughtful enough to indulge their prisoners with such trivial concerns. No sun, no sundial.

As James got lost in the thoughts of somehow introducing watches and clocks to Aqui, one of the arresting lexers from the night before marched in and unlocked the cells without a word.

"Where are you taking us?" Leo demanded.

"The Rex has requested an audience with you," the lexer answered curtly.

"Are we free to go after that?" Leo pried.

"I cannot say," said the Riser, who would have been a fine policeman on Earth. There was such a finality in his tone that even Leo did not dare press further.

They followed the lexer along a corridor surrounded with similar cells left and right. Only a couple of these cells were occupied. Apparently, a few teenagers had become some of the most wanted criminals.

Two other lexers with broad shoulders and frozen expressions waited to drive the horse-drawn carts outside the high walls of the lexer command. One by one, the prisoners found their places to be taken wherever the self-declared king of Aqui wanted them to be. James could not believe that people could be arrested without cause, simply with the word of a man. Maybe Kaya was not as perfect as he thought it was.

James had assumed that the lexers were taking them to the center of Xavi, where they had first met Rex Cathan, but instead the horses dragged the prisoners out of the city towards what appeared to be the middle of nowhere, nothing but wheat fields and fruit orchards beyond bright green rolling hills.

Soon after the city of Xavi disappeared behind golden wheat fields, the horses made a sharp right turn, following a rougher and less-traveled path. James looked to the others to see if anyone else had a clue where they were being taken, but only detected confused looks on the faces of all. Yet another moment for the game of wait-and-see. The entire situation was getting out of hand. What had started as an innocent discussion of traveling beyond the Ambit had turned into being arrested and taken into unknown places. James hoped that Cathan was not willing to have blood on his hands for the "greater good."

The Kayan sun had been descending to the west for a while now, and shadows were already as tall as they would get today. Soon, the forest would be enveloped by darkness, where sinister affairs could be hidden.

Right before the horses needed torches or lamps to see the road, two lexers jumped out of the carts to open tall iron gates that looked too much like prison bars. The kissing gates yielded to a high stone wall that successfully blocked what laid behind. When the lexers and their entourage passed through the iron bars, a magnificent mansion, three times bigger than the Inn, appeared in the middle of a well-tended garden. But, instead of heading to the luxurious house, the cart once again made a right turn and halted in front of a small, two-story cottage hidden within the woods beyond the mansion.

All three lexers leaped down with intimidating agility to lead the prisoners into the dark cottage. The door creaked open on its rusty hinges, revealing a man clad in black robes. A small torch in the man's hand gave weak light. When the man lifted his head, the hood slid down. The face of Rex Cathan greeted them with a smile that was more eerie than anything else.

"Thank you very much, lexers. You served Aqui well today."

Cathan dismissed the dutiful lawmen who did not dare or care to question their orders.

James and the others reluctantly filed into the cottage behind Leo.

The humble cottage was much more spacious on the inside than one expected just by looking at it from the outside. The entrance door led directly to a cozy living room, where a cold hearth and wooden table with chairs received the newcomers. Another man sat on a short stool, facing the ashes of the dead fire. When James looked around, he spotted two other lexers, standing tall and motionless in the kitchen.

The Rex's black satin robe was embroidered along the sleeves and hems with sparkling gold geometric patterns. The triangles and pentagons twinkled every time the light hit the threads just right. His long fingers adjusted his hood as he walked towards the quiet man in front of the fireplace. His salt and pepper hair appeared perfectly combed.

"Turn around," he commanded the motionless man.

"I will not do your bidding," replied the man almost in a whisper. James recognized the voice and looked at Leo, who looked as petrified as James felt.

Cathan nodded over to one of the rather muscular lexers. The obedient Riser came over immediately, lifted the silent man off of the floor with little effort, and turned him around against his will.

The man kept his face concealed beneath the hood of his robe.

"Dear children," Cathan started with a fake sweetness in his tone, "I have no desire to see any one of you harmed. I do what I do for the people of Aqui and their good. This man here has been conspiring against the elected government of Aqui for as long as I have known him."

"Elected?" Joan chortled. "How is it possible to have been elected over and over again while your rivals mysteriously keep pulling out of the race?"

"Life is full of surprises, little girl. Sometimes good and sometimes bad. I am merely making sure that you will not find yourself in the middle of a bad one."

He walked towards the man who persistently left his face covered, leaned over, and jerked the man's chin up. The silent prisoner's hood fell off, revealing the familiar face of Brother Aelred.

But instead of the soft, smiling eyes that belonged to a man who had cooked clam chowder for them only a night ago, eyes filled with rage and fear stared up at their captor. The bottom half of his right cheek and most of his mouth were severely disfigured. The flesh appeared to be melted off and healed soon after, probably over and over again. It looked like a chemical burn, more likely acid. A talented Healer had tried to mend the damage, but healing did not mean returning to the original.

Brother Aelred moved his rage-filled eyes from his old friend Cathan to James. Part of his mouth was fused shut after being melted and then healed, but the Abbot was still able to talk even if it was only in a whisper:

"Do not yield."

The Rex slapped the Abbot in the face with such force that the disfigured man stumbled across the room, eventually falling on his back. Intense pain and unbearable humiliation had weakened him. Leo stepped forward to help him up, but the big lexer had a different idea. While the Abbot crawled backwards to lean against the wall, the Rex retrieved a small vial from the inner pockets of his black robe and stood over the fallen monk. Their benevolent ruler unstoppered the vial, his face contorted in disgust and satisfaction at the same time.

"You will learn to obey, old friend."

The Rex lifted his arm to line the vial over the Abbot's face and spilled a tiny amount of the clear liquid inside the monk's mouth. The gut-wrenching wail could not escape. Brother Aelred seized in his place, groaning, writhing, trying to find something to hold on to. His screams were imprisoned behind the melted flesh of his mouth as the liquid sizzled even deeper into his face. The monk crawled on his back until he hit the wall and passed out in shock, covering the rest of his face with his right arm His Servus shackle gleamed in dull light. The flesh around his mouth including his lips was melted off revealing teeth and jaw bone in many spots. The burn still let out faint smoke, along with a nauseating smell of seared flesh.

For the first time in his life, James felt paralyzed with fear as he beheld the severely-disfigured face of the man who had given him counsel only two days before.

Once he came out of the fogginess of disbelief, James heard screaming and sobbing. Claire was yelling at the Rex, as a collapsed Joan sobbed on the floor. Elgar was already moving towards the fallen monk to Heal, clearly having forgotten about his own servus.

Cathan motioned towards the large lexer again, and the deadpan Riser stepped forward to remove Elgar's shackle. James watched his friend's hand hover over the Abbot's unconscious face. Slowly and imperfectly the muscles and skin started to weave together. James could tell that Elgar was trying hard to cover the exposed bones and teeth, but the task was almost impossible. Elgar worked patiently, concentrating hard to help the man he so admired. Almost half an hour passed before the Healer's hand dropped to his side.

Brother Aelred's face looked considerably better. Dark pink healing skin replaced the raw redness. Elgar had managed to enclose all of the teeth and bones behind flimsy patches of recovering tissue. But the Abbot would never be able to talk again. The damage was too severe. Even the legendary Healers of Kaya were not miracle workers.

Elgar arranged the Abbot to a more comfortable position and sat on the floor next to him. The lexer returned with the Servus and put it back on Elgar's limp wrist. The drained Healer kissed the disfigured monk on the forehead and rejoined his captive friends.

Cathan looked at each of them with a stare that could melt through a concrete wall and headed for the door. At the threshold, the torturer turned around to address his prisoner one last time.

"You will not prevail."

The Rex left with the blood of his former mentor on his hands. It was difficult to think about what else the Rex had done to ensure his greater good.

James, Leo, Joan, Claire, and Elgar were left with two lexers and the disfigured Abbot.

After a while, the muscular lexer picked up Brother Aelred off the floor and slung him over his shoulder as if the renowned Weaver was nothing more than a sack of flour. The limp body folded over without resistance. The lexer left the house, and the other captives followed the monk's limply swinging hands that had scribed so many books and drawn so many illuminations.

The other lexer brought up the rear. The silent company walked into the depths of the dark forest for another hour. Finally, the large Riser stopped in front of a wall of ivy that covered the mountainside. He parted the leaves and entered into a cave. The place smelled of animal urine and musk. It was about the size of Kea's cave room, but without any cozy and comfy cushions or warm fire. The only creature comfort was a bucket of water in a corner. The big lexer propped the Abbot up against the rough wall. They both left without a word, but not before making sure to cover the entrance with a rock that was too big to move without a Riser.

The unconscious and mute Abbot was trapped in the darkness with five youth who chose to be as quiet as he was.

Day 16: Earth

James sat up and put his face in his hands, not believing what he witnessed only a few hours ago. His homeless life had now become more desirable than his life on Kaya, which now included imprisonment and torture. His piece of heaven had turned into hell, making him wish for the first time that he did not wake up on Kaya the following morning.

The pain he felt for Brother Aelred was eerily familiar to the pain he felt after Jake's accident. The helplessness and darkness embraced him like an old friend who had not been in touch for a while. He did not want to talk to anyone or do anything. All he wanted was to be perfectly still so that his heart would stop aching, and his brain would not wander into lost places.

"James! James! Are you alright?" came Maggie's voice from a distance. He did not want to talk to her. She was nothing more than a distant memory. Not a friend, not a sister, just another nuisance. Loneliness was all he craved.

"James!" Maggie shook him hard and pulled his hands off of his face. Her fingers gently wiped off the tears that had been rolling down his cheeks without his knowledge.

"What happened?" Maggie asked gently, as if her mere breath could break him into pieces.

Words were useless.

James shook his head, laid down, and rolled over to face the cardboard wall.

She did not insist.

Hours later, he woke from a fitful sleep that was laced with nightmares. It took a moment before the events of the previous day overtook his memory, paralyzing his emotions once again. If it was not for the thirst in his throat, he would not have gotten up.

The shelter was empty, but half a loaf of bread and a cup of coffee sat sadly on the floor. James downed a few sips from the cold, bitter liquid and picked up the bread.

Out to bum. Hope you're feeling better.
the note under the coffee mug with Maggie's slanted rushed handwriting read.

He bit into the stale loaf, chewing and chewing. The small piece seemed to multiply in his mouth. He felt hollow, not unlike an oyster who has lost its precious pearl, left only with a fragile shell. How could he care this much about a man he had known less than a month? Why was it not possible to tear one's heart out and cast it aside? Surely, it would be much less painful.

James wallowed in self-pity. He tried to sleep again, but peaceful slumber avoided him at all cost. All he could do was stare at the flimsy wall and ponder about the unfairness of it all. What bothered him the most was his powerlessness to change anything. Brother Aelred would never have his face or his voice back, and their perfect lives at the Inn and the Academy were lost forever. He felt useless and weak.

The morning and most of the afternoon passed as he lay inside the box house, hidden from the whole world. Maggie was understanding enough not to bother him and did not show up all day.

Slowly, a dark heavy sleep engulfed him. A dream formed from the darkness and turned into a day with his family when James and his brothers played ball in the backyard. It was ages ago. He ran after the well-used baseball and tackled his brothers. The warmth of the sun beat down on them, making all of the colors faded, but somehow more alive. Then in the corner of the yard, hidden in the shade of the old oak tree, he saw his mother, standing, motionless. She did not belong to the happy family picture. Her deep green eyes were red and swollen from the tears still flowing down as if coming from an endless stream. Long brown hair looked neglected, matted like she had not showered for weeks. She was much slimmer, even sickly under her old nightgown. If she were not standing and staring at James, he would have thought she was dead.

The laughter of his brothers died, and a deafening silence took over. The sun left. The green backyard faded. It was only James and his mom in the middle of darkness, staring at each other. The nothingness was terrifying.

James woke up in cold sweat, breathing hard like he had been running. Maggie was sitting on her make-shift mattress, looking at him with eyes full of concern.

"I brought you some more food," she said.

There was a spread of chili, Fritos, fruit, and a pint of ice cream. She had even bought a can of root beer for him. It must have been an entire day of bumming to make this happen for someone who did not even want to talk to her. James felt the stab of guilt in his heart, and his eyes welled up.

"Thank you," he said and swallowed the tears, not wanting to cry twice in the same day.

Pecan cluster ice cream awaited his attention, so he dug in with one of Maggie's silver spoons.

"I dreamt of my mom," he mumbled in between heaping spoonfuls of frozen deliciousness. "She looked dead, but she wasn't."

Maggie did not say anything. What was there to say, anyway?

"Cathan tortured Brother Aelred with some kind of acid. Half of his face is melted off now, and he can't talk." That was all he could manage to get out without letting the tears flow freely. Maggie at least deserved to know why he had been acting distant all day.

"I am sorry," she whispered. "Are you alright?"

"Not really, but better than this morning," James replied, putting the ice cream aside and crumbling some Fritos in the cold chili.

Soon the food dwindled down. In between bites of much-needed sustenance, James told Maggie every single detail about his day of captivity on Kaya. As words flew out of his mouth, a stream of poison that threatened to darken his being oozed out as well. He ate and talked for almost an hour, unloading the emotional burden.

Maggie sat across from him, her knees pulled to her chest, shedding tears for the people of another world.

Day 16: Kaya

If his internal clocks on Kaya and Earth had not been painfully accurate all these years, James would have thought it was still night. The cave was pitch-black even in the morning. He could not tell whether his eyes were open or closed. Still, it was possible to feel his way across the damp floor on all fours until he bumped into someone else.

"James?" asked Joan's voice.

"Yes, I'm awake. Is everyone alright?"

He felt much lighter after the monologue Maggie had suffered during dinner yesterday. Who knew talking had healing powers?

"We're alive, if that's what you're asking," Claire's voice replied, clearly still shaken from the events of the previous day. Living an entire day on Earth had given James some time to gather his thoughts and process Brother Aelred's torture, in addition to Cathan's threat that a similar fate awaited them.

Yesterday, James had not had a moment to tell them that he had solved the puzzle with Maggie's help. Maybe that was a good thing. Maybe not all of them were willing to risk their lives or at least their faces for the sake of taking the Ambit down. Before breaking the news, he decided to figure out if everyone was still on board. No reason to risk any of his friends being harmed for something they were not interested in pursuing.

As for himself, the choice was a little easier. Even if he was incarcerated for the rest of his days here on Kaya, he would still have a life on Earth, regardless of its imperfections. Also, if he quit now, Brother Aelred's sacrifice would mean nothing, and he would remain a disfigured mute for the rest of his life just for not having told Cathan about Kea and Claire. If the Ambit came down, there would, at least, be some meaning to his suffering. Whatever destination their current path led, James was willing to follow. At the same time, he was grateful that the end was unknown, since he was not sure if he was prepared to suffer like Brother Aelred. Courage was not an easy prey.

In the darkness, James sat up and crossed his legs on the cold and slightly humid cave floor. He was positive that nobody listened in on their conversations or knew that they were in the middle of nowhere in an obscure cave. Yes, they were all alone.

"I am sorry everyone, but I have to ask you something," he started, wishing he had Leo's talent to make motivating speeches or ease at finding the right words without getting a headache. The pause in between his two sentences was heavy.

"I understand if any of you wants to go back," he said finally, words clumsy on his tongue.

"Go back? How and where would we go?" Joan asked. "We're trapped in a cave with a giant boulder at the entrance, with servus shackles suppressing our marks. Nobody's going anywhere."

"You know what I mean," James said, wishing again Leo would be the one doing the talking.

"Yes, we know," Claire said. "How can we quit after having witnessed what Cathan is capable of?"

"I never had to Heal something that terrible before," Elgar said, almost too quiet to hear. James had forgotten that the Healer felt some of his patient's agony during the Healing.

"We cannot let him do that to anybody else."

His best friend had not spoken.

243

"How about you, Leo?"

"I can't believe you have to ask!" said Leo's voice. "How could you possibly think that I can go back to the Academy or to the Inn while that monster is in charge of Aqui?"

Despite being chastised, James felt a wave of relief relaxing his whole body.

A hand grabbed his arm, startling him almost out of his clothes as if he was a cartoon character. It was, of course, Brother Aelred, whom he had wrongly assumed was still unconscious. The Abbot made some sounds but was not able to produce any intelligible words. James did not know what to say to the man who had refused to give up Kea, Claire, or that they were close to discovering the Rex's secret, so he did not say anything. The mute Abbot found James' hand and put it over whatever was left of his lips. It was a gesture of gratefulness.

James didn't know why any of them deserved being thanked but assumed it was because none of them had bowed down to Cathan's threats.

He pulled his hand away in haste, since only the young kissed the hands of their elders as a sign of respect and submission. It was not James' place to be respected by the head of an order that had educated and guided the Aquites for centuries. He was humbled and filled with a sense of duty.

"So, how do we get out of here?" Leo asked from his left.

"After you fell asleep last night, James, we touch/searched every inch of the cave. There is no way out," Claire summarized what happened while James spent a day with Maggie, homeless, but free to roam the world.

There was no way out of the cave, unless someone else rolled the rock. They would have to wait until the next time the lexers came to bring them provisions, then somehow overtake them without marks. As implausible as it sounded, that was their only plan.

They spent hours trying to come up with ways to overpower two possibly T7 Risers in addition to their other marks while imprisoned with Servuses. The plan was not perfect, but worth a try. It was time to play the waiting game again. James wished they were back at the lexer command where they could at least see each other.

After forever in the unyielding darkness, they heard the giant boulder that covered the entrance of the cave move ever so slowly. The girls took their places on both sides of the entrance after a still weak Brother Aelred was moved closer to the escape route. They would have to knock the lexers unconscious if there was a chance of making a clean getaway, because Brother Aelred was not yet up to running.

The small window of opportunity before the guards reacted to their attack approached fast, so as soon as the sunlight started seeping in, James, Elgar, and Leo jumped out to trap the lexers.

However, instead of overpowering big Risers, Elgar and Leo were captured easily by a startled and on the edge Kea. James' fate was no less humiliating as he was sprayed in the face with a forceful wave of water that was brought over from a nearby creek by none other than Zoe Rose.

The exact moment they learned that their plan would be entirely useless against actual lexers was also the moment Kea and Zoe came to their aid. James was going to hug them both, once he stopped coughing out water.

Claire hugged her sister, and Joan almost toppled Zoe over to express her gratitude. Once put down by Kea, Elgar and Leo helped Brother Aelred out of the dank cave. At the sight of the mostly-burnt face of the Abbot, Kea's and Zoe's smiles froze on their faces.

Zoe brushed off the tears as if something got into her eye, while Kea led the way to the opposite direction of the Rex's mansion.

"How did you find us?" Claire asked.

"Once Wombat Claire took me outside and would not let me return, I knew something was wrong. I hid and waited until after the lexers left with you. I've been following you since then. I tried to move the rock earlier today, but it was too heavy for one Riser. Zoe helped me with her Waving."

"How do you know Zoe?" Joan asked Kea, clearly having a hard time figuring out how Zoe Rose fit into the crazy picture life had been drawing for them the last few days.

"I spend a lot of time in the forest," Zoe said. Even though that explanation did not give many details, it gave an idea where the two might have met.

"She was practicing Reading nocturnal animals, and I was picking herbs. I followed her around a little bit and introduced myself. Mom was alive back then, and she encouraged me to make at least one friend," Kea explained further.

She avoided making eye contact with Claire. It was one of the rare times the topic of their mother had come up since James and the others joined them.

James wanted to talk to Zoe after being humiliated. Hopefully he could remedy the situation.

"Where is Basil?" he asked with as much coolness as he could muster.

les, and ink pens were placed along the table, waiting for
r next task. Everything was made of similar kind of raw
d, screaming sturdiness and durability. James wondered
long all of these had been hidden here.

On the left side, three hearths were carved into the
ntainside, equal distance from one another. The closest
was surrounded by kitchen items like cauldrons and
es along the wall. Pots, pans and plates piled up on a
ll kitchen island across the fire. In contrast to the careful
nization of the library, the kitchen was messy. Utensils
dishes were placed all over the place haphazardly.

Two long and slender dining tables were spread near
second hearth. Each would accommodate about twenty
ple. The one closest to the fire had nine places set, with
ls of fruits and vegetables in addition to rye bread and
cheese. James' stomach protested the delay and
dered why it was not already digesting some of the
dness that lay before them.

The third hearth was the focal point of a comfortable
ng area. Divans and fluffy cushions sent everyone an
invitation to sleep. At least, that was what James heard.

A sudden movement startled the whole party while
yone except Brother Aelred admired the best safe house
. Brother Cadoc ran towards his abbot through a door at
back. A look of pain spread across his face as he
ined the quiet man's disfigurement.

"Cathan?" Cadoc asked. Aelred nodded.

"Painful?" Cadoc asked again. Aelred shook his head.

"Healers?" Cadoc asked one more time. Aelred
ted towards Elgar.

The monk who could be their grandfather went to one
in front of Elgar and kissed his hand.

"I didn't know you knew his name," Zoe looked back
at James, with the smile that made James' stomach twist
inside his ribcage. He blushed, hoping nobody noticed.

"Who doesn't know Basil the Iguana?" he said,
brushing off the discomfort uneasily.

"He's sleeping in my satchel," Zoe said, pointing at
her bag that was embroidered with bugs and lizards along
with butterflies and flowers. It was, beyond doubt, a Reader's
satchel.

"So, what's the plan?" Leo asked, always the man of
action.

"The plan was to get you out of the cave," Kea said.
"Not good enough?"

"No, no. Thank you," retreated Leo. "I meant, where
are we going?"

"We don't know. Just wanted to put some distance
between the extra muscular lexers and us."

James heard a groan, trying to rise above the
incessant chatter. Brother Aelred, who was now walking
without help, pointed at his own chest.

"Do you know a safe place where we can hide from
Cathan?" Kea asked.

The Abbot nodded and hastened his strides to catch
up with Kea. Soon, the man who could not walk without
assistance two hours ago was leading the group. A sense of
purpose must have given strength to his muscles.

They walked hours and hours and hours. James
wished the servus shackles away, so he could just Pace the
distance, but the shackles were stubborn. The Ambit had to
be close by now, so they should be arriving at their
destination soon. The sun was threatening to leave the
fugitives in the dark, which meant that James's time on Kaya

was coming to a close. He hoped that his friends wouldn't have to carry him.

Another half hour passed before Brother Aelred suddenly stopped in front of a triangular rock. One of the corners of the smooth rock was pointing towards an ancient maple tree. He passed the tree, faced east, and started taking deliberate steps, counting each step with a nod of his head. Then, his hooded figure leaned over and started to push an overgrown bush around, finally pulling something out. He produced a spherical black rock the size of a honeydew melon. He kissed the rock with what James assumed a smile on his face and replaced it back deep in the bush.

Their leader beckoned the confused-looking teenagers to where he stood and grabbed James' and Zoe's hands. Everyone then knew what he was doing. They all joined hands and followed the monk as he took a slow step forward. Five more steps and the sensation of walking through a sheet of icy water embraced them. A moment later, an entirely different forest unraveled before them.

They all looked around to recognize the woods, but other than Kea and Brother Aelred, confusion prevailed on all faces.

"We are close to the Castle of Kaans, aren't we?" Claire's older sister asked.

"But don't you think that would be the first place the Rex would search when he finds out we're gone?" asked Leo.

Brother Aelred shook his head enthusiastically, and made hand gestures again, asking them to follow him.

Another hour and a sunset later, they were still walking. The castle was nowhere to be seen. James was about to wish he fell asleep right there and then. He did not like not being able to pace or getting tired easily like the non-

Pacers. Apparently, he was spoiled. May learn this muscle-aching lesson.

While James was too busy with himself, Brother Aelred stopped walking a around a wall of moss that covered o formation protruding out of the Zita Mo whatever his target was after a minute and perfectly spherical stone at the bottom of t

The moss that had been peaceful mountain range slowly moved and parted a thick, heavy theater curtain, revealing y James and his friends. However, unlike was glad to see this cave.

As soon as they walked through darkness enveloped them. The mountain thick moss once again for any onlooker. hidden from all unwelcome eyes.

Brother Aelred broke the darknes near the entrance. Holding the fire abo group, he started walking down a tunne that led to Kea's cave room. James had s last him a lifetime.

The tunnel was long and windin way into an opening that should not be w

This cathedral of a cave, twenty three hundred feet wide, greeted them lit along the rough walls. Two football f in this magnificent sanctuary, if the football was. On the right side, rows wooden shelves carried hundreds of bo alphabetical order.

At the end of the impressive li table that could seat at least thirty pec

"My brothers and I are eternally grateful to you for healing our Abbot. I am at your and your friends' service."

Elgar tried to pull his hand out of the old monk's grasp to no avail. He was an orphan who was taken care of by others his whole life. The honor the old monk bestowed on him by kneeling and kissing his hand was overwhelming. With apple cheeks, Elgar mumbled a few words inaudibly, and Brother Cadoc let his hands go.

"Come and eat," he said, "you must be exhausted and famished. Please, accept my apologies. I didn't have time to prepare anything warm."

They did not have to be asked twice. In ten minutes, everything on the table had disappeared. After a day filled with hunger and a long hike, everyone sprawled on the puffy cushions, enjoying the warmth of the crackling fire.

James wanted to stay awake to talk to everyone, but when he saw that Joan and Kea were already asleep, he gave in. The last thing he remembered was Zoe playing with burnt down wood pieces lazily with an iron stick, Basil snuggled against her feet.

Day 17: Earth

When James woke up, he was not greeted with the hopeless void from the day before. Brother Aelred was still scarred, and they were still fugitives, but finding possibly the best hideout on Kaya had considerably lifted his spirit. There was much to tackle, but at least they were not prisoners in a forsaken pitch-black cave, waiting to be tortured or killed by the Rex. Yes, it was a better day.

He laid on the hard bed for a while, his eyes closed, feeling the bumps in the folded-up material, the chill of the morning seeping in. Despite the draft, the current weather was much more agreeable than usual for February in Seattle. It had been a particularly cold winter, and there were more than a few homeless that had given into the bite of freezing temperatures. For a while, almost every day there was an ambulance carrying out yet another elderly person who had died of hypothermia. James was grateful for his youth, their relatively robust shelter, and the space blankets that a family with six kids had brought at the end of the fall.

He rolled over to let the blanket shield his back from the draft. Soon it would be warm enough to sleep without a cover.

Maggie surprised him with a smile and a couple of stale glazed donuts. For some reason, he had thought he was alone.

"Good morning," she said with the chirpiness of a bellbird.

"Maggie!" James said, feeling even more rejuvenated at the sight of the girl who did not hesitate to share his pain. "Thank you for everything you did yesterday. Also, sorry for being such a jerk," he said. A heartfelt apology was overdue.

"No problem. What are annoying sisters for?" She looked pleased that the old James was back. "I am glad you're feeling better."

"I am better," James said and recounted the events of the previous day after snagging one of the donuts out of her hands.

Without interruption, Maggie listened to their escape from Cathan's cave, the long and arduous walk through the woods, and the pleasant evening at the Kings' Den. James' life on Kaya had been a fairy tale up until a week ago. She was one of those people who wanted to believe that there always was a happy ending, and the monotonous life James and his friends led at the Inn and the Academy could be the definition of "They lived happily ever after." The recent turn of events, however, had proven to both that there was no such thing as a fairy tale.

"What was your dream about?" she asked, catching James off-guard.

He had almost forgotten about the dream, even though waking from it had felt like he could breathe again.

"It's really nothing," James mumbled, despite the fact that every time his mom's pale image came to mind he shuddered.

"It didn't sound like it was nothing," Maggie insisted.

James knew that she would not give up until she got some answers, so he obliged

"It was a very happy dream at first, with me and my brothers playing. Even Dad was there, drinking beer and laughing. Then I saw Mom and she looked like," he hesitated for a moment, "well, like a zombie."

"A zombie?"

"Not the flesh-eating kind. It was as if she was dead, but still standing. Drained out of life, her eyes were listless, her soul missing. I don't know, Maggie. It was really weird. I hardly ever have nightmares, and this one felt so real."

"Why do you think you dreamt of her?" Maggie asked, her eyes troubled with sadness.

"I am not sure, but I think I had a glimpse of the pain she felt after we lost Jake. I haven't known Brother Aelred long, but his suffering was very hard to bear for me. My mom, on the other hand, lost a child. I cannot imagine how desperate she must have felt. I think, when it happened, I was too young to see anything from her perspective."

A hopeful smile spread on Maggie's face who had probably known all along that James would come around.

"So, are you ready to forgive her?"

"I don't think I am ready to forgive just yet...but it wouldn't hurt to talk."

Talking was a start.

A promising start.

Day 17: Kaya

James woke with one thought in mind. His body rested, his mind was already racing. Now that they had escaped Cathan's clutches, it was time to get to work.

The cozy sitting area in front of the third hearth was empty. Everyone was awake already.

Good.

He felt movement and heard chatter behind him. The busy and happy workings of his friends reminded him of the Sixday meals at the Inn. Everyone contributed in the process even if it was as simple as setting the table. The company and the food were better for it.

Zoe was bending over the cauldron, tasting its aromatic contents. James was sure it was delicious. Joan was slicing bread, her tongue stuck out in concentration. Elgar was getting plates and bowls out. Kea and Claire were putting utensils on the table. James watched them from afar. He felt peaceful for a moment before the memories of the previous days clouded his mind.

Leo and the two monks walked over from the library side of the cave, carrying books and discussing something animatedly. They saw James awake and walked towards him before joining the others at the long slender table.

"Good morning!" Leo said with an extra shot of cheer in his voice. "I must say, as far as prisons go, this place is the best."

"I thought it was more like a hideout. What's this place anyway?" James asked.

"It's a safe house for the Kaans and their family to hide, in case of life-threatening situations. Many times, princes, princesses, or other members of the royal family hid here for weeks at a time during wars or sieges. It's called the King's Den. Only a handful of people know about it," Brother Cadoc explained.

"Where do the food and water come from?"

"The water is a constant supply from an underground stream that trickles down from the mountains. It's a little creek that runs through the far side of the cave. The brothers keep the Den stocked with enough food to feed about thirty people for a month."

James was impressed and grateful for the Kayan version of doomsday preppers. The four of them walked towards the dining area, since breakfast looked ready.

After everyone took a seat, the majority of the chairs were still left unoccupied. Theirs was not a big fellowship.

Zoe ladled steaming rice pudding into red clay bowls. The smooth porridge-like dish was spiced with cinnamon and vanilla beans. It reminded James of his mom's kitchen on Earth. A powerful longing in the pit of his stomach bugged him, but he dismissed it as hunger.

They all ate in a much better mood than yesterday. Once all of the rice pudding was licked off the bowls and there was not one slice of fruit to be consumed, Brother Aelred picked up a parchment size blackboard Brother Cadoc had found for him in the library and wrote on it with a short chalk stick.

"It's time to talk" appeared on the small board.

Reading, instead of hearing, the words in the Abbot's practiced handwriting, unloaded the severity and dimness of their situation on their shoulders, like a hammer of silence.

It was finally time to break the news. "Maggie and I solved the puzzle," James said.

All heads turned to him.

"May I?" James reached for Brother Aelred's blackboard and started drawing the circles Kea had shown them a few days ago. This time he only drew the top half, turning the diamond into a triangle.

"On Earth it's called Pascal's Triangle. It's a mathematical array of numbers. Once we found out that the Rex taught math and chemistry, Maggie and I were able to narrow down our search. This puzzle actually is not a well-recognized version of the Triangle, because it's in Chinese."

"What's *Chinese*?" Elgar asked.

"It's the language of another advanced culture on Earth." He waved his hand to regain his train of thought.

"This is how it works."

He turned the blackboard towards the table so everyone could see it, and started filling in the rest of the circles, first in the Chinese fashion and then in Kayan numerals, with the bottom row reading 1,4,6,4,1.

"The only different thing Cathan did was to turn it into a diamond to make it more complicated."

"That would have never occurred to me," Leo said.

"It's because Cathan wanted to make sure that no one from Kaya would be able to figure it out. It's a human phenomenon. I am sure he thought that he was the only one who lived in two worlds at the same time."

"What does this array do?" Joan asked.

"We still don't know what it means." Kea said, not ready to get excited just yet.

"I think the puzzle and the riddle would complete each other and direct us to the location of the Manual." Claire joined the discussion. "Joan and I have an idea about what the riddle might mean, but we need your help," she added, looking at the Maelites.

"Joan thinks the fathers in '*Fathers counsel at the heart of the triads*' is the founders of your order?" she half-said and half-asked. All heads turned to Joan momentarily before seeing the reaction of the monks.

Brother Aelred reclaimed his blackboard, eyes widened, turning it over so as not to erase James' Pascal triangle and quickly scribbling what he wanted to say. Brother Cadoc obviously knew what his Abbot was about to explain, but he patiently waited for the mute man to finish writing.

"The first twenty monks of the order are called the Fathers," read the blackboard.

"Also, Claire thought, maybe the word counsel means that they continue to teach somehow. Maybe their books or writings," Joan said.

"All their writings and books are in the library at the Castle of Kaans," Brother Cadoc said.

"But the Rex would not have placed the Manual at a place someone might accidentally stumble upon it," Leo said, eliminating the library suggestion.

"Where else could the teachings of the Fathers be found?" Joan asked Brother Cadoc. The older man thought for a moment.

"The Academy, the University, and probably the Rex's personal library."

James hoped that it wasn't in Rex's personal library. He had no desire to see the man again, let alone break into his house.

"His library could not have been that big when he was with my mother," Kea said, throwing out the last library as the possible location of the Manual.

"So, the libraries are out," James said.

"I think the Academy and the University are too public as well," Claire added.

Another bout of silence overwhelmed the King's Den. There were no other ideas where the Fathers' writings could be. James did not want to believe that they had come this far just to hit a wall. Maybe it was time to look at these writings themselves and see if they hid some clue within them, as far-fetched as that theory sounded.

The only person who had not joined the deliberations yet broke the silence,

"The tombs."

The only people who did not seem to be confused by Zoe's sudden mention of the dead and their resting place were the monks.

"What do you mean?" Joan asked.

"Fathers of the Maelite order are buried in tombs whose inner walls are inscribed with their most important contributions to the society, so that those who visit them after death would learn, not mourn," explained Brother Cadoc to the confused crowd.

"That's it!" James stood up, ready to raid these tombs and find the coveted Manual.

"Well, that poses a few complications," offered Zoe again.

"Such as?" Leo asked, getting a little impatient.

"First of all, there are twenty tombs, each bigger than the next as all are devoted to the lives of men who had accomplished much for Kaya. So, it would take days to search all the little nicks and crooks where the Manual could be hidden," Zoe explained calmly. James wondered if she ever lost her cool, but at the same time, her being grounded anchored all of them to serene waters.

"Well, we do have days to search for it," Claire said. "We can't go back to school or the Inn anymore."

"We don't have days."

"The tombs are located beneath the University, because the Fathers founded the first university on Kaya," Brother Cadoc added.

It was indeed bad news, and they would not have days to search the place, merely hours.

The University was located in Xavi, the same place where Cathan had most likely stationed every lexer available. Also, if he had alerted the Council of Ministers, then probably every willing and able Riser had volunteered to catch the traitors. Everyone was sure that the Rex failed to mention their desire to take the Ambit down.

A collective sigh, then a blanket of hush followed.

"We can do it," Brother Aelred wrote.

"How do you suggest we break into the most protected place in Aqui?" Joan snapped.

"With planning and help."

For the lack of a better option, everyone shrugged and accepted Brother Aelred's proposition. Seeing that everyone was on board of the only ship in the sea, he jotted down another sentence.

"First we need to know where exactly it is."

He erased that with the hem of his habit to write more in its place.

"We won't have much time to look for it."

"I was thinking," Elgar mumbled hesitantly, "*heart* might mean center as well. First, I thought it meant maybe in the tombs itself, near where the actual heart would be, but that would be unlikely."

"Couldn't triad mean triangle, like your Pascal's triangle?" offered Kea.

Nobody knew that the puzzle was about a triangle before today, so no one had linked the words triangle and triad.

"So, the center of the triangles would be the number six," Elgar completed the train of thought looking at the back of Brother Aelred's board where James had drawn the Chinese version of the famous mathematical array.

"Brother Elian," wrote down Brother Aelred.

"Brother Elian's is the sixth tomb from the entrance. He is also the most renowned chemist out of all the Fathers," Brother Cadoc explained.

Despite the impossibility of their task, smiles spread all around.

Now that they knew where the Manual was, at least the first part of the obstacle course was overcome. The next challenge, however, might prove to be much harder and possibly end with them either being acid-tortured by the Rex or thrown in prison for the rest of their lives. Neither was appealing.

Whatever the outcome, the lives as they knew prior to the night at Kea's cave were forever lost. James hoped that at least they would find a way to take the Ambit down and give the people of Aqui their freedom. Then, maybe, imprisonment or a disfigured life would be more bearable. Still, as he looked at Brother Aelred and saw where his warm smile once was, he could not bear to imagine a similar burn on Claire's, Leo's, or Zoe's faces.

One by one, they all rose from the table. It was going to be a long day at the King's Den as each one of them would use all available brain cells to conjure up a plan to overcome the Rex's forces.

Brother Cadoc left to return later in the day with plans of the city and the blueprints for the university building. Meanwhile, the rest of them would put their feet up and think hard.

Elgar, Claire, and Kea headed to the library, while the rest of them washed the bowls in the underground creek Brother Cadoc mentioned. Melted snow meandered through the mountains, eventually surfacing inside the Den. By the time everything was clean, James' hands were shaking from the ice cold water, sending shivery pulses up his arm. A nice, warm shower sounded wonderful, even if it was invented by the Rex.

Hours later, Brother Cadoc arrived with all the resources they might need and more bad news than they wanted.

"The Castle of Kaans is taken over by the lexers. Nobody is allowed to enter or exit without the knowledge of Rex Cathan himself." he said, unloading the contents of his extra-large Maelite size satchel. "All of your names, except Zoe's, Kea's, and mine, are posted around Aqui as treasonous fugitives. Of course, the Abbott is charged with attempting to force the Rex out of office so that he could take control."

No words could explain the horror on their faces. They were now all known as enemies of the state. Quite a change from their humble origins as orphaned teenagers less than a week ago.

"How did you manage to escape with a huge satchel?" Leo asked.

"They have their ways, and we have ours," said Brother Cadoc, rather mysteriously, looking at Brother Aelred whose eyes smiled in return.

The last two items he retrieved from his enormous bag, which was almost as spacious as Hermione's beaded bag, were curious: a clear bottle filled with something purple and a cutting tool. Brother Aelred must have known what they were, since he approached the older monk and offered his wrist carrying the Servus shackle.

Brother Cadoc poured a small amount of the sparkly purple liquid with the consistency of tree sap on the sharp edges of the tool, which could be best described as a bolt cutter. Purple sap covered the gleaming blades of the cutter, glowing ever so slightly.

The Abbot put his wrist on the table and waited for Brother Cadoc to place the shackle in between the gooified edges. The older man stepped forward, held the bolt cutter over his Abbot's wrist, and cut the indomitable shackle with one easy motion. The bolt cutter went through the metal like hot knife through butter.

"That's impossible!" Elgar exclaimed, but still eagerly placed his own shackle under the monk's glowing purple tool. Soon, everyone was free to use whatever marks they wanted. James and Joan even Paced around the cave, before the others got annoyed with them for accidentally knocking things over.

"I thought only the person who placed the shackle could remove it?" Claire asked, once everyone settled down.

"The Maelites have always opposed the use of Servus shackles," Brother Cadoc replied. "A few years ago, one of the brothers formulated a compound that reacted with the shackle metal. The ingredients are very rare, and the formula is extremely complicated, but the end result is potent."

"Thank you, Brother Shackle-Remover!" Leo said, and bowed.

Now that they had gotten their marks back, planning did not seem too hard.

For a short while.

Alas, that optimism slightly dimmed when Brother Cadoc unrolled the blueprints to the tombs through the university. It would take a miracle to enter the catacombs without being detected.

During the afternoon, everyone took a turn to study the blueprints and the layout of the city. Maybe one of them would find a weakness.

Thanks to Brother Aelred, the Rex did not know about Kea, Claire, or that his beloved wife had Seen the location of the Manual. Because of the Abbot's resilience in the face of torture, the catacombs would not be guarded as heavily. Quite a few lexers would be guarding outside the university, but not too closely. The Rex would not want to raise suspicion by deploying excessive amounts of force in a peaceful land.

The area around this ancient building also hosted the only government building of Aqui where James Knox had met Cathan Zoss for the first time. Their impossible task started with at least two problems, first getting into the university, and then entering the building.

"We need a diversion," Elgar said.

"I think I have an idea how to create one," Claire said with a twisted smile. James wasn't sure if he wanted to know her idea.

He would not be able to hear it anyway, because time had flown in the midst of discussing important items like ten foolproof methods of taking a lexer down, the possibility of Striding through the ground into the catacombs, and whether flooding the whole city would be acceptable.

James fell asleep on the divan across from the third fireplace with an empty bowl in his lap, surrounded by the most important people in his life.

That night could have lasted a lifetime as far as James was concerned, because come morning, duty called.

Day 18: Earth

"I *cannot* wait to take a shower!" Maggie said as soon as James indicated that he was back to Earth. "You know, your cousin spoiled us. Before we bumped into her, I was lucky to shower once a month."

"I can smell myself," James agreed.

"I can smell yourself too," Maggie agreed even more.

James mussed up her disheveled hair and crawled out of the shelter. "Let's go then, lazy bum!"

He did not know why he felt this cheerful, despite the lack of a plan and his current status as a traitor on Kaya.

On the way to Sarah's, they talked as if they hadn't seen each other for weeks. Maggie seemed more than pleased to see James uncharacteristically chatty.

When a stack of pancakes with blueberry syrup greeted them in the kitchen, the day got even better. Thoughts about showering and untangling hair disappeared at the sight of fluffy sticky goodness. Both Maggie and James took their seats around the table without a word, and soon the pancakes disappeared, leaving two satisfied and content faces in their wake.

Extra-long showers were in order, not to mention laundry. James smelled of lavender and ylang ylang instead of sweat and other unmentionable bodily odors. Clicking through television channels and lazily turning pages of Sarah's books about dentistry made the morning even more carefree and relaxing. But one of Sarah's roommates would soon come home for lunch, and they needed to leave.

James grabbed the brown bag Sarah had left on the table for them and placed a note on the counter.

I will be at the Greenlings Park on Thursday at noon.
Could you tell my mother?
Thank you,
James.

Maggie read the note as she grabbed her brown bag and gave him an approving smile. James knew that she, too, hoped to leave a note for her mother one day, but not while her mom lived under the same roof with that man.

The rest of the day, neither James nor Maggie wanted to talk about the upcoming meeting. Neither of them knew what to say. Some things were just plain awkward. So they left earthly troubles aside and focused on the goal of reading as much as possible about various ways to break into high security places. Maybe one of the infamous criminals of Earth would help James and his friends to sneak into the catacombs without being detected.

Thanks to Sarah, the brown bags contained enough food to last them all day, leaving the two researchers to freely skim through bank robberies and other heists.

When the evening rolled around without any revelations about deceiving a city-full of lexers, James decided not to think about the impossibility of their task come morning.

Day 18: Kaya

Unfortunately, the night of pseudo-planning and light-hearted chatter was over, as was the day of being surrounded by books about bank robberies. James hoped that their extreme interest in ways to break into high security places would not get them into trouble on Earth. He could only handle the adventurous life on one planet at a time.

He yawned and stretched his back. Since there was no shower and still no coffee, a splash of cold water would have to help him with the rest of the waking up. Looking around, he saw that the remainder of the Den's current occupants had already gotten busy. Seven in the morning was clearly not an early enough a start when you needed to figure out how to defy the most powerful man in your country.

The cave looked a lot less crowded than last night. Some people were missing.

"Where are Claire, Elgar, and Leo?" he asked Kea. She carried a bowl to the table from the cauldron. Rising steam danced over the food as Claire's sister dipped a wooden spoon in her breakfast.

"Good morning to you too," Kea said.

It was shameful that someone who grew up in isolation had better manners than he did.

"Sorry, Kea, good morning," he remedied.

"I'm being silly, James, no need to feel bad," she smiled. It was amazing how much the two sisters looked alike. Not only did they share similar physical appearances, but their kindness and gentleness were singularly precious virtues they must have inherited from their mother. Because their father did not show any sign of either quality.

"They're the group in charge of creating a diversion, so they left to divert."

James bolted up. "We are going into the catacombs today?"

"No, no, no. Relax. We're going in tomorrow after lunch. They needed some time to get ready. Anyway, you had better eat some breakfast. You're with Zoe and Brother Aelred. They're taking out a few books from the library for your part of the plan."

"I didn't know we had a plan," James said.

"The plan is to have three groups, and each group is going to find a way to complete their part of the mission. After we retrieve the Manual, we will all meet here, if we don't get caught or die."

Kea mentioned "dying" as a matter of fact. Her approach to life and death revealed much about the recluse girl. Long, lonely years of hiding and waiting were about to bear fruit. The more James looked at Kea, the more he realized that she was more than ready to bring this business with the Manual to an end. Until now, she lived to keep the puzzle and the riddle safe. They were her burden, just like her mother's. Now that she had fulfilled her duty, Kea could finally start life anew at the age of twenty-one. Tomorrow was going to be the last day of her former life. James hoped that being caught or dying would not be the season finale.

"What's our part?" he asked as he got up and folded the woolen blanket that kept his unconscious body warm all night.

"Well, while everyone's being diverted by Claire and the others, the three of you are going to get into the catacombs," Kea said.

"How about you, Joan, and Brother Cadoc?"

"We're the back-up team. Joan is going to hide in a Readable distance, in case we need a quick getaway with the Manual. Since nobody knows that Brother Cadoc and I are involved, we're going to act as if we're visiting the University for educational purposes and assist you if needed."

It was as good of a plan as any. The details were hatched while he lived his day on Earth. James was glad that the burden of retrieving the Manual was not on his shoulders alone.

After cleaning up the sleeping area, James grabbed one of the wooden bowls and ladled some oatmeal. The sweet taste of dried apples and raisins made waking up easier. He washed his breakfast down with sour cherry juice and once again missed caffeine. Approaching footsteps pulled him from his reminiscence about the bitter smell of coffee beans. He swallowed the last sip of the tangy juice and was ready to face the day.

The other members of his group walked towards the long dinner table carrying books and scrolls of parchment. They put the hefty tomes down next to his empty breakfast bowl. Brother Aelred wrote on his tablet and turned the small blackboard around.

"Are you ready?"

James nodded.

Zoe carefully rolled out the parchment, a detailed map of the Catacombs. James had thought the hardest part would be entering the University and then sneaking into the Catacombs undetected by the finest lexers in Aqui. But one glance at the map proved that the journey in the ancient tombs would not be as easy as he had previously hoped.

Once entered, they would have to zigzag through a tunnel that was marked as "The Reverie." Zoe pointed at the slender line marking a miles-long tunnel on the map.

"This is where the monks and the visitors are encouraged to walk silently and reverently as they contemplate the teachings of the Fathers. That way, their minds would be open and receptive when they reach the actual tombs. It's two miles long."

That meant, if they stuck together, which they would, it would take up to forty minutes to walk the tunnel. The fact that the Reverie was the only way in and out did not escape James' attention either. Once inside, they would be trapped.

Brother Aelred pointed at a spot towards the middle of the map, a little over a mile into the catacombs itself. "Tomb of Brother Elian, noted chemist and Healer" read the insignia where the Abbot's finger indicated. Each tomb was a circle, spiraling into a center where the sarcophagus itself was located. They would have to walk more than three miles just to get to Brother Elian's final resting place and then find the Manual within the tomb itself.

"How big is the tomb?" James asked.

"Brother Aelred thinks we would need at least an hour to search, if we are lucky," Zoe replied.

"That means, we need two to three hours after we get into the university."

The Abbot nodded, and Basil the Iguana wrapped his tail around Zoe's wrist as if he wanted to take her away before it was too late.

"We need a long and convincing distraction then," James said, wondering what Elgar, Claire, and Leo could do to occupy the lexers' attention for that long.

"Claire seemed to think they could manage it."

"We have another problem," Brother Aelred wrote.

"What now?" James said, shoulders drooped.

"Your sleep tonight."

James slapped his forehead with his palm. To reach Xavi from the Kings' Den, they would have to walk at least ten hours. After that long of a walk, no one would have the energy or clarity of mind to search the tomb. As if that wasn't enough, James would be asleep through the night. Just to make it to Xavi in time, they should have started to walk two hours ago. Why did he not think of that?

Realization hit James in the face like a cold glass of water. He jumped off the chair and toppled some of the books over. Zoe put her hand on his arm to stop him from knocking the Abbot over as well.

"Don't worry, Brother Aelred has a friend who is going to help us through the woods. We're going to ride horses for most of the way." Her words dispersed some of his anxiety as her touch made the room a little warmer than before.

Again and again, James was glad that he was not in charge.

"We have another hour before the horses arrive. While you were sleeping, Brother Cadoc and I prepared the supplies we might need on the way and through the night," Zoe moved her hand. Part of James was glad that her touch stopped taking his breath away, and part of him wanted to take the small delicate hand into his hands.

Not a good time to dwell on silly things like that.

"Meanwhile, we read," wrote Brother Aelred and pushed a small stack of handwritten books and ancient scrolls towards James.

The three of them read everything they could about the builders of the Catacombs, the University, and Brother Elian. There was no way of knowing how much of this data overload their brains would retain. But they kept on reading, memorizing pictures, learning key words, and hoping that their memories will not fail when needed.

At the end of the hour, James rose up with a slight headache, a side effect of trying to shove too much information in an already busy mind. Hopefully, he did not push anything important out like multiplication tables or how the Hobbit ended.

It was time to bid goodbye to Joan, Kea, and Brother Cadoc, who seemed as carefree as if they were on an all-expenses-paid cruise ship, sipping tea and nibbling on cookies.

"See you tomorrow, Outsider," Joan said, punching his arm with a smile on her face and burying herself back in the cushion with another cookie.

"Yes, see you tomorrow," mumbled James.

"Take care of the Abbot for us," Brother Cadoc said without getting up. "Nobody keeps the books like he does," he added with a wink. James was amazed to see that the old monk had a sense of humor. Every world was indeed full of surprises.

Zoe and Brother Aelred were already waiting for him at the entrance of the Den with satchels on their backs and walking sticks in their hands. Another satchel leaned against Zoe's legs. James grabbed one of the sticks piled at the entrance, picked up the satchel, and followed Brother Aelred into the dark tunnel.

The trio strolled without a word. James thought about Earth and his earthly problems. Everything and everybody in Seattle felt out of place in Aqui. Even the memory of skyscrapers and cars felt dizzying. It was akin to remembering a day when you had the flu, throwing up all day, your head in the toilet.

Brother Aelred pushed another rock button to part the mossy curtains, blinding them with the blazing sun. It felt good to smell the forest and bask in the sunlight again, even though his time at the Kings' Den had been more than pleasant. His Reader side always pulled him to nature one way or another. He was sure Zoe felt the same way.

The older man stepped into the sun and lifted up his face as if he wanted to soak the sunrays into his skin. James could almost see a smile on the disfigured face. But in reality, no one would see the Abbot smile ever again.

Brother Aelred led them into the woodland just like the day before. The Reader in James could not help but enjoy the waking up of berry bushes and wild peach trees. Bugs, bees, and butterflies flew about without a worry in the world and spread some of their cheer. Nature's rebirth eased the weight of their task, letting the travelers feel a little lighter and a little less worried with every step.

When they reached the Ambit, a different spot this time, Brother Aelred took their hands once more and stepped through the icy water that wasn't there. The invisible cage spat them out at a place closer to Xavi than the Kings' Den, but still they would have to travel at least until sunset through the forest, making sure to avoid highways.

Shortly after going through the Ambit, they heard bushes rustling and horses neighing. The voices came from two mares, drinking out of a nearby creek while a monk kept an eye on the animals.

The young monk stood up and lowered his cowl as soon as they emerged from the woods. The distracted monk James saw when he broke into Maelites' private quarters at the Castle smiled at their approach.

Without a word, the younger man bowed to kiss the Abbot's wrinkled hand. He must have been warned about

Aelred's disfigurement, because he made no comments nor did he show any sign that he noticed anything different on his Abbot's face.

After giving the dutiful monk a blessing on the forehead, Brother Aelred propped his walking stick against a cascading willow tree and fished a piece of chalk out of his pocket.

"Brother Faro, the youngest of Maelites," he wrote for James' and Zoe's benefit.

The monk, who could not be more than twenty, blushed from ear to ear and promptly hurried towards the horses to hide his red cheeks. He ushered two dark brown mares with long manes and gleaming coats. The Reader who took care of the Castle's horses had done a wonderful job at grooming these gentle and magnificent animals. Zoe approached the one closest to her and looked into the beast's eyes intently for a moment. The animal picked up its hoof as acknowledgement and bowed his head. It was always amazing to watch a master Reader deal with animals. James' own skills were far below Zoe's.

Because of the Readers and their connection with animals of service, horses or elephants did not need reigns on Kaya. In a way, they worked for food and shelter like everyone else and always did as they were bid by their Readers.

Brother Faro looked into the other horse in a similar manner as Zoe. The animal lowered his massive body to the ground for the Abbot to mount. The young monk settled himself on first of the double saddles. Kayan horses were much bigger and stronger than their relatives on Earth because of their Riser blood. Two people could travel on a Kayan horse for as long as a day without the animal needing any rest or food.

Zoe and James mounted the other horse. The beautiful mares turned around and slowly headed downhill. The sun had already passed high noon. It would be almost dark by the time Xavi was within reach.

"I will leave you outside of the mountain villages near Xavi," Brother Faro explained, reading James' mind. "You will have to walk about two hours before you can reach the city walls." After a while, they would have to continue on foot, since the horses were too big to get close to the city without detection.

"Thank you, Faro," wrote Brother Aelred on his board and showed it to the younger monk, who smiled and bowed his head.

The colossal animals moved through the spring woods with a grace unexpected of their size. With the gentle sway of the horse's steps, James watched Zoe's braided hair swing above her hips. He was grateful that there was a satchel between their two bodies, as the urge to touch her hair might have been too overwhelming to resist. He held onto the brown bags tighter and contented himself with staring at her shoulders and the occasional profile of her face. There were more important matters to attend to at the moment. James scolded himself and tried to remember the many accomplishments of Brother Elian in chronological order to distract his thoughts.

Traveling on horseback was enjoyable at first, but after a while it began to be painful. James would give anything to Pace the distance instead of staying another minute on the mare. He tried to be grateful, but his butt objected to being squished against treated leather for endless hours. From the uncomfortable shifting of the rest of the travelers, James assumed that everyone was experiencing similar levels of pain except Brother Faro, who was probably used to being on horseback for long periods of time.

Finally, after about another hour, the forest started to thin. They would have to leave the easily-noticeable animals behind and continue their journey on foot. James had never been more grateful for having to walk. They all dismounted in a small clearing next to a pond, lotus leaves floating lazily on its surface. As soon as James' feet hit the ground, it became clear that walking was not going to be as fun as he imagined. Being saddle sore had made the inside of his thighs unusable for other activities. His muscles did not want to assume a more natural position and left him standing as if he was sitting on an invisible bar stool.

Not comfortable.

Brother Faro held up his hands against Brother Aelred's chest, palms facing the older man who was also sitting on an invisible stool. A few moments later, the Abbot straightened his back and shook his legs, his whole body relaxed.

Thank heavens Brother Faro was a Healer. James could not have appreciated another mark more at the moment. Perhaps teleportation, if it existed.

The young monk walked towards Zoe first. After making her feel brand new, he came over to James. The only Healer among them gave James a smile and lifted his hands up, palms facing forward. Slowly, the pain eased, and James sensed his muscles revitalize. In less than a minute, he felt as if he had just woken up from a long and restful nap.

"Thank you," he said. Insufficient words.

"I must leave you here, Abbot," Brother Faro turned to Brother Aelred, who was ready to continue the journey, holding his walking stick in one hand and his leather water flask in the other.

"I need to rejuvenate and then bring the horses back to the Castle before anyone notices we are missing. The outer walls of Xavi are two hours away from here. I suggest you camp in that abandoned barn tonight and continue tomorrow morning," he said, pointing at a dilapidated structure about a mile away from the cheerful pond.

"We'll stay with you until you're ready to travel," Zoe said and settled herself on the soft spring grass, sprinkled with bluebells and buttercups.

Healers needed time to regain their strength after restoring others. For something as minor as saddle sores and tired bodies, Brother Faro needed no more than ten minutes.

James was more than ready for a small picnic. Brother Aelred, too, put his walking stick aside to enjoy the sight of spring without thinking about tomorrow. Soon, ominous thoughts of the night would overwhelm the green lightness of the young leaves.

Thanks to Brother Faro's healing, the hour-long walk in the dark turned out to be enjoyable even though it was near the end of the day. By the time they reached the old barn, set up camp, and prepared dinner, James figured he still had a few hours left before the mandatory slumber took him away.

They used the rest of the time going over the plan a few more times and talking about contingencies if anything went awry. It seemed like there were so many things that could go wrong that they decided to have contingencies for their contingencies. After a while, the chatter and chalk scratches calmed down. Well before James, Zoe fell asleep with Basil curled up against her legs, facing the crackling fire.

While the two youth were getting ready to get lost in the dream world, Brother Aelred remained awake, flames dancing in his thoughtful eyes.

Day 19: Earth

Some days were waiting days. This Wednesday would qualify as one of those days, during which the seconds and the minutes seemed to pass slower. Time was indeed relative. Since the moment he fell asleep in the torn-apart barn and woke up to a chilly spring day in Seattle, nothing James did made the time go faster. The midnight did not rush so that the mission which had turned their lives upside down could be accomplished.

Another part of him was looked forward to seeing his mother the following day. The meeting had the potential to become one of the most awkward conversations of his life, but the possibility of his mother returning to her former self was worth all the awkwardness in the world. Still, James had no idea what to say or where to put his hands. He had been living by himself for years now and so much had been lost between the mother and son. Soon after he first left the house that was no more than a structure four people shared, he had realized that life had been kind to him up until then. The hardships and evils of the world had stayed at bay, mostly because of his parents.

Difficulties of the homeless life descended upon him shortly after he arrived in Seattle with only fifty dollars in his pocket and the clothes on his back. The cash did not last long. Soon enough hunger and desperation led him to do things he would not have otherwise dreamt. It was a good day if he did not get cornered by drug-pushers or bothered by bullies or muggers. Slowly, he started to lose his sense of self-worth and did not care about petty things like body odor or education. Every day was a struggle, and there was no room to worry about tomorrow. Today was all he could handle. He was sure that numbing his body and mind with drugs and alcohol would have become appealing if Maggie had not come into the picture and put some color into his otherwise bleak life. The ordeal became entirely different once they decided to look after one another.

Soon, James and Maggie put together their shelter on the recently-vacated spot next to Mrs. Jackson and John with cardboard boxes, styrofoam sheets, and discarded tarps they scavenged during their daily exploits. It took almost two months to find all the material, but their new home was a shelter that kept most of the northwestern cold out, despite a few drafty spots.

Since the completion of their shelter, James and Maggie developed some form of a routine to keep the blues away as much as possible. Thugs and muggers left them mostly alone at their new place. They did not know why until a few days ago when John the comic book guy beat the living daylights out of the big dude. Theirs was a bizarre arrangement with peculiar characters.

Now having his rough edges smoothed by years of fending for his own, James did not know how it would be to see his mother again. Was she dead inside like his dream? Would he able to respect her after all that had happened following Jake's death?

Time was a formidable enemy, one that did not forget. Something was broken between James and his family, and no matter how much glue was applied, there would always be a weak spot, ready to fall apart again. Things could never go back to the way they were, but maybe, just maybe, his family could build something new from the broken pieces. For the first time in a long while, he hoped.

So, James wished the day away as Maggie sketched her version of a futuristic city and its occupants. He tried not to dwell on the things he could not control, but his mind was persistent. Even as they asked perfect strangers for change, sometimes getting a dime or a nickel, sometimes getting the cold shoulder, James thought about his parents and his one chance to end the captivity on Kaya.

When the night came, his head welcomed the bumpy pillow made of folded clothes. Sleep would chase the worries away.

It was time for action.

Day 19: Kaya

The glorious smell of sausages and scrambled eggs with herbs tickled James' senses before he even opened his eyes. Nothing was as refreshing as waking up to the smell of skillfully-cooked breakfast. Well, maybe waking up to the bitter aroma of freshly-brewed coffee might tie the race. Thinking about coffee made him think about the mornings with his mother on Earth, who downed at least two cups of coffee with cream and sugar before she even thought about waking up. He smiled at the memory and rolled over to enjoy the tasty breakfast that made his stomach feel like a bottomless pit.

Brother Aelred was stirring the eggs, cooked on a sheet of cast iron. Near the fire, patties of sausages begged to be eaten. James did not want to disappoint his favorite breakfast food and put two whole sausages in his mouth.

"Can you believe Brother Cadoc packed these for breakfast? It's a miracle that the eggs survived the horseback ride," Zoe said, filling cups with some kind of sweet-smelling tea. Chamomile? Sage? Nobody cared.

James ate a few more sausages, while Brother Aelred dished out fluffy, bright yellow eggs onto thick leaves functioning as plates on this sunny morning in yet another hiding place.

Over easy eggs on James' leaf plate disappeared to the depths of his stomach in a minute as an amused Aelred and Zoe watched him eat at an incredible speed. He was almost full after having devoured three additional slices of bread and dried figs. The tea Zoe had steeped helped everything settle down into his belly.

James leaned against the red wall with peeling paint and watched the other two finish off their breakfasts. Brother Aelred finished last since half of his burnt mouth was fused shut, and he had to eat through the half Elgar had healed. James wondered how the monk still retained any joy despite everything that had happened over last the few days. Other than the disfigured face, he was the same man who took pleasure in cooking clam chowder and apparently going on dangerous missions with clueless teenagers. If the Abbot were able to talk, surely he would point out the lesson that needed to be learnt.

When Brother Aelred folded up the leaf after the last bite, Zoe started to pull out yards of soft bright green fabric from her satchel. That shade of green was familiar, but nobody wanted to make a comment just yet.

They needed a disguise to walk from the city walls to the University incognito, and Zoe had volunteered to find a solution. James was afraid to ask, but Brother Aelred was having a hard time holding his silent laughter at the sight of the green fabric. He clearly approved of their disguise, in addition to being amused.

"Are those Hider robes?" James could not wait any longer.

"Yes, they are," Zoe answered and unraveled another length of cloth.

"Do I want to know your plan?"

"No, probably not," Zoe replied and tossed a rolled-up robe to James. Brother Aelred caught his in the air, his body shaking with silent laughter.

Since the Dispersal, there lived the descendants of people who were exposed in close proximity to whatever radiation Haydar had created through the explosion. These victims did not die, but their DNA was altered so unnaturally and haphazardly that over the centuries, all their children continued to possess severe physical abnormalities. Tired of being shunned and ostracized, the descendants of this group formed a village of their own. In this sanctuary, no one paid them any attention or avoided looking at them. They kept to themselves, raising their own food and traveling to other parts of Aqui only rarely. They came to be known as the Hiders.

Once in a while, Hiders would come to one of the cities to trade or meet with a minister. Everyone else left them alone, respecting their desire to live apart. Even though it was uncommon to see Hiders in Xavi or Faus, it happened at least a few times a year. The fact that they traveled in threes made it the prefect disguise for their mission, albeit a slightly embarrassing one.

A Hider delegation always consisted of women, which was what made the Abbot laugh so hard. Hider men never left the village. The women always dressed in bright green silk robes and covered their heads and faces with veils.

James concluded that having worn the same habit for decades must have gotten old, and the monk was ready for a change. Green silk would bring out his eyes. The great abbot of the scholar Maelites posing as a woman was indeed a once in a lifetime opportunity to witness. However, James did not think the same was true for himself. He felt unusually self-conscious.

Zoe walked out of the cave and came back in a few minutes, wearing one of the shiny robes that was stuffed in her satchel. The soft silk made her curves more pronounced. James had a hard time looking into her eyes, so he turned to Brother Aelred.

"It's our turn," he said, no eagerness whatsoever in his voice.

Zoe produced a length of canvas and a small bag of cotton out of her satchel and put them next to the pile of green silk.

"You will need hips and breasts," she said, trying to stifle her laughter and left the cave to give the two men some privacy.

Brother Aelred and James wrapped some of the lose fabric around their waists and helped each other to smoothen out the bulks and kinks to make the curves look natural. Creating fake breasts was a little harder, but thanks to Zoe's preparedness, soon the old monk and the young Pacer had cotton stuffed ta-tas that would be the envy of many women. Brother Aelred pulled the silk robes over his brand-new hips and boobs. And voila! A new Hider was born! James could not help but chortle at the transformation. Still chuckling, he pulled the green robe over his own head and down his fake bottom. It was the Abbot's turn to laugh. He grabbed his board and scribbled in between chuckles, "You are much prettier."

"Thank you," James said and curtsied.

They helped each other with the veils and called Zoe back in the cave. Her forced resolve to not giggle lasted about two seconds before she had to steady herself against the cave wall because of the overpowering convulsion of laughter. Brother Aelred and James waited patiently for her to compose herself with the dignity of wise old Hider women.

"You look much better than I thought," she finally said.

"I am not sure if that's a compliment," James replied, smiling at Zoe and thinking that her eyes wrinkled in the most beautiful way when she laughed.

When the hysteria came to an end in a few minutes, they packed their satchels, put out the fire, and left the old barn for Xavi. A gentle downhill slope swallowed their steps for two hours, and to James' surprise, the green robes were rather comfortable, making the balmy day more bearable.

Three Hiders passed the outer city walls around noon. It was another half an hour before they could reach the university. The rendezvous was at one o'clock. They had made good time.

Nobody knew what the signal for the rendezvous was, but apparently Claire assured them that it would be impossible to miss. The disguises Zoe came up with made a quick getaway possible if they needed if things went south.

As the Hider trio approached the city center, sightings of lexers became more frequent, but not at an alarming rate. Hosting a much smaller population, the Aquite government did not need as many law enforcement officers as the United States government. James assumed most of the lexers were concentrated around the University and also closer to the Rex himself.

People nodded politely to the Hiders, but no one initiated conversation, for which James, with his booming male voice, was grateful.

When they arrived at the city center, there was still half an hour to kill. The closest touristy or time-killable place was the Dispersal memorial on the opposite side of the University. What was more natural than three Hiders reminiscing about the day that condemned them to a life of isolation and veils?

James' hands started to sweat and the number of butterflies in his stomach increased as they headed to the Dispersal Memorial with the solemnity of maimed people. Every passing minute made the waiting harder. He wished they had arrived later, but Zoe's prudence to arrive early in case Claire's signal came before the rendezvous could not be trumped.

Through the mesh of his green veil, James spotted Brother Cadoc and Kea entering the University, carrying stacks of books in deep conversation. One of the lexers at the door stopped them for a few moments and let them pass without a problem. Another fifteen minutes and the signal would be heard or seen, whatever it was.

As he stood in the memorial, pretending to read the names of the fallen on the day of the Dispersal, James was overwhelmed with the thought of a hundred things that could go wrong. He wished the whole thing would just start so he did not have to endure the delay another second.

Patience was not a virtue he had acquired just yet.

Another ten minutes.

Another five minutes.

The watched pot was insistent on not boiling.

The rendezvous time came and went. The trio in bright green silk moved towards the University entrance as slow as possible without attracting unwanted attention. Nobody bothered the Hiders unnecessarily, but they did not want to push their luck. James started to wonder if Claire, Leo, and Elgar had been discovered by the Rex. The thought of them being tortured by the man who believed ends justified means sent chills down his spine.

The agreement was to wait fifteen minutes before aborting the plan. It had been almost ten minutes past one o'clock. Time had come to a stop now. Nothing happened.

James nodded to the other two to signal that it was time to leave and come back another day, with another disguise. He turned around to head for the city walls again, head down, discouraged. Lexers running in the opposite direction towards the sundial tower caught his attention, snapping him out of the gloom. People from all directions came to a stop at the bottom of the tower. James heard Zoe gasp. When he looked up, the source of all the commotion and their distraction was all too clear. Three figures clad in black stood on the ledge, right above the giant dial itself. The sundial tower was no Big Ben but was over ten stories high. Gravity from that height would still do its job of crushing the bones of those who were defiant.

"It's the Goners!" Zoe whispered in disbelief.

Now that she said it, James could see that Sadwen, Eoban, and Fina were the ones who were looking down on the crowd, hands on hips, waiting for their audience to get bigger. They didn't have to wait long. In no time, almost everyone in the buildings around and the nearby marketplace flooded to the circle where the sundial tower was located. A great number of Risers in the area came running in their charcoal vests to diffuse the crowd, but Aquites were used to neither public stunts nor crowd control. Everyone was adamant to see what these troubled teenagers were about to attempt.

"Get off the roof, at once!" a lexer shouted, "or you will be arrested!"

The Goners dutifully ignored them.

A few moments later, even the guards at the University entrance had left their posts. Sadwen plunged down, and Eoban and Fina followed him right behind. It was the perfect moment to sneak into the University.

Three fake Hiders moved swiftly.

James glanced back to see what happened to the Kayan thrill seekers and saw that all three of them had become flying squirrels as their wing suits filled with air. It would be wonderful to watch their glide over the crowd to a hopefully smooth landing, but the window of opportunity was closing fast. Without a moment to lose, the women in green darted for the entrance of the catacombs that remained unguarded. Before disappearing into the stairway spiraling down to the two-mile-long Reverie, Brother Cadoc and Kea watched them from the second-floor landing.

Everything had gone according to the plan.

So far.

James still had a hard time believing that the Goners had been willing to help them. Not long ago, Claire and Leo got detention because of their stupidity. That was going to be an interesting story to hear.

The stairs took them three levels below ground before leading to the long tunnel, the Reverie. Torches flickering with green flames led the visitors to the catacombs through a circular tunnel whose walls were decorated with twisting and twining branches of the tree of life. Raised leaves, filled with intricate webs of veins, covered the branches, leading the visitors to the tombs where eternal knowledge could be found. The women in green should be contemplating about how one's death became another's life in nature and how eternity of self could not be found in the physical realm. But these visitors were so disrespectful that all they did was to run and look behind to make sure that they were not being followed.

Jogging through the tunnel was much more pleasant than James had thought. Eerie green light danced on the endless branches, following the visitors as they traveled, giving the impression of a stroll in the woods during a moonless night.

They progressed much slower than James wished because of Brother Aelred, who could not run as fast the two teenagers, even though fit for his age. After all, as Readers, both his companions spent considerable amount of time outdoors. It was going to take another thirty minutes to reach the catacombs themselves.

Before the final resting places of the first Maelites came into sight, the Reverie expanded gradually like a funnel and the carvings of leaves turned into thousands of blossoms. Green torchlight turned white. A breathtaking depiction of spring unfolded with each step, carved in stone, preserved for eternity.

Without losing their focus, they progressed through the first tomb, a hallway spiraling toward the crypt in the center. The works of Brother Viator were written in calligraphy along the walls, and the memorable moments of his life were depicted as detailed reliefs.

The spiraling tunnel eventually led to the crypt, in the middle of which stood a sarcophagus that contained the remains of one of the most noted Maelites in Kayan history. If a visitor wanted to see just Brother Viator's tomb, then he would go back to exit the catacombs. If not, a short shaft led them even lower into the ground to the next tomb, and so on and so forth. They proceeded and briefly witnessed the lives of another four brothers and wasted twenty minutes before finally Brother Elian's name appeared above the entrance of the next tomb.

Since they entered the catacombs, almost an hour had passed. James doubted that the Goners' stunt would hold off the lexers long enough for them to make a clean getaway, but he hoped. There was too much hoping and counting-on-luck going on nowadays.

As soon as they entered the hallway of Brother Elian's tomb, each of them started to search for nooks and crooks or secret buttons, anything and everything. Even though the carvings were well preserved, it should be relatively easy to spot anything that had been added centuries after the tomb was built.

Each of them ran their fingers over every writing and every picture, making sure to check the floor and the rounded ceiling that led to the crypt. No switches. No handles. No buttons. No secret compartments.

By the time the search party reached the center of the circle where Brother Elian was laid down for his final rest, James had started to lose hope. If the Manual was in the sixth tomb of the Fathers' catacomb, it should be here, unless Cathan figured out their scheme and removed it before they arrived.

The search of the crypt did not prove any more fruitful than the rest of the tunnel. The slow realization of having risked all their lives on a wild goose chase was dawning on James. He was so sure that this was the place the Rex had hidden the Manual. There was no way for him to know that they were aware of the Manual's location. They had moved fast, not giving him much time to relocate it out of caution.

They had thought through everything.

When another thorough search of the crypt left them empty handed, all three gathered around Brother Elian's sarcophagus looking at each other, hoping one of them had an ingenious idea to save the day.

"I am sorry. I thought it would be here," James whispered, making sure to keep the dead sleeping.

"We all did," said Zoe.

Brother Aelred fished his board and chalk out of the depths of his satchel and wrote in haste. "There is one more place to look," read the chalk letters as the Abbot eyed the sarcophagus.

James did not want to open it. He did not. Zoe seemed to agree with him, since she recoiled as soon as she read the Abbot's board.

Seeing their hesitance, he wrote something else down. "The dead do not care."

James knew that they could not leave without exhausting every possibility, so as reluctant as he was, he nodded. Even though disturbing those who had passed away was considered one of the worst offenses on Kaya, Zoe approached the marble box where Brother Elian had been sleeping for centuries.

All three of them lined up against one of the long sides of the sarcophagus to push it open enough to search the inside. Both James and Zoe were more than willing to let Brother Aelred do the searching. It would have been wonderful if one of them was a Riser, but alas Pacing, Waving, or Reading was utterly useless when one was faced with heavy stone plates.

They pushed with all their might until it was clear that the lid was not willing to oblige. Right as they were about to give huffing, puffing, and pushing another try, James suddenly became aware of the presence of another. Zoe must have felt it as well, because they both looked up at the same time in the same direction.

Rex Cathan stood at the entrance of the tomb, blocking their only escape route, taking in the fruitless efforts of his next victims.

"It's not there," Cathan said, his clever eyes twinkling in the milky white light. "I removed it long ago."

James might not be as good of a Seer as Claire was, but the Rex's mind was blood red with each word he uttered. Even though the events had taken a rather unfavorable turn in the last few minutes, a rush of hope and purpose ran through James' body at this blatant falsehood. They needed time to search the sarcophagus.

As if he saw the new found hope on James' face, Brother Aelred unstoppered the gallon size leather bag of water he had been hauling around all day. Water swirled out as if alive. The master Waver brought the clear liquid into the air like a snake rearing his head for attack. A noose of water wrapped itself around the Rex and tightened.

James and Zoe kept pushing the stubborn lid. The water prison would not hold Cathan long.

"I see you don't have anything else to say," Cathan said, not bothered by the water ropes. "It is refreshing to see you, and not endure a lecture on the importance of free will and choice. I should have used that acid sooner."

James looked at him with disgust. "How did a school teacher from Ohio turn so evil?" he said in between grunts.

"You are too young and too naive to know about the world, boy! Don't talk to me about evil!" Cathan replied, the amusement turning to rage in an instant.

Zoe and James pushed a little harder, but the gap was only a couple of inches wide. The sarcophagus was still too dark to see the inside. Zoe leaned against the lid one more time.

Cathan broke of his water chains. Being a T7 Riser, without a Servus shackle, the Rex would be impossible to subdue for long even by an expert Waver. Leo or Claire should have been here, but nobody had quite expected the Rex to chase after them himself. Then again, men of secrets do not have many friends. Cathan probably did not trust anyone else.

"I think I am done with your meddling, Abbot!" Rex Cathan took three long strides and reached for the Abbot's throat, lifting him off the floor as if the older man weighed nothing.

"Leave. Him. Alone!" James screamed and pushed.

"I don't think so. Once he and you are out of the picture, nobody will ever know that there even was a Manual. The Ambit is our life line."

"We're all going to die in this prison!"

"We *will* find a way." Cathan pushed Aelred a little higher, his shiny black robe still soaked.

Because they were a few moments away from witnessing a murder, with a swish of her hand, Zoe gathered up the water that had splashed all around the floor and encased Cathan's face in a sphere. As the liquid found its way into his lungs instead of air, Cathan released Brother Aelred, struggling to get rid of the death trap.

Unlike their Rex, Zoe was not a murderer. She splashed the water against the cave wall once the Abbot was free. Cathan coughed and gagged, trying to dispel the liquid out of his lungs to replace it with life-saving oxygen. Using the Rex's momentary distraction, together they pushed the lid with all their might one more time.

The lid gave in and exposed the bones of one Brother Elian who enjoyed his eternal rest in his habit, hands folded over his chest. The right hand of the dead monk held a scroll symbolizing the importance of the pursuit of knowledge, which was the charism of his order. In his left hand, there laid a two-headed arrow pointing opposite directions, symbolizing the significance of free will.

A quick glance in the sarcophagus did not reveal the Manual. It would have been too easy if the Rex was considerate enough to place it gently next to the bones, preferably with a sign pointing to it.

It did not take long for Cathan to recover from his coughing fit and make his next move. There was still no sign of the Manual. They were running out of time. The Abbot lifted up Brother Elian's robes as gently as possible under the circumstances. The fabric had deteriorated over time, ripping in places despite the gentle touch. Still, a quick search around the skeleton yielded no fruit.

But James had seen the deep red in their leader's mind when he said the Manual was not in the sarcophagus. It had to be here.

The Rex reached into inside of his skillfully-embroidered robe. When his hands came out, one clutched a painfully familiar vial and the other a short, curved silver dagger whose well-honed edge gleamed even in the dim light.

James had hoped that the Rex would not go as far as murder to keep his perfect little kingdom captive under the Ambit. Deep inside, he knew better.

Watching Cathan move in the periphery of his vision, James touched around the black marble sarcophagus to feel for any irregularities. Zoe did the same, but she kept staring at Cathan directly, just using her hands to look for the Manual. Brother Aelred was almost done checking under the robe. It wasn't there. Somehow Cathan must have learnt to deceive a Seer. James thought that was impossible.

"Move away!" the Rex commanded with a voice that chilled James' blood.

As he took a step towards the long-dead Brother Elian, Cathan removed the little cork that held the destructive contents of the vial at bay.

"Move, or it will be your eyes this time, Abbot!"

The silent man pushed James and Zoe aside, placing himself between the youth and the Rex. One of his hands was still reaching around the bones for a final attempt to make this whole mission a success.

Cathan reached over the lid and poured some of the clear liquid on the Abbot's fingers. The old man screamed silently and pulled his hands out in vain, knocking the bones around in the sarcophagus.

Zoe's wail of agony filled the air as if it was she whose hands were bathed in acid. She lunged towards the Rex to stop him from inflicting more harm. As her smaller but still strong body collided with the Rex, whose attention was fixed on the Abbot, the vial flew out of his hand. The clear fluid spilled, forming an arch in the air. James watched the deadly liquid slowly give in the call of gravity, helpless to protect either Brother Aelred or Zoe. Everything unfolded in slow motion. He could do nothing, trapped in time. A useless observer.

A stream of droplets landed on Zoe's face.

She let out another howl, this time for her own agony. Both Brother Aelred and James lunged forward. James caught Zoe before she hit her head. She writhed in pain, tears flowing down her cheeks freely. At that moment, all he wanted was to be a Healer and take her pain away. His wish did not come true. Zoe curled into the fetal position and shook violently for a while. Slowly, the seizing stopped and her beautiful eyes looked at him, red, covered in tears and anguish. Once the initial shock passed, she whispered. "Go!"

The Rex and the Abbot struggled to overpower each other. Water that was splashed against the wall was now weaving through the air towards Cathan who had captured Brother Aelred again. As the Waver motioned to take the Riser's breath away, the hand that held the dagger moved towards the monk's middle. James could see what was about to happen. Again, in slow motion. But even as a Pacer, he was too late to stop it. The dagger disappeared under the bright green silk. The happy color of the Hider garment was soon bathed in the dark red blood of the head of the Maelites.

James jumped on the Rex with all his weight and pushed him away from the Abbot. They both tumbled around the tomb that was supposed to be a place of contemplation and learning. James wanted to hurt the man, who had been selfish and cruel for his whole life under the disguise of benevolence. Now, the simple teacher from Ohio had hurt two of the people he cared for. It was payback time.

But neither on Earth nor on Kaya had James learned how to fight. All he could do was to make sure that the strong Riser did not get a hold of him. Years of rough-housing with Leo was about to pay off. After a few moments of skirmish, James was able to push Cathan off so hard that the ruler of Aqui hit his head on a bronze sconce and fell on the floor unconscious. A pool of blood surrounded his head.

Out of breath, James turned around to find the old monk bleeding freely on the cold rock floor. Zoe was trying to press on the wound to slow the blood loss, but they both knew that it was too late to save the Abbot.

With a final effort, Brother Aelred pointed towards the sarcophagus.

The master Waver, the Abbot, the humble monk exhaled his last breath as if he had accomplished his life's goal and did not inhale again. Zoe reached down and closed his eyes gingerly as if he could crumble at her touch. They both sat there, silently crying for having lost a friend and a father whose last act was to save both of them from the rage of a mad man.

James stood up after a while to close the lid of the sarcophagus. They had risked their lives, lost Brother Aelred, and scarred Zoe for nothing.

He leaned against the lid from the opposite side. Just as the rectangular marble slab was about slide back to its place, he saw that the bones of Brother Elian were misplaced. Out of respect for one of the Fathers of the Maelites, he reached in to put the bones where they belonged. The skull had rolled over as well. Even though he hesitated to touch the bones that once contained a great mind, it would be even worse to leave it as was. James gently lifted the skull up, but his fingers brushed against a hole at the top of the occipital bone.

What was a hole doing there?

Reluctantly, James picked up Brother Elian's skull and placed it on top of the lid. Zoe looked at him with horrified eyes, as if the worst thing that had happened so far was him moving the skull of a monk out of its resting place.

"There is a hole here," James explained, pointing at lower back of the head. Zoe gently placed Brother Aelred's body on the floor and leaned over to join James.

When they turned the remains over, there appeared a perfectly circular opening that was cut with a tool. Disgusted with what he was about to do, James reached inside the hole with his index and middle fingers and pulled out a pencil-thick metal tube. It was similar to long cylindrical containers that were used to carry paintings or drawings. James twisted and pulled the two sides of the tube, revealing what had cost them so much in such a short time. A tightly rolled piece of parchment dropped on the black marble lid right next to Brother Elian's head. Zoe unrolled the paper and spread it open, her fingers trembling. As soon as she looked at the ancient paper, expectation turned into disappointment.

"It's blank," she said.

"No! How can it be blank? Why would the Rex hide it then?"

"I don't know. Look at it."

James reached over, not believing that all this effort, death, and pain were for nothing.

The moment he touched the paper, lines of ink started to bleed through like tiny rivers on the ancient parchment. The two teenagers watched wisdom come alive in James' hands with unbelief.

The invisible ink needed an Outsider's touch.

They had found the Manual.

It was almost impossible to believe that this little piece of paper had caused so much chaos. They stood frozen, staring at the meaningless shapes, until shuffles and quieted chatter from the hallway reached their ears.

James and Zoe flattened themselves against the wall, ready to defend themselves. Two people turned around the corner, and Zoe blinded the first one by splashing her in the face with the remainder of the water from Brother Aelred.

"You've got to stop doing that!" said Claire's thoroughly wet older sister, while Zoe tried to dry off her friend's face as much as she can with Waving.

Brother Cadoc knelt next to Brother Aelred to heal him, but he stopped right away.

"He's gone," Zoe said.

The old monk lingered for a moment next to his Abbot's side whispering inaudibly. Then he moved quickly towards the Rex and started Healing him.

"What are you doing?" James yelled. "He is the one who killed Brother Aelred!"

"We are not murderers," Brother Cadoc whispered with the stern tone of a father who corrected his child.

"Leaving him here to bleed out when we can help is akin to murder. Don't worry, I'll leave him unconscious."

"Brother Cadoc, you should take a look at Zoe's face as well," Kea called out.

The monk turned abruptly, having just noticed that she also needed medical attention.

"I am very sorry, dear," he said, kneeling down next to Zoe, who had refused to leave Brother Aelred's side once it became clear that the Rex was arrogant enough not to ask for the help of other lexers. As Brother Cadoc's hand hovered above her head, the tension on her face relaxed. The pain was gone at last. She was having a hard time forming words amidst tears. A nod and a smile were all she could manage.

A long chemical burn, starting from her cheekbone, ran down to her right collarbone thinning at places, but still visible with wrinkled pink skin. A desire to strangle Cathan for causing so much pain overtook James' whole being, for killing Brother Aelred, for having the audacity to think that he knew better than everyone else. Maybe it was good that Brother Cadoc was there. Otherwise, James would be more than happy to watch the Rex bleed out in agony.

"Have you found it?" asked Kea, who had been holding her tongue out of respect for the dead.

"Yes, yes, we did," James replied absentmindedly, still staring at Zoe's scarred face. He opened his hand to expose the tiny tube that contained the Manual.

"We need to leave," Kea said, picking up the Abbot's limp body as if he weighed no more than a sleeping toddler.

James did not know why the run back through the tunnels felt much longer than before. Time was playing tricks with his mind again. All he wanted was to get everyone to safety without getting killed or scarred by a psychopathic leader.

When they finally approached the end of the tunnel, Zoe and James put their bright green veils back on, and Kea covered Brother Aelred's perfectly still face with the other veil. As they emerged from the tunnel, James saw that the lexer guards at the University entrance had returned to their posts despite the on-going commotion outside. It was impossible not to be impressed with the efficiency of the Goners' diversion. After all these years of planning ways to annoy the Goners, James had never thought he would be eternally grateful for their adrenaline junky ways.

Brother Cadoc took the lead, Kea following close at his heels with the Abbot's body in her arms.

"Is there a problem, Brother?" the guard asked, suspiciously eyeing the limp body Kea carried.

"We have a medical emergency. We need to take this Hider back to her village," Brother Cadoc replied.

Despite the extensive cautions he was asked to exercise, the lexer still had great respect for the Maelites and the Healers. He was reluctant to ask further questions about how they came to be in the catacombs. The Riser struggled between duty and reverence. Every passing second gave the Rex the chance to catch up. Doors to freedom stood within reach but for the two lexers. In that moment of uncertainty, gravity came to their aid by slightly sliding the veil down, exposing Brother Aelred's scarred face. Against his better judgment, the lexer recoiled at the sight of the disfigured features and moved aside to let them pass.

Without running, but with the speed required by a medical urgency, they passed the crowds who were still talking about the events of the last hours. Words like "flying" and "explosion" got thrown around. James would have been excited to hear the whole story, if the price of the Manual was not Brother Aelred's life. He felt as if nothing would amuse him ever again.

No one else paid them any attention after they left the city center. The combination of three Hiders and a Maelite monk was enough for everyone to stay at arm's length.

They found Joan waiting with three horses beyond the city. The journey back to Kings' Den was disturbingly quiet. The afternoon came and went, and then the evening. The solemn party stopped and ate in silence. James held the small bronze tube tightly in his hands and hoped that he could fulfill the Abbot's dying wish.

Midnight approached with the silence of death, but with the speed of light. James' body begged for the relief sleep would bring. Not just physically, but mentally and emotionally, every aspect of his being was exhausted. He had not felt this tired since Jake's accident.

Still on horseback, he fell asleep, thinking about his little brother's and the wise monk's dead bodies.

Loss had connected the two worlds space could not.

Day 20: Earth

James inhaled the humid, chilly morning air of Seattle and knew at once that no longer warm, Kayan air filled his lungs. It was good to take a break from the emotional roller coaster of the day before. The guilt of getting to distance himself from the pain while his friends had to endure a night of grieving Brother Aelred's death overwhelmed him momentarily. But still, James could not help but feel relieved to live a day away from the running and the crying. Was it possible that his cardboard shelter had become a refuge? Life had such strange turns and twists.

Since the chase for the Manual started, it had been hard to pull his mind back from the happenings on Kaya. When all was calm and monotonous in both worlds, the transfer from one to the other was seamless, but recently he needed a few minutes to focus his thoughts to Earth instead of dwelling on his life on Kaya. Maybe the impossibility of stuffing two lives into one mind was catching up to him finally.

"How did it go?" asked Maggie's voice gently, as if she sensed the feeling of loss that shadowed James since the catacombs. This time, he was aware of the need to talk about what the Manual had cost. The wound had already started to fester, and the only way to heal was to get rid of the infection. He told Maggie about his long day on Kaya. There was not much emotion in his storytelling. Their journey through the forest and the fact that they had to dress up as women had all become insignificant details. The distractions Claire, Leo, and Elgar conjured up with the help of the Goners was nothing more than setting the scene. In the colossal shadow of death, so little mattered.

Even when James was able to find the breath to tell what happened in Brother Elian's tomb to a speechless Maggie, there were no tears. Once again in his life, James had to experience what death meant. Once again, he felt numb, as if death was darkness. The absence of light was the absence of life. When all the words were said, he stopped. Maggie put her arms around him. It was one of those occasions when talking did nothing to improve the situation. Again, she silently cried for James until the time came for him to shed his own tears.

By mid-morning, James had told Maggie all that there was to tell. Even though the pain in his chest did not cease, its companionship became dull and nagging rather than whiny and loud. It was a presence he had known well since Jake's accident. Two different worlds, two different losses, and two different people who were so far apart settled in James' heart right next to each other. He hated the familiarity of it all.

Once the talking was done, the reality of the meeting with his mom came crashing down. Why did these life-changing events have to happen at the same time?

A seed of doubt about the wisdom of seeing his mother after such a loss on Kaya started to grow in his mind, despite the fact that he understood what she had been through much better now. James had always taken his mom's withdrawal personally. The sting of being abandoned by his parents when needed most had poisoned him in the aftermath of the accident. The nights of no food and no parental supervision had increased in number, as his parents' marriage strained under the weight of the loss of a child. Then the fights ensued, as if they did not have two other children who needed their attention more than ever. Then his dad stopped coming home. His mother spent her days and nights in her bedroom holding Jake's clothes in one hand and a liquor bottle in the other.

His dad was as guilty as his mom, but for some reason, maternal betrayal caused a much deeper wound. That, or James was not ready to see his father yet, the man who left his family stranded at the first sign of trouble.

"Stop!" James scolded himself, "if you keep thinking like that you are going to spiral down a dark hole." He did not want to keep stewing over what should have been. Not after what had happened to Brother Aelred. The regrets of his life drove the Abbot to become a recluse. James wanted to hope for tomorrow, instead of obsessing over yesterday. Today was the first day of that future. If he learned anything from Brother Aelred's death, it was how short life was.

"Are you gonna be able to meet with your mom?" Maggie asked, knowing what was bothering him. She would have made a wonderful Seer if she had been born on Kaya instead of Earth.

"I think so," James replied. "It can't be worse than this, right?" he asked, gesturing towards the rest of their cardboard home.

"Well, we still have a couple of hours. Did you wanna get donuts from the youth shelter?"

James had forgotten that as much as Maggie loved hearing about Aqui, the stories were nothing more than fairy tales for her. This harsh and unforgiving life was all that she had, with hunger and cold. Despite all that, as James wallowed in self-pity, Maggie had fed both of them for days. He felt ashamed, but did not say anything. Yes, he would get donuts for the little girl who liked drawing castles from other worlds and taking care of whiny older brothers.

"They'd better have more than enough left," he said with an enthusiasm he did not feel. It was a cloudy but mild day, without the usual suffocating humidity. Perfect for a walk to the shelter and for a reunion meeting. Maggie did most of the chattering during their leisurely stroll, while James nodded and made affirmative sounds once in a while, but in reality, he was lost in thought. The remaining hours went by like a dream as James followed Maggie around mindlessly until noon. Then, the two homeless teenagers walked towards the park where Mrs. Knox was waiting to repair the severed relationship with her son.

Part of James was afraid that his mother would look like the zombie in his dream, lifeless and lost. If she was in such a state, would James be able to trust her? He didn't know.

Maggie decided to sit this one out. The little duck pond was the perfect place to kill time with happy ducklings vying for attention. James headed to the benches near the playground where his mother brought her three boys to run around when they visited the city. She would sit at the same bench and read, checking on the boys every other paragraph. James knew that she would be there again, possibly with a book and a cup of extra sweet creamy coffee.

Squeals and laughter of children exploring the tunnels and monkey bars of the playground were a welcome melody that drained the seriousness from the situation. James circled around the swing set to make sure to approach his mom from behind. The walnut-stained wooden bench with cast iron frame faced the blue twisty slides. There was someone sitting there, but he was not sure if it was her. He tried to focus, taking slow, deliberate steps, squinting his eyes. Was it her? James couldn't tell. It was just embarrassing to realize that you could not recognize your own mother. So much was broken, so much needed to be healed.

Forgoing his desire to see his mother first, James walked toward the two toddlers who shoved fistfuls of sand in their mouths. As he passed the bench to check the lady watching the girls lick their shovels, the woman looked up.

This stranger had short hair, parts of which were held back with colored hair clips. A thick pair of light pink glasses hid her eyes. His mother had long flowing hair and always wore contacts. This lady looked comfortable in loose-fitting blue jeans and a yellow floral blouse that was more summery than springy. His mom almost always wore dresses or skirts. Finally noticing that someone was watching her, the lady looked up and smiled at her watcher. James' mother's eyes twinkled at the sight of her son, despite the short hair and the pants.

Mrs. Knox got up from her seat and tried to find a place to put her hands. They were strangers now.

"Hello, James."

"Hi, Mom."

Awkward silence.

"You've grown tall," Mrs. Knox said, hoping to break the ice.

"Your hair has grown short," James said, trying to help her break the ice. Mrs. Knox combed the short hair with her fingers.

"Do you like it?"

"It's different, but I like it," James said with a smile. The ice was broken.

"Do you have time to sit down a little bit?"

Yes, James had time, and lots of it.

Mother and son settled on the wooden bench right next to each other, watching the sand-eating toddlers. Mrs. Knox reached into the depths of her huge purse that always contained what was needed and retrieved a plastic container.

"I made the cookies you like."

James pulled the lid open, letting the sweet aroma of peanut butter fudge no-bake cookies escape. It smelled like his childhood. He picked up one and savored the familiar and safe flavor. Everything got better.

"I am sorry," said Mrs. Knox's...his mom's...voice, waking him up from the gone-by days of trying to steal one of the coveted cookies.

"I am sorry for everything."

James could hear the pain and the remorse in those few words. In the midst of bittersweet memories and friendly cookies, the sincerity and humility of the woman who had raised him so well for so long touched his heart and put a dent in the wall that had gone up between him and his parents. Just a dent, but it was a start.

"It's alright, Mom," he managed to say, swallowing hard, cookies and tears.

"I know it's not alright, James. I neglected you and Jesse in my grief. There was no excuse for my behavior. Will you ever be able to forgive me?" she begged.

"You were in pain, I understand," said James, realizing that today was the best day to see his grief-stricken mother.

"So were you."

"Not like you, Mom...I think, I was too young to understand what you were going through."

"You grew up, James...and I wasn't there to see it. I am sorry," she said one more time, and her silent tears turned into a sob.

James put his arms around his mother as she cried for her children. The woman he held was not the woman he had left drowning at the bottom of a liquor bottle. The drunken, neglectful recluse was gone, leaving behind the broken woman who cried in his childhood playground. It was too much to handle.

James' mom wiped her face with a tissue that appeared from one of the many pockets of her purse. "Sorry," she said again. James smiled to reassure her.

"Will you come home?" the mother asked her almost grown-up son.

"Not yet," said the son. "But I'd like you to meet someone."

James took her mother's hands in his own much bigger hands and was amazed at how much smaller they felt. Together they walked towards the duck pond.

"Maggie, this is my mom," James said.

"Pleased to meet you, Mrs. Knox," Maggie said, shaking bread crumbs off of her hands.

Two homeless teenagers and the woman spent the day together, eating, talking, and eating some more. It was good to be cared for once more, and it must be good to be a mother once more. James and Maggie told Mrs. Knox about their lives in the company of the freely-flowing tears the older woman shed. They lost count of how many times she said, "I am sorry."

By the time the sun set, signaling the end of their time, James had not asked his mother about Jesse or his dad. His mom did not volunteer the information either. One parent at a time.

Still, James was pleased to see that his mother wore her engagement ring and wedding band on the same finger.

Not that it meant everything was peachy, but at least not all was lost.

"When can I see you again?" his mom asked, when their last stroll led them to the subway station she needed.

"I'll call you," James replied. "Soon," he added quickly when he saw the discouraged look on his mother's face.

Mrs. Knox smiled and touched her eldest son's face with the tenderness only a mother can muster. "Here, call me whenever. I mean *whenever*," she put a folded envelope in his pocket. Then she gave Maggie a hug and kissed her on the forehead. "Thank you very much for taking care of my boy."

A painfully beautiful day.

Day 20: Kaya

Throbbing pain seared the left side of his head when James woke up. He touched his head, sitting up in front of the third hearth in the Den. The smell of bacon and the warmth of crackling fire made him almost forget the events of the previous day. Almost.

A few moments later, Zoe walked over holding a cup, releasing the steamy sweet smell of the tea she had steeped the other day. James felt at home.

She put the cup on the floor and ran her fingers over the side of his face, making him grimace.

"You fell off the horse at midnight. Joan Healed you right away, but it will sting for a while," she said with a look of concern that was uncharacteristic of her easy-going, non-worrying self.

"It's nothing," James said and reached out to touch the scar on her face. "At least, nothing compared to what you suffered."

"An Ambit-free life would be worth it."

"I'm sorry."

"There is nothing to be sorry about."

The intimateness of the conversation left both of them blushing.

Joan saved the moment by coming to check up on James' wound.

"You'll live," the Healer declared, trying to cheer things up, but even the sarcastic Joan was listless at the face of death.

"Where is he?" James asked.

"We laid him next to the creek. Brother Cadoc said the monks would want to bury him according to Maelite rituals," Joan answered.

"Are Claire, Leo, and Elgar back?'

"Only Elgar," answered Zoe reluctantly.

James sleepy eyes shot wide open. "Wait, what happened?"

"Claire and Leo were captured along with all three Goners," Joan explained.

James could not believe his ears. Not only did they lose the only person who knew anything about the Ambit, Claire and Leo were gone too. Thanks to Brother Cadoc, Cathan would feel well enough to torture them soon. The Ambit asked for too much. James did not know how he could possibly continue without Leo's steadfast presence.

"We need to rescue them," he said, not wanting look at Zoe or Joan.

"We will," came Elgar's voice. "But first let's make sure all was not for naught."

James knew that it was time to see the Manual. He retrieved the thin bronze tube from the pocket of the green robe he was still wearing and handed it to Elgar, the man who had the vision to take the Ambit down. With utmost care, he pulled the two sides apart revealing the tiny scroll that had cost so much.

"It's blank," he said with disappointment.

Having forgotten that only he could read it, James touched it with the tip of his finger. "I need to be touching the parchment to make the ink visible," he explained to a confused Elgar.

They all gathered around the elusive Manual that had changed all of their lives forever.

The parchment was no bigger than his palm. James' hand lingered over the edge, and the markings slowly became clear as if somebody had drizzled ink over it. After a minute, the lines stopped twinkling, and the Manual became still, revealing to them the instructions on how to take the Ambit down.

At the top of the page, James spotted three suns and a number of planets orbiting them. The largest of these suns had eight planets, and the other two had only one. The big sun shared one planet with each smaller sun. It looked like a solar system with three centers.

There were no titles, headers, or footers. Simply the picture of the strange system. They all looked at each other. Everyone had a version of confusion and frustration written all over their faces.

James touched the solar system. As soon as his fingers traveled over the page, letters started to appear below the picture. They all leaned in closer to read the tiny poem that accompanied the weird planets and their three suns.

Brother Cadoc, who joined the spectacle without anyone noticing, started to read aloud the nonsensical riddle with eight lines written in a pyramid.

- Sacrifice
- Yourself
- to Restore
- the lost freedom.
- Burdened with the royal ingots,
- bearing the suns and the moons of life

• prepare to shed the blood of the perfect number of the perfect people.

• Unite the red with the ancient magic in the golden order where the vanishing door appears with the touch of darkness.

"Wonderful! Another puzzle and a riddle!" Joan threw herself down on the divan with exasperation.

"You don't understand it," Elgar said. "We finally know how to take the Ambit down, after all these centuries. This is nothing but a small hurdle. We will solve the puzzle

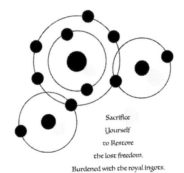

Sacrifice
Yourself
to Restore
the lost freedom.
Burdened with the royal ingots,
bearing the suns and the moons of life
prepare to shed the blood of the perfect number of the perfect people.
Unite the red with the ancient magic in the golden order where the vanishing door appears with the touch of darkness.

and the riddle, just like we did the other one, and finally set the Aquites free."

His renewed sense of purpose was contagious.

"Yes, we will solve them," Zoe said, "for Brother Aelred."

James looked at her scarred but still beautiful face and the brightened faces of the ragamuffin orphans and the old monk.

"Yes, we will," he said. "But first, we save Claire, Leo, and the troublemaker Goners."

To be continued...

with

Two Fallen Worlds:
Found

Day 21: Earth

When his shoulder blades flattened against the make-shift bed on the concrete, the sensation of sinking enveloped him for a moment. Good thing he was young and healthy. Otherwise, bed sores would have covered his entire body for being unconscious through the night, every night. What was going to happen when old age and frailty arrived? He did not know. Nor did he care, especially in the current state of things on Kaya.

His legs and arms felt grateful for the stretch in the pleasantly chilly spring morning. The air could be classified as fresh, since a newness, an excitement lurked in the dark corner of their lost street. Maybe it was because of what happened with his mom, or maybe because the elusive Manual was finally in their possession.

As his toes and feet stuck out of the blanket, relishing the blood flow, memories of what it cost to possess the Manual dampened his bubbly spirit.

"Any new developments?" Maggie's voice came.

"Oh, good morning, Maggie," James said and rolled over to face his roommate, if their cardboard shelter could be called a room. Maybe a street-mate?

"Yes, yes, it's a good morning," Maggie said, one eyebrow raised in impatience.

"You're not gonna like it. It's another puzzle and a riddle."